BAD BLOOD

A DETECTIVE JACK BRODY NOVEL

J.M. O'ROURKE

INKUBATOR
BOOKS

Published by Inkubator Books
www.inkubatorbooks.com

Copyright © 2023 by J.M. O'Rourke

J.M. O'Rourke has asserted his right to be identified as the author of this work.

ISBN (eBook): 978-1-83756-223-7
ISBN (Paperback): 978-1-83756-224-4
ISBN (Hardback): 978-1-83756-225-1

BAD BLOOD is a work of fiction. People, places, events, and situations are the product of the author's imagination. Any resemblance to actual persons, living or dead is entirely coincidental.

No part of this book may be reproduced, stored in any retrieval system, or transmitted by any means without the prior written permission of the publisher.

PROLOGUE

Her eyes snap open, and she stares into the darkness, forgetting for a moment where she is. Then she remembers. She listens to the sound of his breathing next to her.

The curtains haven't been drawn in the hotel room, and in the grey, predawn light, she pulls back the cover and gets out of bed, pads across the carpeted floor to the ensuite. She goes in and locks the door, the marble floor tiles cold against her feet. She pulls down the toilet lid and sits. He'd left it up. Just like Jeff used to do. This annoys her. This is her room, not his. She invited him here. Not the other way round. He is her guest. As she begins to piss, she gingerly touches her neck. He'd been a rough lover too, liked to squeeze it, his grip tightening in rhythm to his thrusts. She hadn't liked it, not really, but went along with it anyway. Her ex-husband used to tell her she was as exciting in bed as a cold hot-water bottle. Well, she'd show him, the bastard. Not that it mattered, because he no longer cared. But she did. Maybe she needed to loosen up, maybe rough sex was the way to go? Maybe when they did it again, she'd be the one on top? That'd be a first.

Maybe she'd squeeze his *neck? She giggled and stood to dry herself off, wondering what might have happened if rough lover boy had been able to last just a little bit longer. Would he have gone on squeezing her neck until she'd passed out? And what if he'd lasted even that little bit longer again? Would she now be dead?*

She shuddered.

Surely not.

She was tender down there too.

Still, she smiled, because apart from constricting her windpipe at critical times, he'd been one great fuck. Yes, sir. Just what she needed. So, take that, Jeff, you old bastard, and stick it where the sun don't shine, where I know you always wanted to take it – right up your own arse.

HE HEARD THE TOILET FLUSH, *standing by the window, watching as the pale yellow smudge of the new day broke through the night sky above the Liffey estuary, like a brush stroke in an unseen ecclesiastical painter's hand. He didn't turn. He heard the bathroom door open and her footsteps cross to the bed and the sound it made as she sat down, like a gentle sighing. He knew she was looking at him, admiring him, could feel her eyes rummaging over every inch of him.*

He allowed that silence to percolate through the room, enjoying it, enjoying the power it gave him, knowing it made her feel uncomfortable: it always made women like her feel uncomfortable. He knew to her it wasn't just a silence, rather it had a sound all of its own, the longer it continued, the louder it became, until it was a pulsating, screeching symphony of white noise.

He waited, listening to the soft sighing of the bed again as she began to fidget, knowing she wanted him to turn and say something, anything, to at least look at her.

But he didn't. And he knew that, in the normal run of things, with normal people, so to speak, she might speak, say something, maybe even demand, What the hell's up with you? Speak!

But she didn't.

She couldn't.

That was the thing.

She couldn't.

As she silently sat there, he knew. It was complete. He could do whatever he wanted.

If only.

He had the time.

But he didn't.

He turned slowly, revealing himself, feeling her eyes taking him in, taking in how pulsating, quivering, excited he was.

She was so busy looking it took her a moment to see what he held in his hand.

But by then it was too late. Not that she could do anything about it.

She couldn't.

Pouf, pouf.

The silencer caused the handgun to sound that way. It didn't so much as buck in his hand – modern handguns had gone beyond that – as quiver, like jelly in a bowl when a truck passes. But by then the round had already left the chamber, travelled along the barrel and exited out the end, on a laser-straight trajectory, hitting Lindsay once in the centre of her forehead. The second pouf *hit her in the upper chest. But she was already dead.*

The second shot was merely from habit.

1

Detective Sergeant Jack Brody was dressed the part, that of a successful businessman staying at the exclusive Herbert Park Platinum Hotel, room prices starting at €800 a night. He had on a hand-cut, blue wool Italian suit, a patterned navy silk tie, and brown loafers. He was sitting at the counter in the Patrick Kavanagh bar, stirring a €30 mojito cocktail. On his ring finger was a wedding band, on his wrist a €30,000 Rolex. Even in a room full of beautiful people, Brody stood out. Which was the whole idea.

The woman came in through the lobby door, dressed in a short black dress, black high heels, a small handbag hanging from her shoulder on a shiny metal strap. She walked with a supreme confidence, her long legs moving her like a stalking cat. She was slim and big breasted, with straight black shoulder-length hair, her walk merely adding another octave to the silent siren blaring through the room. Although there were other empty stools along the counter, she chose the one next to Brody. She didn't so much sit as slide onto it, crossing those long legs of hers, resting one graceful hand onto the countertop, the fingers tipped by expensively manicured red nails. She raised the index, discreetly catching the attention of the bartender.

She turned to Brody and gave him a coy look, her big doe eyes taking him in in an instant, right down to the colour of his socks – sky blue with white stripes. Her appraisal was so fast he almost missed it. But he didn't. She smiled: perfect, even, dazzling white teeth. Up close, he guessed she was no more than mid-twenties. She wore little make-up. She didn't need it. Her appearance was what might be called classically beautiful.

'Hello,' she breathed, her voice out of synch with her appearance, the voice of someone older, a voice that belonged to a smoky jazz club.

Brody glanced at her, a glance that was both inquisitive and wary at the same time, one fitting the occasion when a beautiful young woman says hello to a complete stranger at a bar. Playing the part. She smiled again, like she could read his mind, like she was attempting to reassure him that it was alright, that everything was alright. Brody went along with it.

'Hello,' he said, returning the smile.

The bartender placed her drink onto the counter. He was dressed in a red half jacket with *Herbert Park Platinum* embroidered onto the breast pocket, a white shirt underneath and black bow tie. His right sleeve rode up as he did, revealing the edge of a tattoo, what looked to be a bird's claw. Brody felt certain something passed between them, a look.

Her drink was whiskey on ice, with a thin, short straw sticking out of it. She picked up the glass and pushed the straw between her luscious lips, her cheeks contracting as she drew the liquid in.

'You a regular?' Brody asked, stirring his drink again. He'd only taken one sip. He didn't like it. In fact, he wanted to spit it out. But it looked the part. What a successful businessman such as he – maybe after closing a big deal – might drink in a place like this.

Brody could tell the question had taken her by surprise.

'A regular? Why'd you ask that?'

'Your drink? You didn't order. The bartender just placed it down without you asking.'

Brody wondered if he hadn't overplayed his hand. Was this the part where she got up and slunk away? He thought she seemed to be considering it. But then again, if she really thought he was a cop, a guard, then she'd also think that would be the last question he'd ask. Brody threw her a wide, innocent grin.

She didn't slink away. No. She uncrossed her legs, then crossed them again, changing position, picked up her glass and took a long sip, leaving nothing but coloured water behind.

'I suppose you could say that,' she said. 'I like it here. What about you?'

'Me?' Brody replied. 'Yes, I like it here too.'

'Well, of course, everyone likes it here. No, what I meant is, are you a regular too?'

'So that must mean you are, because you just used the word *too*. Are you on business as well?'

Her eyes narrowed.

'You ask a lot of questions, you know that. Are you a cop?'

'And if I was?'

She laughed.

'You don't look like one. What would you be doing in a

place like this if you were? Undercover? I don't think so.' She laughed again, holding his gaze. 'I am. On business. You asked if I was on business. Yes, I am…if you get me.'

She raised an eyebrow mischievously, at the same time bringing up her leg a little, offering him a view into the mouth of a dark, sensual chasm.

'Oh, I get you,' he said.

Her eyebrow came down, knitted together with the other one.

'Why don't you buy me a drink, and I can tell you all about it? We can take it to your room if you like.'

Brody was silent, like he was thinking about it. All part of the show. Then: 'I like the sound of that. Why don't we do just that.'

THE FOYER where they were standing as they waited for the elevator was busy. A loud group of uppity student types, fresh faced, in tuxedos and evening dresses, were sitting around, half cut, drinking in the centre. At other tables the business types, dressed like Brody was dressed, sat. Through it all rumbled bell carts loaded with suitcases, pulled by porters trailing the latest batch of new arrivals. It was just gone 11 p.m. on a Tuesday night, but the place had the feel of a busy VIP airport lounge. Brody had the distinct impression he was being watched. The concierge, maybe, who seemed to be looking his way, so too one of the desk agents, standing at his station along the wall just inside the door.

The elevator arrived, and she stepped in first. Brody was about to follow when he spotted the man emerge from a door to his right. As the door swung closed again, he saw it had *Staff Only, Otherwise For Emergencies Only* written on it in block letters. Something about the fella caught his attention, set Brody's cop's nose twitching. The fella walked quickly but calmly across the foyer towards the main entrance. *Click,* as Brody took a mental snapshot, and looked at his watch, 11:04, then *click* again. He filed both away.

'Come on, baby,' she said coyly, the elevator doors starting to close.

'You never told me your name,' Brody said, stepping in.

She flicked a hand through her hair and made a twittering sound, came right up to him until they were touching. She didn't smell of perfume. She didn't smell of anything, simply fresh air.

'Does it matter?'

She touched his crotch without warning. Brody froze. She stepped back, laughing, normal service resumed.

'Call me whatever you want, big fella...hm.'

Brody reckoned she was high, or acting as if she was. She began a pole dance routine but without the pole, miming shimmying up and down it, one hand holding the imaginary column of metal, running the other across her breasts. The elevator pinged the third floor, and the doors opened. She straightened, laughing, stepping out, draping an arm around his waist as she slinked along next to him, making that twittering sound again, like she was laughing at her own private joke. Maybe she was. Maybe the joke was him?

They went into the room, and she closed the door and leaned against it, observing him.

'Hm, all alone at last, big fella?' She pulled one of the dress straps from her shoulder, did the same with the other one, tugged at the top of the little black number and lowered it to just beneath her breasts, cocooned in a black lace bra. They weren't so big after all, not as they'd appeared when she'd walked into the bar. She actually had small breasts, Brody thought, but she made the most of them.

She stepped towards him, pressed her lips against his, giggled, and walked by.

'Unless you want to do it on the floor – I don't mind, baby – but where's the bedroom?'

He pointed, but she'd already spotted it and was heading in its direction.

'The menu,' she said when she went in, turning on all the lights until the room resembled a doctor's surgery more than it did a boudoir. She moved to the bed and sat down.

'The menu?' Brody, knowing what she meant but acting like he didn't, lingered in the doorway.

'Yes, the menu. What you'd like. Oral, covered or French, swallow or catch, full sex, ditto, half hour, one hour, two, all night if you want, whatever. No anal. A girl's got to have standards, after all. But I'm open to anything else. Ha, ha, open, you get it? Come on, big fella, what's it to be? The meter's running.'

'Um...' Brody knew that *um* would sound good. Authentic.

She lay back, to help him make up his mind, it seemed, the short dress riding up her thighs, all the way to her waist. She wasn't wearing any underwear.

'Um,' Brody said again, and this time he meant it; he wasn't acting.

'Could you step closer, baby? Come on, I don't bite...not unless you want me to, that is.'

Brody stepped closer.

'And *closer*. Come on. What's a girl got to do? Jeez. Or

maybe you just want to stand there and gawk? Some do. That's fine too. I can do that. You like what you see, baby?'

'Um...'

'Or maybe you don't like what you see.' She sat up, reclined back onto her elbows. 'Maybe you want me to pull my dress back down again and leave? Do you want that, baby?'

Brody shook his head. 'Um...I didn't say that, did I?' He was careful of his words, knowing that whatever judge this ended up before might decide he had somehow invited her to stay when she'd expressed a wish to leave. Which might mitigate her role in this caper, might see her walk free. Brody didn't want that. No way.

'Okay,' she cooed, 'you want me. That's good. Come on, big fella, take your clothes off...'

'Um...'

'Hm, I think you're a little shy. That's cute. I can touch myself first. Look. Hm. Get you in the mood, yeah. You like?'

There was a knock on the door. Sudden and loud. It came again. Louder this time. She didn't seem in the least surprised. That was because she wasn't. But Brody had to act like he was.

'Who the hell's that?' Authentic.

'I ordered a bottle of champagne. On me, baby. That's room service. Call it an appreciation of your business...Hm, come on, baby, go get that bottle of champagne and join me.'

'Um.'

'You say that a lot, sweetie, *um*, you know that?' She stopped what she was doing. 'I'm getting a little fed up with it, to tell you the truth. It's beginning to grate on my nerves. Now, will you go and open that fucking door, please?'

Brody did and had to act surprised when the two goons

rushed in. They didn't look like your average goons, being young and slim, wearing designer tracksuits and sneakers, sporting buzzcuts. But goons they were, nonetheless.

'W-what's this? Who're you?' Brody was impressed, if he said so himself: pass basic acting skills, show surprise building to alarm in situation of sudden jeopardy.

The smaller of the two, he had a nasty glint in his eyes, pulled apart his tracksuit top so Brody could see the handle of what he had in there; it looked like either a large knife or a small machete. Brody guessed small machete. The other fella looked suspiciously like the bartender who'd served him in the Patrick Kavanagh bar. Brothers?

'Cindy,' Nasty Eyes said. Brody didn't believe that was her real name. 'Call the pigs.'

Despite the circumstances, Brody wanted to laugh. Like seriously, the *pigs*?

Cindy probably-not-her-real-name was on her feet, straightening her little dress, pulling the straps back into place, as she delivered her line. 'The pigs.' And then she looked at Brody. 'You don't want me to do that, do you, Mr Businessman? I mean, you being married and everything.'

'Also,' the bartender's – possibly – brother said, 'you're a dirty little paedo. You know what age Cindy is, do you?'

Brody said nothing, looking suitably distressed.

'Okay, I'll tell you then. Fifteen, that's how old she is. Yes, you dirty little paedo you. Anyway, you're well fucked now, so you are. Cindy, go on, call the pigs.'

'Wait.' Her tone held a commendable earnestness. 'Let's see. I mean, we don't want to ruin this man's life, not unless we have to, that is. Maybe he's learned his lesson. Have you, Mr Businessman?'

'Oh, y-yes, yes,' Brody stuttered. 'I've learned my lesson.'

Thinking, *really, I ought to be onstage at the national theatre, the Abbey, remarkable performance, bravo, bravo.* 'Truly, I've learned my lesson. Now, if you could just all leave? I'll pay you...Cindy, of course. This won't happen again. Ever. I can assure you all of that. Don't know what I was thinking, to be honest, just got carried along with everything, I suppose. I mean, a girl like you, Cindy, you really are quite beautiful. Fifteen? No, no, I can't believe that. I'm not a paedo, as you put it. So, yes, thank you. Now, thank you too, but can you all just leave.'

Brody pointed to the door, as if that would do it.

Nasty Eyes slow clapped.

'On-fucking-core,' he said.

Brody looked surprised.

'What do you mean?'

The bartender's – possibly – brother approached him. 'I mean, are you really that stupid? Or do you take us for complete eejits?' He extended his hand. 'Hand it over. The Rolex. Give it here.'

'My Rolex?'

'And the ring. What, you thought there wouldn't be a price for all this, did you? A successful businessman such as yourself can't be that stupid. I mean, that's impossible. You can't just take a little fifteen-year-old girl to your bedroom like that and get away with it. No, you dirty little paedo, it doesn't work like that. There has to be a price. So hand them fucking over. Now! Call it a down payment. And be grateful I don't smack you around the room either. Come on, get a move on.'

'Oh, I get it,' Brody said, because the fella had a point. He couldn't be that stupid, or he couldn't appear to be anyway.

'I know what he's thinking,' Nasty Eyes said when Brody

made no effort to remove the watch. 'It's what they all think, he's thinking why? They've nothing on me. Show him, Cindy.'

Cindy reached into her handbag and took out her phone. 'See,' she said, and held it up, a video beginning to play.

But Brody didn't need to see it. He knew what was on there. A recording of what had gone down in the room: with a little editing, enough to blow apart a successful businessman's life, and some. He heard her voice drifting from the phone...*Come on, big fella, the meter's running.*

'Well now,' Brody said, 'I think you've all had quite a run of it, don't you? Look at this.'

He took out his Garda ID wallet from a pocket of the hand-cut Italian suit, and, as he opened it, an armed response team rushed into the room – without any sound, like the TV had been turned to mute during an action movie.

The hotel duty manager had been insistent: guests at the Herbert Park Platinum Hotel must not, under any circumstances, ever be disturbed.

ONCE THE REALITY had dawned on the girl and the goons that Brody had been wearing his own miniature surveillance body camera, they began to understand their little caper was over.

Still, Marty Sheahan, sitting alongside Brody on the other side of the table in the interview room where all three of them sat now, let it be known, in case they still clung to any fairy tales: 'We've compiled twenty-five injured party statements; just to be clear, that's twenty-five people who are willing to testify against you in court, twenty-five very disgruntled men who've lost a lot of money and dignity, twenty-five men you've been blackmailing. They're pissed off, big time. Understandably. And they can't wait to testify.'

Which was a lie. In reality, it was just five men who were willing to testify, and of these, three had the jitters and couldn't be trusted to take it over the line. That left two whom Brody felt he could trust. Enough.

Marty pointed to each of them in turn. 'That's you, Shisha Burke; you, Josh Rock; and you, Bartley Thompson... why look so surprised? You think we haven't worked out who you are? And Shisha, you're pushing it a bit, aren't you, girl? You'll be twenty-five next birthday. Come on. And the barman. Who's he? Is he involved in this? He looks just like you, Bart. A brother?'

All three sat in stunned silence.

'I never said I was fifteen,' Shisha said, 'just so's you know. That's on Bartley, okay?'

'Don't land this on me, bitch,' Bartley shouted. 'I want a solicitor.'

'You,' Marty said, pointing at him. 'Calm down.'

'Hey.' It was Josh Rock's turn. 'We were just passin' by outside. The door was open. We heard Shisha. We thought she was in trouble. Honest.'

'Just passin'?' Brody enquired.

'Out for an evening stroll, was it?' Marty added. 'Along a residents' corridor in one of the best hotels in Dublin? Jaysis, taking us for right eejits yourselves now, boys, aren't ye...? I for one have heard enough. Boss, what about you?'

'Yes, Marty, I agree. I've heard enough too.'

'Wait.' It was Shisha. 'A word.'

'We're all ears.'

'No, in private, I mean.'

'What? Shi?' Bartley whined. 'No fucking way. What you up to?'

'In private,' Shisha insisted.

Bartley jumped to his feet. 'No fucking way. Shi, you can't. It's not fair.'

'No, you bollocks,' Marty said, 'what's not fair is running a honeypot scam on unsuspecting poor plebs for God knows how long. We'll never know. That's what's not fair. But you're all stupid, of course, every one of you. You posted it all, the cars, the bling, on Instagram and Facebook. The only fair part of this is that we got all of you.'

Bartley looked at him, then sat down heavily, like a boxer slumping onto his stool, having gone twelve rounds.

'This way,' Brody said, getting to his feet. Shisha stood as well, and he led her out of the room.

THEY WERE in Store Street garda station, the nearest one to the Herbert Park Platinum Hotel. At the end of the corridor outside the interview room was a discreet seating area. Brody led Shisha here. He told her to sit with her back against the wall in a corner. This way, Brody was satisfied she wasn't going to try to leg it, even if she still was wearing high heels. Brody had learned the hard way; you couldn't be certain of anything in this game. If she did try to make a run, she wouldn't get far.

'So, the other night,' Shisha started, 'I got this weirdo, right. You need to know about him.'

'That's it. That's what you have for me?'

'A right weirdo he was. I said you need to know about him. He needs to be removed from the streets.'

'You think? How very civic minded of you.'

'Yes, I do think.'

'And why do you think?'

'Because of what he said.'

'And what was it he said, Shisha?'

She smiled, her face suddenly like that of a sly fox.

'Well, that's just it. You know, I could say I was…what's the word? Coerced, yes, that's it. I mean, okay, I'm not fifteen, but I never…'

'I know, you never said that you were.'

'Well, I didn't. I mean, what exactly did I do? Nothing. I never did anything to those men.' She dropped her voice. 'It was Josh and Bart, especially Bart. They did it. You'll see.'

'Of course. Nothing to do with you. Come on, Shisha, I didn't come down with the last shower, you're just trying to save your own skin, me girl. This weirdo nonsense is all made up, isn't it?'

'No, it's not.'

'Then talk, tell me.'

'In a minute, right. I'll tell you in a minute. Swear to God. But first. I want you to know I had nothing to do with this tonight. Like I told you, I was coerced. I'm a victim, me.'

'This could be dangerous for you if you are. Those boys, Thompson and Rock, they won't like it.'

'Well, I've told you now; you're going to have to keep me protected, aren't you?'

'Am I?'

'Yeah, it's the law. You do. And the way I see it, those two boys will be going away for a few years. Me, I'm going to Dubai.'

'You are?'

'Yeah, I've met somebody.'

'Shisha, can you not talk about yourself, just for a moment?'

She folded her arms and pouted.

'This weirdo you said I needed to know about, Shisha. Tell me about him.'

She smiled. 'It's a pity.'

'What? What's a pity?'

'You and me. We never, you know…it's still not too late, you know.' She grinned. 'What about it, big fella? And then you let me go, yeah. I promise, you won't be disappointed.'

'Okay, get up, Shisha, we're going back to the interview room right now.'

'Wait, wait, okay, okay. I'll tell you. We were in the room, his room, last…' She looked to the ceiling, then down again. 'Sunday night, yeah, or maybe it was Saturday night, one of them, yeah, I'm not certain…' Her voice trailed off.

'And,' Brody said, 'go on. Shisha, my patience is beginning to wear thin.'

'Just give me a chance. It's like this, only for Josh and Bart were passing by outside…'

'That again.'

'Yeah, that again. But it's true. Only for them passing by and hearin' it an all, he would have killed me, he would. Honest to God.'

She looked at him, and her face displayed a searing honesty that was all the more powerful he guessed because she seldom, if ever, looked that way. Brody knew she was telling the truth.

He spoke softly. 'Okay, Shisha, tell me what happened.'

She looked to the floor and up again, a burning anger in her eyes.

'So,' she said, 'we were in the bar, just the way it was tonight when I met you. It's not something I want to do for the rest of my life, by the way, but for now...'

She paused, looking at him.

'I'm not making any judgements.'

In truth, Brody wondered why she even cared.

'And...well, you know the next part. Anyway, we're in his room...'

'What number?'

'Um, I'm not certain, six two, maybe five two...Josh or Bart'll know. Ask them.'

'Why should they know?' he asked. 'If they were just passing? That's what you said. You were the one who was actually there, in the room.'

That sly-fox look returned to her face as she shrugged.

'They just would, that's all, okay?'

'Okay, because they were watching, isn't that right? Because they knew exactly what room you'd gone into, because they needed to know what room to call to later, after you'd made yourself comfortable...'

'Look, you want to hear about this, or don't you?'

'I want to hear,' Brody said, 'but just so as we understand one another. I don't believe in unicorns.'

'Whatever. I ran through things the same way I did with you. Everything was cool right up to then. But just like that, things changed. Once in the room he said he didn't have to pay for it. He said he never had to pay for it. And what was it about him that made me think that he might pay for it. He started getting angry, really angry, and I started getting scared. I've had shite in the past, people get mad from time to time, you know, it comes with the territory, but I can handle it. This, this was different; he looked like he was going to kill me. I thought he really would.'

She fell silent. Brody didn't say anything, giving her time.

'He grabbed me by the hair, the bastard, can you believe that? Pulled me up off the bed, taking down his fly, shoving my face into his crotch, saying I was going to blow him, and that I was a filthy whore, and then he was going to give it to me up the ass, because that's all I deserved. I screamed and tried to scratch him, but I only caught his shirt. He caught my hand, he was really strong, and he flung me across the room, the bastard. I landed on the floor. But I didn't move. You know why? Because he had a fucking gun in his hand, and he was standing over me, pointing it at my face. I've seen guns, sorry-looking yokes, hundred years old, stuff like that. But this was a proper yoke, a big gun with a silencer on the end, like you'd see in the movies. It would've blown my head clean off.'

Shisha fell silent again, a new look on her face, one of vulnerability, fear and anger all mixed together. If she was telling the truth, and every instinct Brody had told him she was, then this was serious. A nut running round with a piece of artillery like that. Serious.

'And then what happened, Shisha?'

'There was a knock on the door. Thank Christ. I was about to scream. He went and opened it, laughing like it was a lovers' tiff. Thank Christ Josh and Bart came in. When he knew they weren't about to leave again, he let them see the gun. They nearly shite themselves. And then, you know what was the scariest part?'

'No, Shisha, I don't. What?'

'He said nothing. He just closed the door and didn't say

another word. He held the gun in both hands. I could see the look in his eyes. I knew he wanted to kill me, kill us all. I knew it wouldn't bother him one bit either if he did. But something stopped him. It was like he was battling with himself, wanting to kill us but not wanting to at the same time. Then he flung the door open and nodded towards it. We legged it. And that was it. But Jesus. There could be a body up there in that room. Really. Maybe some poor bitch who wasn't as lucky as me.'

Brody wanted to tell her that she wasn't exactly lucky either, but he didn't.

'You should've reported this at the time.'

Shisha began to tremble. 'I know. But I didn't. I couldn't...'

And this man would have known that too, Brody felt sure; otherwise he wouldn't have let them walk away like that. Either way, he was out there now, somewhere. Not a weirdo like she'd said, or not just a weirdo. Because carrying a gun the way she described meant a whole lot more. If everything had gone down the way she said it had, well then, it was only a matter of time before Brody heard about this man again. And that news would not be good, guaranteed.

'Okay, lads, tell me, what room was it in? The weirdo with the gun the other night. I need to know.'

'Didn't Shi tell you?' one of them muttered. Brody guessed it was Thompson. 'You were talking to her for long enough.'

'No. She didn't. She doesn't remember. But one or both of you will.'

The two of them were slumped across the interview table. Neither of them moved. Brody was standing just inside the door. A uniform was with him. Just in case. He walked to the table and banged his palm down onto the surface.

'Fuck off,' the one who had muttered muttered again.

'Lads, not a good attitude, seriously. Tell me the room number, and I might be able to do something for you. Otherwise, it's not looking good.'

'Where's my solicitor? I asked for my brief ages ago.'

Yes, definitely Thompson, the lippy one.

Brody didn't know anything about a solicitor; this case belonged to Store Street now. He looked at the uniform, who just shrugged.

'They usually don't do call-outs,' the uniform offered, 'not in the middle of the night, that is, not unless it's a matter of life or death. Otherwise, it waits until the morning.'

Thompson sat up abruptly. 'That means I'm going to be here all fucking night. Fuck's sake. No way. Get lost. I'm telling you nothing, Mr Pig Man.'

The other one, Rock, who seemed to take his cue from the big dog, Thompson, sat up too.

Brody worked on him.

'You tell me, then, do yourself and your friend here a favour. If you do, I'll get my uniformed colleague here to get that lazy solicitor out of bed and have him come down here right away. We might even send a car round to collect him. Otherwise, you wait until morning. In here. Because there's no cells. That's what I hear.' Brody looked at the uniform. 'That right?'

The uniform didn't flinch. 'No cells, fellas, that's right. You'll both be stiff as a week-old corpse after spending the night in here.' He smiled.

Terrible analogy, Brody thought, *but it seemed to do the trick.*

'Aw, bollocks,' Rock said, 'seventeen two. There. That's the room number.'

Thompson folded his arms, but didn't say a word.

Bingo, Jack thought.

BRODY ASKED Marty Sheahan to contact the hotel and speak with the night manager. The man's name was Roger Halloran, but he refused to talk on the phone. 'How do I know you really are who you say you are?' he asked. Marty thought that was a fair point. 'You could be anybody, a member of the press fishing for a story maybe, I don't know. We get that a lot, by the way.'

Marty might have asked him to look up the number for Store Street on the garda webpage, but he didn't. The hotel wasn't far. Instead, he told him he'd drive over. When he hung up, Brody was standing next to him. He told him he'd go along too; it was looking like there was a lot more to this case than a honeypot scam, a lot more.

It was just gone 1 a.m. when they rolled up in front of the Herbert Park Platinum and parked in a drop-off/pick-up bay just down from the main entrance. They went in. It was deserted except for a member of cleaning staff swinging a polishing machine back and forth across the marble floor. The machine made a humming noise that echoed through the empty, high-ceilinged foyer.

A man was sitting behind the dark wood of the long reception counter, hunched over a computer, a notebook beside him, seemingly ticking off a list against what was before him on the screen. He wore a dazzling white shirt with yellow, gold-edged embroidered braces. The two detectives stared at the top of his head, where a bald patch was spreading out from the centre of his crown. After a moment he looked up.

'Yes?' His face was square, falling seamlessly into the donut collar of blubber below that was his neck. He wore tiger-stripe plastic-rimmed glasses, behind which two tired, bloodshot eyes stared out at them, glancing from one to the other.

'Detective Garda Martin Sheahan.' Marty reached into the inside pocket of his sports jacket. He showed the man his ID. 'And this is Detective Sergeant Jack Brody. Are you the night manager, Roger Halloran?'

'Yes, that's me, glorified night porter is what I am, if you want to know the truth...You know, I always wanted to be a guard.'

'You did?'

'Yeah, but it's my club foot, only slight, mind, so slight you'd hardly notice, but it was enough.'

'Sorry to hear that,' Marty said, wondering why the man was bothering to share this information in the first place.

'Anyway, what's this to do with?' Halloran wanted to know.

'Maybe nothing,' Marty said. 'Room seventeen two. That would be a start. Who's staying there?'

'Let me see.'

Halloran tapped a couple of keys on the keyboard, scrolled an index finger across, tapped once. 'Seventeen two, you said. Guest checked out yesterday morning. Name Matías De León. A Chilean national.'

'Anyone in there now?'

'Mr Scott Anderson should be, except his flight from Atlanta was cancelled. Technical issues, he said. He's arriving later this afternoon.'

'Can I take a look, please?'

'Around the room?'

'What else? Yes.'

'What's this all to do with? I mean, we had that commotion this evening. It was like an episode of *Cops*. Anything I should know about?'

'No,' Marty said, 'nothing you need to know about…for now.'

'And' – it was Brody – 'a question. Tonight. In the Patrick Kavanagh. The bar staff. Have they all gone home?'

'Who? The bar staff? Are you referring to anyone specific?'

'Tattoo on his right arm, medium build.'

'That wouldn't be so easy to spot. The tattoo. He always wears a jacket. That's why you're a guard, I suppose. You're talking about the deputy head barman, Matt Thompson, he…'

Well, well…

'Thompson, you say?' Brody interrupted.

'Thompson. Yes. What of it?'

'Is he still around?'

The night manager who thought he was nothing more than a night porter tapped his computer keyboard a couple of times. 'Should be. He hasn't cleared out his tills yet. So, not gone home. He's still in there. Or should be. Will I call him for you or what?'

'No,' Brody said. 'How do I go in there? Is the bar locked?'

'Not locked, because the keys haven't been handed in yet either. Everything goes in the night safe. He might still have residents in there, drinking; he can't close until they've all gone.'

'Thank you. I'll go and have a look once we finish here.'

'Gentlemen,' Roger Halloran said, 'can you tell me what this is all about? Has to be something important if it's got you two coming in here at this time of night. Is it to do with what happened earlier or not?'

Brody gave him the answer police officers the world over always seemed to give at a time like this.

'Routine investigation,' he said.

'Routine investigation,' Halloran repeated, not looking like he believed any of it.

'Room seventeen two,' Marty said, 'can you give me a temporary room card, please? We need to move this along, thank you.'

'It would be quicker if I just went with you, if that's alright.'

'That's alright.'

'Meet you back here, Marty, okay,' Brody said. 'I'll go talk to the barman.'

'Sound, boss, meet you back here.'

Brody set off across the foyer towards the Patrick Kavanagh bar, leaving Marty to go check out the room.

WHEN HE PUSHED OPEN the door, the bar lay mostly in darkness. Except, that is, for a strip of light like a yellow fog emanating from behind the bar. Brody stood stock-still just inside the door, listening. He could hear nothing. He made his way between the tables and chairs towards the counter. There were no residents in here drinking. There was nobody in here; the place was deserted. At the bar, Brody could see that the cash register was open. It lay on a shelf opposite, set within in a cocoon of liquor bottles topped by silver pourers. A bar in a hotel like this wouldn't deal so much in cash as in room and credit card charges. But it would deal with enough, especially at €30 a pop for a mojito.

Someone was in here, Brody knew it, someone who didn't want him to know they were here. He turned and walked back towards the door, opened it, like he was about to leave, but instead stepped quickly to the side, pressing himself into the corner by the door, lost to the darkness.

And waited.

He didn't have to wait long.

THE NIGHT MANAGER who considered himself really a night porter led Marty from the elevator on the seventh floor to room seventeen two. He slid the room card into the security slot on the door, a light turning from red to green as it pinged once.

He pushed the door open and turned the room lights on. They stepped in.

'What's this cost per night?' Marty asked.

'Depends,' Halloran answered. 'Mr De León paid €950. Mr Anderson will pay more, over a thousand, something to do with the computer algorithm. Don't ask me. I don't need to understand; they just tell me what to charge.'

The room didn't look anything special to Marty. It was just a hotel room, a bed, a dresser with a mirror above it, the usual, maybe a trouser press in a wardrobe. Nothing unusual. Just a hotel room.

'I won't ask,' Marty said, 'but I didn't think hotel prices could fluctuate like that.'

'Well, they can. Now you know.'

'Now I know,' Marty agreed. He crossed to the window and looked out. At least the view was nice. He could see over Herbert Park in the near distance, a ribbon of streetlamps about it like a necklace.

He looked around, not sure for what, but anything to back up Shisha's story: in the bathroom, under the bed, in the wardrobes, even pulled the trouser press – yes, there was one – out and looked behind that. Of course, there was nothing here. The housekeeping staff would have found anything if there was. Maybe they did. In any case, all traces of De León were gone, though something might be found if they forensically combed it. It was a hotel room, after all; fingerprints would be revealed by blue light everywhere. Take your pick. But that wasn't going to happen. There was no reason to. Other than the word of Shisha that something happened here, that is. And that wouldn't be enough.

'Thank you, Mr Halloran,' he said. 'I've seen all I need to; we can go now.'

THE SOUND WAS like that of a scurrying mouse. It would stop for a moment, then start again, stop start, stop start. But Brody knew it wasn't a mouse. His eyes searched through the darkness, and he realised it really wasn't that dark at all. His pupils, fully dilated, squeezed every last scrap of light there was, diluting the darkness, giving everything except the darkest nooks a pale, translucent sheen. He pushed himself further into his nook by the door.

The scurrying mouse sound had a beat to it. As Brody listened, the sound seemed to change slightly, very slightly, becoming duller. He decided what it was; it was someone tapping, like on a keyboard but not a keyboard, because a keyboard had a distinctive sound all of its own. No, this was a tapping sound on something smaller. But while they were tapping, then they wouldn't be looking for him.

Brody stepped out from his nook, made his way silently and quickly between the tables and chairs, the obstacle course visible to him like he was watching it through a night sight. He reached the corner of the bar and peered along it behind the counter to the other end. There he could see the shadowed outline of a figure standing in an alcove, behind it stacks of boxes against a wall, black wording, *200 Napkins Plain*, visible on some of them, other shelves taken up by bottles of liquor and stacks of glasses. It was a small storage area for the bar. The shadowed figure leaned forward, and Brody could make out a man's features in the smoky glow of light like a ghostly apparition. He guessed the light was from the display on a credit card payment console.

He reached out his hand and felt along the corner wall on the other side of the counter. This is where they usually placed electrical switches, out of sight. Sure enough, he felt a metal faceplate and the outline of plastic switches, straining to reach the top row. He paused. What to do if he turned these on?

He could see the apparition still hunched in the glow of light ahead. He didn't know who this person was, maybe it was Thompson, and maybe this was all completely legit; maybe it was just the way this person liked to work, having all the lights off. Maybe, but Brody doubted it. In any case, he didn't have to worry about turning the lights on. Someone else did.

They flooded the room, dazzling him, as a voice boomed, 'You in there, boss.'

There was the sound of footsteps.

Brody turned. Marty was standing there.

'Boss,' he said.

Brody caught a movement in the corner of his eye and looked again along behind the counter just as the figure leaped over the wooden countertop, landing onto its hunkers on the other side, squatting briefly, its hands touching the ground, like a startled wild primate. In an instant the figure bounded up again and bolted forward across the bar towards the door.

'Stop him,' Brody yelled, scrambling in pursuit.

But Marty didn't move. Not right away. He was a good mule, but studying law the way he was and almost now at his final destination, that of bar-registered, fully fledged solicitor, had made him contemplative and circumspect. Which had its uses, but not now. The figure was almost at the door before he even seemed to register.

The figure pulled the door open, disappearing through to the foyer. Brody followed, emerged just in time to see him tearing towards the main door, almost at it when…

The figure's arms sprang up in a reflex as his upper body shot forward, but his feet remained firmly rooted to the spot as he sprawled onto the polished marble floor, the flex of the polishing machine trailing behind like a tether, twisted around his ankles. The figure cursed and tried to stand again, but in doing so only served to wrap the flex tighter around his ankles as he toppled to the floor again.

By then Brody had reached him and was standing above,

peering down. The deputy head barman wasn't wearing his red jacket with *Herbert Park Platinum* embroidered on the breast pocket now. His white shirt was short sleeved, so Brody could clearly see the tattoo. He'd been correct. It was indeed that of a bird's claw, from an image of an eagle, its wings outstretched, talons extended as it swooped in for the kill.

As Brody was doing now. He reached down and grabbed the collar of Thompson's shirt, twisted it and said, 'Come on, fella, on your feet.'

A PATROL CAR was summoned from Store Street to come and collect Matt Thompson. He did not answer any questions while they waited in the foyer, staring blankly at Brody when he asked him if he was the brother of Bart Thompson. But they were related, definitely; you only had to look at them to know that. He said nothing either when Brody pulled the wad of cash, mainly €50 and €20 notes from his back pocket, a total of €1,555, give or take, as well as a printout of credit card numbers taken from the card machine. Thompson had been breaking for the border with whatever he could carry, it seemed. The numbers would be milked for all they were worth until the card holders became aware and cancelled them. Brody wondered why Thompson had even bothered. If he hadn't, it wouldn't have been so easy to pin anything on him. Outwardly, he'd done nothing wrong up until now. Yet, Brody imagined, it was only a matter of time before the others ratted him out anyway, and he knew it. So it probably made no difference. With dens of thieves, it was always the same. Anyway, this was Store Street's baby now. That was the arrangement.

'I could have been quicker,' Marty said, 'instead of standing there looking on with me gob open. Sorry, boss.'

'Lucky we had backup, then.' Brody pointed. 'The polishing machine, I mean.'

Marty glanced to it sheepishly.

'What about the room?' Brody asked. 'You find anything in it?'

Marty shook his head. 'Nothing.'

'No surprises,' Brody said.

'You think there's something in Shisha's story? I mean, being threatened with a gun like that.'

Brody looked at Thompson. 'You hear anything about that, sunshine?'

Thompson maintained that blank stare of his, but spoke. 'Don't know what you're talking about.'

'I didn't think you would,' Brody answered, then looked at Marty. 'Quite a tale, though, to roll off her tongue if there's nothing to it. CCTV might tell us something.' He yawned. 'But that can wait until tomorrow.'

Marty yawned too, an involuntary movement that seemed contagious.

'That's a plan,' Marty said.

Outside, the Store Street marked unit rolled up.

2

Brody got back to his home in Drumcondra at a little after 2:15 a.m. He was pleasantly surprised to see Ashling Nolan's car parked against the kerb. Six months into their relationship, they'd recently exchanged house keys. She'd already shown up a couple of times like this, unannounced. There was one bad relationship in her past that Brody knew of. Something told him she showed up unannounced to reassure herself both that she could do it, and also that Brody wasn't seeing anybody else.

Ashling Nolan was lying on her side in Brody's bed. She turned on the light as he crept into the room.

'Sorry. I tried not to wake you.'

'That's okay, I was only half asleep anyway.'

He yawned. 'I'm wrecked.'

'You know, before you got home, I was thinking, what if Jack comes back with someone...?'

'Someone?'

'Okay, another woman. That would be awkward.'

'Ashling, seriously? Come on?'

'You're later than I thought.'

'A fifteen-year-old tried to seduce me, that's why.'

'W-what?'

Ashling watched him undress as he told her of the honeypot scam. He hung up the hand-cut Italian suit in his wardrobe and took off the Rolex. All to be returned to the seized property storeroom at HQ, as good as any TV prop department. He slipped under the duvet next to her, and she poked him with a finger. 'Fifteen years old. I didn't know what you meant. God. Anyway, I thought I'd surprise you by showing up. You're not mad, are you, that I didn't tell you?'

'How could I be mad? It's nice. Really nice. I'm flattered, actually. No, not mad.'

She smiled. 'Good.' And kissed him gently.

Brody pulled her close, holding her, breathing in her fragrance, feeling her soft skin against his. Didn't this woman know how beautiful and wonderful she was? It seemed not. It seemed she didn't believe it. They kissed, their lips lingering, neither wanting to pull away. Jack's tiredness began to melt like ice beneath a hot sun as he forgot about everything, lost in the moment.

They made love slowly and afterwards lay on their sides facing each other. Jack stayed awake for a while after her eyes closed, listening to the gentle rhythm of her breathing telling him she had slipped into sleep. And then he closed his eyes too, and drifted off, listening to that gentle rhythm, like ocean surf gently lapping to shore.

3

Matt Thompson was sitting on a hard wooden bench next to the uniform who'd arrested and taken him to Store Street, awaiting his turn to be processed by the custody sergeant. Thompson rubbed his right wrist where a welt had formed from the cuffs the arresting guard had just removed. Although it was Tuesday night – well, actually, it was early Wednesday morning now – Store Street was living up to its official title of being the busiest station in the country. At the custody desk a prisoner was kicking off, a big strapping lad with a strong country accent. No doubt he was normally the epitome of good manners and politeness. Not now. 'You can all fuck off...' he shouted. 'I've done nothing wrong, d'ya hear. You're persecuting me like Enoch Burke.'

Enoch Burke was a teacher who'd lost his job and took to standing outside his old school every day. For a time, the country was obsessed with his antics. The man believed he was being persecuted for his beliefs.

The custody sergeant said he begged to differ, that head-butting a pub doorman and kicking in a plate-glass window didn't meet his definition of having done nothing wrong. The country lad, his face like an overripe tomato and fit to burst, roared something unintelligible and dove across the counter, writhing and squirming about like a beached catfish (he had a moustache), as a bunch of uniforms ran and piled on top of him, pinning him down. One of them was the uniform who'd arrested Thompson, leaving the prisoner on his own. Thompson looked on at the melee and, after a moment, casually got to his feet and stretched, turned and sauntered over to the door he'd just come through a short while before from the car park. He expected at any moment someone to shout or run down and jump him. But they didn't. The country lad was strong as an ox. He was keeping everyone busy. Thompson reached the door and stood to the side. It was locked, of course, he knew that, but it wouldn't be long before it opened again and a couple of cops came in with another prisoner. He stood there, his face to the wall, his back to the custody counter, keeping his cool, knowing by the sounds of the commotion that the uniforms were still struggling to land their catfish. He distracted himself from thinking that he was going to be noticed at any moment by considering that they weren't the same anymore, cops, that is. You could find some of the smallest, puniest specimens of humankind wearing a garda uniform these days. Size didn't matter, that's what they said, but everyone knew that was a load of bollocks. It did; size was everything. It suited him just fine now, though. He waited, looking at the wall, expecting someone to shout, *Hey, what's that prisoner doing there? Get him!*

But still nothing happened. It couldn't last much longer, just couldn't. He took a deep breath and held it, pushing it down, down, as far as it would go, held it until he couldn't hold it any longer. He released it again, forcing himself to keep the outtake slow and steady. Still, nothing happened.

Then he heard it, the sound he'd been waiting for, the metallic rasping of the lock mechanism being released as someone punched in the security code on the pad on the other side. He stood there, just down from the door, waiting. The two uniforms with their prisoner between them came in, not even glancing his way. 'What the...' one of them said, taking in the commotion dead ahead, while his partner ran to assist, and he waited with the prisoner. Thompson slipped out the door before it had a chance to shut again.

At the top of the door was a small rectangle of toughened glass. Not that they would right now, but if someone were to peer out, they would have seen Thompson tear across the car park, take a flying leap at the metal gate on the other side, scamper up it, shimmy over the top and disappear.

By the time someone did eventually look for him, he was long gone.

4

Brody heard about the escape the next morning when he got to the office. There was no point in getting angry. Prisoners escaped – it happened, rarely, but it happened. Most were quickly apprehended again, as in the following minutes and hours, before the shite hit the fan. Which is what Store Street would want now, and especially before the press heard about it. Embarrassing, yes, but all in house; so far, that is.

Brody moved on. He opened his emails. There was a message from the main switchboard. It read:

Roger Halloran, Herbert Park Platinum Hotel, rang wanting to speak to you. Said he knocks off work at 8 a.m., and if you don't get this message in time, you can contact him on his mobile, 089-423-88765. Says he's come across something of interest.

It was 8:15 a.m. Brody got onto that immediately and rang the mobile number, listened to it ring five times before it connected to an answering service. He left a message, telling Halloran he'd ring him again later, and hung up. He next checked Pulse. The honeypot scam team had previously been on as intelligence listings only. But now they were the stars of their very own show, their names up in lights on an official numbered incident, Matt Thompson included. Pulse revealed that Matt and Bart were indeed related, Matt being the older brother. Every one of them had multiple incidents on their individual Pulse catalogues, but very few convictions, mainly for minor traffic offences and a couple of simple possessions, but nothing major. Brody thought that interesting; they were either new to the caper or very good at what they did. Until now, that is. In any case, all, apart from Matt, had been transferred to Mountjoy prison on remand, to appear before a judge later that day. They'd likely get bail and be released once they'd surrendered their passports and agreed to sign on at their local garda station each day for the duration of the bail time. The case was cut, dried, wrapped and placed onto the judicial process conveyor belt as far as Brody was concerned. They couldn't wriggle out of this. No one could. All that was missing was Matt.

But still, something nagged at him, as he remembered the individual he'd seen exiting the employees' door at the hotel the evening before. Maybe it was nothing; maybe it was just the way it looked, someone knocking off duty and going home after a long shift. Maybe his cop's nose was twitching just that little bit too much. *Maybe I need a holiday?*

Brody considered it. *Not such a bad idea.* A Ryanair flight to the Costas was as easy as taking a train to Westport. About the same price too. Imagine that. He could surprise Ashling. He thought about that too. And smiled. *I like this idea.* Still, he couldn't surprise *surprise* her. Wouldn't she need to know in advance so she could book time off work? Hm, did this mean he was further deepening his relationship with her? Taking it up a notch, as they say. Would that be such a bad thing? Would she see it the same way too? Is that what he wanted? Is that what she wanted? What the hell did he want anyway? And what...?

'Penny for them.'

He looked up. Superintendent Fiona Ryan was standing there in the doorway to his office. He looked at her warily, like he would a dog wagging its tail but one that had once tried to bite him. Ryan was the new unit CO, having replaced the Old Man, who'd been killed, not so much in the line of duty, but on a siding connected to it. Not that the Old Man could ever be replaced. At best, Ryan might put on his shoes, plod about in them as best she could, but she would never, could never, fill them. What Brody was firmly convinced she should try to do instead was not bother wearing them at all, but instead leave things alone, as they were, the way they'd always been. The members of the MCIU knew what they were doing. As the saying goes, if it ain't broke, don't fix it.

But, to give her her due, lately Ryan seemed to be doing just that. She had lost much of that arrogance she'd brought with her when she'd moved from her old unit, the SDU, better known as the KGB. She had sided with them in a recent joint operation, and she had backed the wrong horse. Her wrong call had softened her cough, as they say. Which explained why she was smiling now at him, even if those small, hard orbs of hers weren't smiling at all; they remained as cold as ever.

'Good result,' she said, 'you emptied the honeypot. Store Street are pleased.'

Brody wondered if this remark was an attempt at

humour. If so, he wanted to tell her not to put herself forward for a slot at any comedy club soon. And that was another difference between herself and the Old Man. With his old boss, Brody could throw anything onto the table, it didn't matter, how he felt if something didn't feel right, as with the fella he'd seen scurrying out the employee door (Brody had now decided that was what this person was doing, scurrying). The Old Man would understand that because he believed in instinct. The new CO had shown herself to be a different breed entirely, a person who ran things according to the manual, even if she interpreted the manual to suit her own needs. No, Superintendent Ryan didn't do instinct, not so much anyway. She followed the contents listing for direction and the index listing for verification. This approach was everything to her; that was the way it seemed to Brody; it was her barometer and her compass. Outside of it, as far as he was concerned, she appeared lost.

'Yes,' Brody said, 'we did.'

She was silent. The honeypot was, as she put it, emptied as a result of information received, by Brody that is, specifically from a tout, one who occasionally provided him with information, a tout most officers wouldn't touch with a barge pole because fact and fiction seemed to exist on the same plane for him; he didn't care. What mattered was how much he could earn, that's all, or how much he could get out of it. As it was with any tout. But Brody had a way of reading him. And he'd rarely been wrong. He knew Superintendent Ryan didn't like it, his source, mainly because it wasn't hers. It gave a power to Brody that she didn't like, even if she was doing her best not to show it.

Brody changed the subject.

'Maybe it's time to take a little time off, I was thinking. A week's leave might be good...you'd approve if I did?'

'Of course I'd approve.'

In fact, Brody considered, she seemed delighted at the prospect.

His mobile phone rang. Brody recognised the number. It was the one he'd dialled just a couple of moments ago.

SUPERINTENDENT RYAN LEANED against the doorjamb.

'Something up?' she asked when he placed the phone down again after the call.

'Maybe.' He stood, reaching for the jacket draped over the back of his chair – a five-year-old Canada Goose that still looked as good as the day he'd bought it.

'Want to share, Jack?'

This was the best she could come up with: *Want to share?* And first-name terms now, was it? If there was anything worse than a commanding officer who had difficulty garnering respect, it was one who seemed desperate for it.

'I don't have secrets,' Brody said, and looked her straight in the eyes. He saw one of them twitch. She wasn't the same cocky person who'd presented six or so months ago, loud and in your face, oh no. 'My information will go on Pulse,' he said, 'just as it should do, as everyone's should do. And that phone call was from the night manager at the Herbert Park Platinum. He says a guest who should be checking out this morning has placed a *Do Not Disturb* sign on the door of the room she's been staying in, number 532. He'd spoken to her. She's from Athlone, a woman by the name of Sabina Happy.'

Ryan gave him a funny look.

'Yes,' Brody said. 'Happy. An unusual surname, that's why he remembers it. She told him she had her two Pomeranians in a boarding kennel and had to be back home in Athlone by midday. So she had to check out this morning. If she didn't, she wouldn't be able to make it back in time to collect them; then she'd have to pay for an extra day, at premium rate. She told him all this. He thinks it's unusual, so he rang me.'

'*That's* unusual.'

'Maybe.'

'I don't think that's unusual. Not really. How could that be unusual?'

And there you have it, Brody thought. The reason certain crimes go unsolved, the reason people leave a station in disgust, having tried to report something to an officer who just wouldn't take it seriously. Police officers, Brody knew, were intrinsically lazy. If it didn't click a box, if it didn't fit the criteria according to the manual, if it couldn't be looked up in the index, then it often didn't exist. But it did, of course, that's the thing. They just couldn't see it, that's all. And, unfortunately, that's how it worked. Just like Superintendent Ryan here. Brody wondered again how she had managed to get as far up the totem pole as she had.

'We'll see,' he said. 'I need to have a look at this. It won't take long. The honeypot scam. One of the suspects, the female, Shisha, claims a john pulled a gun on her the other evening in that same hotel; she felt certain he was about to kill her. He didn't only because her two accomplices came in right on cue.'

'You believe her?'

'I didn't say that. I don't know.'

Ryan looked like she was weighing up her options, and said nothing, keeping her powder dry, as it were.

THERE WAS no one in the unit room when Brody called down – it had been a late night, after all, for both himself and Marty. Nicola Considine was dealing with a case of vehicles stolen, officially known as UTs for unauthorised taking, having their front ends cut off and exported to Africa at the back of shipping containers. An unusual one. Seemingly the front end with the engine attached was all the criminals were after. As for Steve Voyle, he was just back from a hiking trip in the north of Spain and was still readjusting in what Brody called the decompression chamber: it took a change of attitude, not altitude, to switch from the solitude and contemplation of the highlands of north Spain to dealing with the dregs of society every day. They'd both be in in their own time.

He rang Marty on the way to the hotel. Marty was driving in. Brody told him to divert and meet him at the hotel. When he got there, Marty was already parked up, waiting for him in the car park.

Now, in the daylight, he saw that there was also a revolving door at the front of the hotel, an intricate affair of brass handles, glass panes and an elaborately carved fascia. He hadn't noticed it last time. But the two detectives went in through the same revolving door as they had the night before. The Herbert Park Platinum exuded a different vibe in daylight than it did at night: no drunken students for a start – such a thing would not be allowed. Instead, it buzzed with a vibrant, subdued energy, with constant activity, as the movers and shakers of Dublin congregated, meeting and sealing deals and doing whatever movers and shakers do.

The desk agent was harried. He was dealing with a book-in, and his telephone began ringing when Brody started to introduce himself. He picked it up and glanced at Brody's ID, his hand pressing down on the mouthpiece. He said nothing, reached under the counter and took out a pass card, handed it to Brody. The detectives went to the fifth floor and midway along the corridor stopped outside room number 532. Hanging from the doorknob was the *Do Not Disturb* sign, just as the night manager who thought he really was a glorified night porter said it would be.

BRODY KNOCKED on the door a couple of times and, when he didn't get a reply, slid the room card into the reader, waited for the light to turn green, and pushed the door open. The curtains were pulled. Brody had taken a couple of steps, Marty right behind him, when he saw it. They both stopped. A wall light was on, casting it in half shadow, the body that was lying draped over the side of the bed.

'My God,' Marty said.

Brody took the Maglite he always carried from his belt and switched it on, directing the beam onto the woman's face and expanding it. He could clearly see in the very centre of her forehead a neat black hole, like a third eye, the size of a small coin, some red smudging along the edges, but not much. The body was naked, and there was a similar hole in the right upper chest. The bedsheet beneath was soaked in blood, nodules congealing on top of the folds like a crimson surf. Her face was frozen and grey, on it a look of complete surprise, like she was saying *what just happened?* The body was slightly arched, the legs folded over the side of the bed, its head turned towards the door, the direction she'd probably been shot from as she'd looked at her killer. In Victorian times, they believed the image of a killer was captured on the victim's eyes just at the moment of death. While optography had never been completely discounted in some quarters, as a forensic science it had been totally debunked.

'Back up, Marty,' Brody said.

They left the room and went back down to the foyer. While they waited for the nomads to arrive – the technical bureau, the SOC, and Dr McBain, forever travelling from one grisly scene to another – Brody went to the back office to speak with the hotel's general manager. While he did this, he asked Marty to go to the bar and see what he could pick up about Matt Thompson.

Unlike the night manager, who thought he was a night porter, the general hotel manager exuded no sense of self-doubt about his role; he was a *proper* manager. His name was Chris Glynn. He looked the part too: mid-fifties, tall, slim, distinguished, with a quiff of grey hair above a tanned face that had now suddenly gone very pale as Brody told him of what he and Marty had found in room 532.

'Dead?' he said. 'What? Are you sure?'

'Very sure.'

'How? Why?'

'She was shot. As for the reasons why, I don't know.'

'S-shot, are you absolutely...'

'Yes, Mr Glynn,' Brody said. 'I am absolutely sure. Yes. Now, listen up. CCTV, I'm going to need all you have, and I want a complete manifest of guests for the past, oh, let's make it the entire week, and staff too...You do know about your barman, Matt Thompson, don't you? You've heard, of course?'

'Yes, I've heard.' Chris Glynn ran a hand through that thick quiff of his and closed his eyes, like this was all a bad dream and everything would be back to normal when he opened them again.

He opened them again, and it wasn't.

He looked like he was about to get sick.

AT THIS HOUR, the Patrick Kavanagh bar was practically deserted. One or two tables were taken up by coffee drinkers, but the midday rush had not yet begun. A female member of the bar staff was leaning over a sink as Marty approached; he could hear the sound of running water beneath the counter. There was no indication anywhere of what had happened the night before. All was normal. She looked up and turned the tap off, straightened, reached for a tea towel and dried her hands on it. She was blonde, and she might have been attractive, but it was hard to tell beneath all the make-up she had on. She smiled, white teeth filling the space between lipstick-red lips trimmed with an edge of burgundy.

'Good morning, sir, what can I get you?'

'Good morning to you too,' Marty said casually, 'how's it goin'?' His law studies module on client liaison and interaction highlighted the importance of an informal, friendly manner, of striving to make clients as relaxed and as comfortable as possible. Similar to the positive bedside manner medical doctors were now being encouraged to adopt. It even had a positive effect on health outcomes, they said. Which in law could mean better client recall and a more honest and engaging dialogue. Ditto for police work. Marty smiled. Her name tag said *Imogen*.

'I'm fine,' she replied, 'thanks for asking, and you?'

'I'm good, Imogen, good. Now, my name is Detective Garda Martin Sheahan. I'd like to ask you a couple of questions? That alright?' He took out his ID wallet, opened it and held it out to her.

Imogen leaned in close and peered at it.

'I really should be wearing my glasses. I tried contact lenses, but my eyes hurt. I don't think glasses really suit me.'

'Take all the time you want,' Marty said.

She nodded, finally satisfied, and straightened. 'Has this something to do with what happened last night? It has, hasn't it? I heard about it this morning. Matty's in trouble, isn't he?'

'Matty? Matt Thompson, you mean?'

'Uh-huh.'

'Yes, Imogen, it seems like it.'

'I always knew it.'

'You did?'

'Yes, he always came across as trouble to me.' She glanced over her shoulder, then left and right, finally leaned in close again and whispered, 'I don't know how he got a job here. He told me once that he was in prison. He was a bit drunk, granted. We were at a party together at the time. He was great craic, though. Next morning, he said he didn't mean it, that he really liked me, he was just out to try to impress me, that it was all shite. But the way he'd gone on about it, like, telling me how he used to work in the kitchens, in prison, you know, and how he used to cook sausages and cut them into small pieces, how he used to freeze them to make them hard as little stones and use them in an elastic for a catapult when there was trouble on the wing. That's *waaaay* too much detail for someone to be just making up, don't you think? Like what, that's supposed to impress me? And then...' Her voice trailed off.

'And then?'

'Well, and then. We, you know...? I knew he didn't like me, not really. It was just a one-night stand to him, nothing else. He ghosted me straight afterwards. But then, a day or so later, after he'd a chance to think about it, I suppose, he came to me at the end of a shift. Just him and me in there.' She nodded to the alcove at the end of the bar. 'Really scared me, he did, got right in my face, told me that if I ever breathe a word about what he'd told me to anyone, about him being in prison, well then...'

'Well then?'

'He never finished that sentence, but I could guess. And you know what...?'

'No, Imogen, what?'

'I found out later he'd done the same with some other girls from different hotels. I met a couple; we all socialise together. I was the only one here at this hotel, though...far as I know. Funny, huh? Well, it's not, but you know what I mean.'

'I know what you mean,' he confirmed, then: 'Imogen.'

'Yes.'

'Did he tell you what he was in prison for?'

'Oh yes. Firearms. He likes guns, so he said.'

'Really.'

'Yes, really. Big-time bad boy?' Her voice held a timbre of excitement. 'What's a girl to do, eh?'

'Anything else you can think of that might be of interest?' Marty asked.

Imogen looked both ways again.

'Hm, well yes, there is something...'

Marty listened as she began to speak again.

'I DIDN'T GET my coffee, Brody, so beware.' The state pathologist Dr Newell McBain flipped the loops of a face mask over both ears. 'To think that one wee coffee machine going kaput can bring a whole Costa emporium down. I mean, what's the world coming to? They offered me an oat milk hot chocolate instead. Heated in a microwave. Can you believe it?'

Brody didn't say anything, merely nodded his head. Dr McBain looked like a trimmer version of Father Christmas, but one dressed in a hazmat suit. Brody knew from his years of dealing with the man that often the best way to actually deal with him was to say nothing at all, merely to nod your head; any questions, just ask someone else.

Not that he was a bad pathologist. He wasn't. He was one of the best in the business. But prickly as a hedgehog, as they say, if you didn't play him right.

Brody put on his own face mask, and they entered the room. Everything was as it had been before, the wall light still on, the curtains pulled, everything except, that is, six technics walking about the bed, in and out of the bathroom, shining blue lights across the walls, floors and fittings.

Brody was satisfied, from perusing the contents of a purse a techie handed him, containing bank cards and a driving licence, that this was the woman Roger Halloran had told him about, Sabina Happy. He wondered what ribbing that name had garnered her during her relatively short life.

When she'd left home in Athlone two days before, she likely had no idea she'd end up naked on a bed surrounded by strangers? And dead.

'Well, cause of death looks obvious enough,' the pathologist said. He stood by the bed, appraising the cadaver; Brody could see his eyes darting about like pinballs. At least he no longer was thinking of oat milk hot chocolate heated in a microwave. His eyes focused like a laser then, as he took a breath, making his mind up on something. 'She was standing when she was shot, in front of the bed. The shot was powerful enough to produce a sufficient mechanical kinetic energy to push her back onto the bed.'

'She was flung backwards, you mean,' Brody said, and immediately regretted it.

'What do I mean?' The doc shook his head. 'What do I mean? You, of all people. Jesus Christ, man, no, that is not what I mean. D'you know how much energy it takes to fling an inert object weighing…oh, I don't know, maybe sixty kilos backward like that? Do you? Have you any idea? Not that she's the biggest girl in the world, granted. She's not. But for every action, there's a reaction, so if she were flung backwards, so too would have been the shooter, and we both know that didn't happen, okay. It would have been a spasm, no more, a push; then she dropped literally like a sack of potatoes, whoosh, gone, onto the bed, her legs plopping over the side, like you see there, torso slightly twisting, head remaining staring ahead as we see it now, a movement overall so fast the expelled matter from the back of her head was angled downward onto the bed as she fell. There'll be quite the mess under the body you'll find when it's moved.'

Brody could argue the point, but he didn't.

Dr McBain studied the wall behind the bed. At about the

same height as where her head would have been if she were standing upright was a hole similar to that in the centre of her forehead, with the area around it spackled in dark-coloured matter: blood splatter droplets.

'The shot went through her cranium and out the other side, lodged there in that wall.' He pointed. 'See it there, the hole?'

'I see it.'

'She was shot dead on.' The doc made a low twittering sound. 'No pun intended. I'd say from a distance of six feet, no more. I reckon her killer was standing just in front of the door. If he meant to shoot her as he did, he's a good shot, an excellent shot; even from that distance, it's not so easy. I don't know where the other round went to, though. You see anything?'

Brody was looking about. 'No, I don't.'

McBain stepped to the bottom of the bed. Brody followed. They looked along the space between the side of the bed and the wall. On the carpet lay slivers of bone, some with tuffs of hair attached.

McBain gestured with his hands. 'See here, Brody...'

'See where? Those.' Meaning the bone fragments on the floor.

'No, man. I don't mean see here as in *see* here. I mean see here, as in, consider this. Which is, the second shot entered the body while it fell backward onto the bed as a result of the first. So the angle would have been different. I surmise the bullet entered the body and travelled *along* as opposed to *through* it, if you get me, crunching and ricocheting off bone, punching through muscle, its velocity steadily decreasing until it was exhausted, and it lodged in there...somewhere.

I'll find quite a mess inside her too, even if her exterior is deceptively intact, don't you think.'

Yes, Brody thought, *deceptively intact*. Whoever had done this had dispatched her with a cynical, brutal efficiency.

'Which one of you is Detective Sergeant Jack Brody?'

The voice came from behind. Brody and Dr McBain turned.

Two hazmat suits were standing there.

'And who are you?' snapped the doc.

'Oh, Dr McBain, is that yourself?' one of the hazmats said. 'Then that means you' – pointing at Brody – 'you're Brody.'

'It's getting very crowded in here,' McBain snapped again. 'Could some of you just please fuck off.'

'And who are you?' It was Brody's turn to ask the question, stepping back from the bed and moving towards the door.

'Inspector Tierney, Store Street, and' – nodding to the other hazmat – 'Garda Jenny O'Leary.'

'Inspector Tierney. Doesn't ring a bell. Did you transfer from somewhere or other?'

'Yes, Fermoy.'

'On promotion?'

'That's it, on promotion; what of it?'

'Nothing, I think I read about it on the Pulse transfer and promotions log, that's all.'

'And you remembered,' Tierney said. 'I'm impressed.'

'Anyway…?' Brody said. 'What do you want with me?'

'Well, it's definitely a murder. And that's what we do.'

That's what we do. The newly promoted inspector sounded like he'd been working in Dublin South Central all his life: he'd just arrived from Fermoy, for God's sake.

A head appeared round the bathroom door.

'Lifted a print from the back of the shower handle. Nice and clear. I'd say this narrows things down for you lads, wha' ya think?'

Tierney nodded energetically. 'That's a positive.'

That's a positive. Jesus Christ, Brody thought. 'There's no point in us all standing here.' Brody took a step back.

'I agree. Not a very efficient use of manpower.' But Tierney didn't move.

'The two shots visible on the victim were likely from a high-powered handgun,' Dr McBain announced to no one in particular. 'Likely a semi-automatic, judging by the entry wounds. The first went clean through the head. Died instantly, had to. Someone who'd used a gun before, knew what they were about, especially with a gun like that.'

'Like what?' Tierney asked.

'Well, sir' – it was his companion, Garda Jenny O'Leary – 'despite what's in the papers and stuff, we don't come across handguns so much. And a semi-automatic at that. Well now...'

Tierney looked from O'Leary to Brody. Brody was already getting to like O'Leary.

'Gangland, you mean?' Tierney said.

Give the man an encore.

'Possibly, but it doesn't seem like it to me,' Brody said.

'What does it seem like to you?'

'I don't know. But not that.'

'Really? And you're psychic?'

Brody didn't answer.

'There's nothing to say this murder isn't anything more mundane than a disgruntled lover, husband, something like that,' Tierney huffed.

'Mundane,' Brody said, nodding towards the body. 'Nothing about this is mundane for her, is it?'

'Ha, ha, funny man. There's no sign of forced entry, is there?'

'Too early to tell. I just got here myself, remember. But no, it doesn't look like it.'

'So, handgun death besides, an *automatic* at that, nonetheless I believe my hypothesis is correct. All too common lately. The initial signs are leading us in that direction.'

'Are they?' Brody raised an eyebrow. 'The initial facts are that the victim was shot dead by a handgun, and the handgun is a semi-automatic, or maybe an automatic, who knows? One of them, anyway. Those are the facts. What you're saying, sounds to me, is that because she wasn't stabbed, beaten or strangled, there's nothing to see here. I beg to differ.'

'For God's sake.' Dr McBain had been shining a pencil torch directly into the victim's head wound. He stood back from the body, the torch still on, the beam dancing about the walls. 'Can you take it somewhere else? You two sound like a pair of old codgers fighting over the half-price vegetables at the finish of a farmers' market.'

A metaphor derived from personal experience, Brody surmised. The doctor was a keen grower of greens and often could be found selling them each Sunday at Blackrock Market.

'I'm happy for you to take this,' Brody said, 'if that's what this is about. Until I hear otherwise, that is. I've enough to be getting on with.'

Brody made to turn away.

'No,' Tierney said, sounding like now that he was getting his own way and had proven his point, he wasn't so certain anymore, 'you run with it, yes, and so will I. We both will and liaise. As you say yourself, not only is it a handgun, but it's an automatic. I'm always happy to take considered advice from someone who perhaps knows better.'

Perhaps knows better. Brody would be impressed if Tierney were genuine in his attitude. But he wasn't, Brody felt certain of it. What he was doing was covering his bases, or, in mule parlance, his arse. Brody resisted an urge to wave his hand through the air to clear away the fumes of blowback repellent.

Brody caught the look from Dr McBain.

'It's okay, Doc, I'm out of here. I'll ring you later, if that suits?'

'Yes, later,' McBain replied, and then again he leaned over the body lying stiff and silent, waiting, it seemed, for the living to stop arguing and to get on with the task of catching the person or persons responsible for what had been done to her.

ON THE WAY back to the ranch, Marty had been telling Brody of what Imogen had said to him in the Patrick Kavanagh bar when the state phone rang on the central console. Brody flicked the Bluetooth on the steering wheel stalk.

'Hello.'

Superintendent Ryan's voice came through the door speakers. 'Where're you, Jack?'

'En route to the ranch. Just arriving now.'

'The ranch? I'd rather you didn't call it that.'

Brody glanced to Marty and grinned. Marty stuck his chin up in the air. 'HQ, then. Does that pass?'

'I want everyone in the unit room in half an hour,' she said, ignoring his comment. 'Contact meeting.' And hung up.

'She called it a contact meeting, Marty.'

'I heard.'

'A contact meeting, well, that's a good one.'

Brody turned off the roadway and approached the gates of Garda HQ, the boom barrier rising as they drew near.

5

'Hello, team,' Superintendent Ryan announced with a smile. She was standing at the top of the unit room, her arms folded. She had a nice smile, one that transformed her face, making her look pretty, lending her an expression that was open and almost kind...almost.

Jack thought maybe she might be all of these things, just that she kept them hidden, down deep, so that you had to dig to find them. Of course, appearances could be deceptive, and Jack could only deal with what he could see before him.

Because of this, he returned the smile, said, 'Hello.'

As for Considine, she merely nodded, as did Marty, and well, Voyle, he did nothing at all. He was still in the decompression chamber.

'You have a nice break?'

For a moment Jack wondered what Ryan was referring to. Had it something to do with the vehicles stolen and their front ends chopped off for export to Africa?

But Ryan wasn't referring to this, nor was she directing

her words to him. She was looking at Voyle. Who was looking at the floor. There was an awkward silence.

'Steve,' Brody whispered, and Voyle looked up. Brody nodded to the super.

'Nice break?' Ryan repeated.

'I was rock climbing; I don't look on that as a break.'

Cue another awkward silence. Ryan's face folded back into its blank, hard look, those small close-set eyes of hers losing whatever sparkle they had temporarily held just a moment ago. It was a PR exercise, Brody understood then, and one that hadn't worked. Maybe if she hadn't made it a PR exercise in the first place, maybe if she had just made it real.

'Okay, down to business,' she said. 'Fine so.'

She was pissed, Brody could tell. But that wasn't real either; that was merely a reaction. Real was somewhere in the middle, and being aware of both.

'We have a body in the Herbert Park Platinum Hotel,' she said. 'Fill me in, Jack.'

Jack filled her in.

'A semi-automatic,' she said when he'd finished. That had gotten her attention. He knew it would. 'Could be a fully automatic too, couldn't it?'

'It could,' Jack agreed, 'but they're not so common. Defeats the purpose really, a handgun on full auto is really hard to control; you'd need to know what you're doing. Might as well trade up to a MAC-10 if that's the case.'

'And a semi-automatic is more common? That what you mean?'

'Yes, it is.'

'I got a phone call,' she said, and pointed to the ceiling,

'from on high. This fella Tierney at Store Street...you spoke with him, Jack?'

'Yes, I did. He rang you?'

'No, no, he didn't ring me. The person who rang me mentioned him, that's all, and mentioned Store Street. And the person I spoke with was very clear...'

She paused and looked about the room.

Yes? Brody wondered, and wanted to shout, "Get on with it already."

'I agreed with the caller,' she said at last.

'And who was the caller?' Brody had had enough of this hide-and-go-seek. 'Unless that *is* a secret.'

'We take the lead in this, more specifically...' She looked like she was about to pause again, but didn't. 'Or you do, Jack. But you still report to me, of course.'

Of course, because what would be the point of you being here otherwise? She hadn't answered his question, he noted. It could only be the commissioner's office. Commissioner McKay had made it part of his mission to stamp out interference, as opposed to cooperation, between various units, to cut the gristle, the overlap and unnecessary bureaucracy. The public liked his approach, as did the media. The brass, sensing the wind, had no choice but to go along with it. But it wasn't working.

'To clarify,' he said, 'this is our investigation?'

'Yes. And how do you want to handle it?' A flicker of a smile crossed her face again, but not getting much further.

'Well, my take is,' he said, 'a semi-automatic, or automatic, whatever, doesn't come in a lucky bag. Even the blaggers spend a lot of time and effort sourcing them. And even at that, the market's bigger than any one gun, so the supplier can pick and choose. Therefore, you can take it that anyone in possession of such a weapon is a serious player.'

'Kind of goes without saying,' Ryan said, 'I would have thought. And your point?'

'That is precisely my point. We're dealing with a serious gouger here. We need to check if we have incidents with a similar MO. Maybe with the same weapon. When we get the ballistics report back, we'll know more.'

'When should we have that?'

'Maybe Marty can chase it up?'

Ryan nodded. 'Okay, I agree.'

'That alright with you, Marty?' Brody said.

'Yes, boss, course. And I'll chase up similar incidents too?'

'Do that, good man,' Brody said. 'I'm waiting on CCTV from the hotel. And I didn't hear anything from SOC about the print lifted from the shower. If there was a match, I'd have heard about it by now. We'll see. Now, the victim, we need a full background check, and we need to interview her husband, partner, whatever. A background check on same. I propose Nicola.'

'I know the craic,' Nicola said. 'I'll look after it, no probs.'

'And I need to speak with Matt Thompson, brother of Bart Thompson in the honeypot scam. I hear he has previous for firearms. There may be a link. How are you with your Africa export job, by the way, Nicola?'

'Sample cases ready for forwarding to our fraud squad and the Nigerian Police Special Fraud Unit. They' – she looked at her watch – 'should be making raids right about now across the port complex in Lagos. You couldn't have timed it better, boss.'

Brody looked at Ryan, a silent communication passing

between them that he was handing the floor back to her. She copped, unfolded her arms and clapped her hands once.

'Right, let's make a start. By the way, press enquires to be directed to either the press office or the media liaison officer at Store Street. That should keep them off our backs.'

Good, Brody thought, *nice one.*

'I have a feeling we can get to the bottom of this quickly,' she added, and Brody blinked in disbelief. 'I really do. It has a unique marker, after all.'

Even if Brody had agreed with her, he knew it was a mistake to ever tempt fate. But he didn't; he disagreed profusely, and for the very same reason – that unique marker.

'Hi, Jack,' the voice on the end of the line said.

A voice that sounded familiar: female, bright, friendly, inviting almost. That was a lot for a voice that had only said two words. Brody couldn't place it. He was sitting behind his desk, having come from the team meeting, or the briefing, whatever, his desk phone pressed to his ear.

'I'm not too bad. Um, who is this?'

'Forgotten already. It's Mandy, Jack.'

'Mandy?'

'Mandy Joyce.'

'Oh shite. Mandy Joyce. I thought you'd retired down country somewhere or other, the arse end of Leitrim, were writing true crime novels and teaching yoga or something… is that right?'

'It was podcasts, Jack, not novels. Supposed to be novels, but I switched to podcasts. Writing novels every day was taking up too much time and way too much concentration. And I bore easily. It wasn't yoga either. It was contemplative touch healing. To tell the truth, I was bored shiteless down in the arse end of nowhere. The silence, you know, it begins to make a noise all of its own after a time, like a scream.'

Didn't say much for her contemplative touch healing, whatever that was, Jack thought. Anyway, he wasn't surprised. Mandy was a city girl through and through. It was after her encounter with a crazed killer that she'd had an epiphany – or so she'd said. Maybe she had, but it hadn't lasted very long. He reminded himself they hadn't exactly been friends in the first place either. Theirs had been a professional relationship, if you could even call it that.

Then it struck him.

'You're back working, aren't you? That's why you're calling me?'

'I rang to say hello. First and foremost. That's all. Yes, I am working, but just a little. Freelancing for the moment. You know, I've got to start almost at the bottom all over again. But that's good, because it's renewal, Jack. Cathartic.'

That again. *If you say so.*

'And what?' he said. 'This contemplative touch healing. You doing that on the side, is it?'

'Oh, no, it's more than on the side, Jack, way more. It's a way of life. I can schedule you an appointment. It might make all the difference.'

'Make all the difference to what?'

'To your life, give you a more, I don't know, even and enlightened, balanced approach.'

'Why you ringing me, Mandy?'

Though Jack was certain he already knew.

'Like I said, just to say hello, Jack, to get back in touch, get reacquainted, that's all.'

Brody waited.

'And there's also that little matter of a body found shot to death in a room at the Herbert Park Hotel.'

'I thought so.'

'Aw, come on, Jack, mostly I want to reconnect too.'

'We were never connected in the first place, Mandy, and you know it.'

'The body, Jack, it was one to the head and one to the chest, that right?'

'It's no secret. That's the way it was, yes.'

'Who's the victim?'

'To be confirmed.'

'I hear it's female, and it was naked, is that right?'

'Who've you been talking to?'

'Well, Jack, that'd be telling, sorry.'

Shit, she was getting right back up into the saddle; someone was already feeding her information. The fact the body was naked was not the type of information that would ever be released, not until *after* the body had been identified, that is.

'You need to refer your questions to the press office or Store Street, Mandy.'

'Aw, Jack, don't be like that. One more question, please.'

'What?' An irritation was creeping into his tone.

'Was she really fifteen?'

'Fifteen?' Taken by surprise, Jack had momentarily forgotten about it.

'The girl at the centre of that other thing,' Mandy said, 'the honeypot scam? Well done on that, by the way.'

Brody felt an invisible force broadsiding him. How the fuck had she known about that?

'Sex with a girl straight off the cover of *Teenage Gossip* magazine is one thing, Jack, but when she's only fifteen, well...you know the rest.'

'Fuck off, Mandy.'

He hung up.

But almost immediately his phone rang again. Jesus, the woman didn't know when to hold back, did she? Her sojourn into the wilds of Leitrim had done nothing to soften her approach, had it? Yes, she was back in the saddle alright, charging her way through whatever it was that lay in her path. He was tempted to not pick up, but he found himself doing so anyway.

'Mandy, I've told you everything I know.'

'Aw, Mandy, is it?' A voice that wasn't Mandy's. 'Mandy Joyce? I heard she's back. Jaysis, a pain in the bleedin' arse, Jack, dat wan, but I wouldn't mind if she were a pain in me dick.' A rumbling laugh followed, like a slow-moving, viscous landslide down the side of a hill.

Brody recognised the voice: Christopher Connelly.

'Christy C. What's up?'

He knew the tout wouldn't be ringing if he didn't have something. The same tout as had told him about the honeypot scam. Whose hit rate was roughly one in five. Brody wouldn't be holding his breath.

'What's up? Yer man, the Matty fella. Dat's what's bleedin' up.'

'Thompson?'

'No, Matt bleedin' Talbot, ya thick? Jaysis, who'd ya think I mean?' Again, a laugh rumbled up from a pair of blackened, charcoaled lungs.

Matt Talbot, a hopeless alcoholic who'd died almost a hundred years before, who'd found the Lord and changed his ways, famous for his piety and mortification of the flesh in self-inflicted penance.

'He was just like you,' Brody said, 'till he changed his ways, that is. They're seriously thinking about making him a saint. There's hope for you yet, Christy.'

'He's in a railway station, no, not Matt Talbot, bleedin' Matt Thompson, saw him there I did with me own eyes, looking at the departures board, going down country, he is. Don't want to lose him a second time, do ya? I heard about dat. Ya'd want to be quick, Jackie boy, so you would.'

'Really?'

'Jaysis, didn't I just tell ya. Yeah, really. What youse goin' to do? Talk about this all bleedin' day or go and get him? Your choice.'

One-in-five hit rate. A double would be a first.

'Which railway station?' Still, there was a first time for everything.

'Drop me in a fifty spot, yeah, and I'll tell ya? I'll be waitin' outside the shelter on the Quays, ya? At half five, after the grub, ya? You can give it to me there, what'd say?'

'Which station?' Brody repeated.

'A fifty spot, yeah, cheap at half the price. Come on, Jack.'

'Okay, a fifty spot. Which station?'

'Heuston, Jack. Went into the jacks, he did, and didn't come out again. S'ppose he'll wait in there till it's time for the train to leave. Whatever train dat is. Safest bleedin' place. Dat's where I'd be if I was him. Lots of coppers down there these days, Jack, tryin' to clean up the place, they are, full of riff-raff so the place is, urban vermin. About time too, wha?

I'm writin' a rap song about dat, the urban vermin. I'll sing you a bit if you want...'

Jack hung up just as the landslide started again, sounding like it was moving faster, like Christy was excited about something. A fifty spot might do that, if only for a little while.

JACK PARKED in a slip road at the side of Heuston station, flipped the visor on the unmarked down to display the sign fixed there:

Garda on Official Duty.

Brody wasn't playing this according to the manual. The manual said that in the event of an incident being attended where there was a possibility of a firearm involved, an armed response unit must be summoned to accompany the responding unit. Which was fine, but in the real world it didn't work like that. In the real world that would give Matt Thompson time to be on a train to God knows where.

Neither Brody nor Voyle was armed. That would have taken time too. And time was something they had none of to spare. Not now. Even if Brody thought the chances of Thompson carrying were slim. Even if he knew that in this job when the weatherman promised sunshine, you always brought your umbrella. Matt Thompson's Pulse catalogue was a lucky bag mix, everything from simple possession, criminal damage, fraud, to possession of a Beretta handgun. The weapon had been found during a drugs search. An old weapon, possibly taken during a burglary and sold on, although there was no record of it on Pulse. And it had been empty, with no rounds in the magazine. With his record, Brody wondered how the hell he had managed to get a job at the Herbert Park Platinum Hotel. Brody didn't know, and Roger Halloran wasn't saying an awful lot to enlighten him either. Probably because his personnel department had been duped by a makey-up CV, verified with a few phone calls to supposed previous employers who, in fact, were probably Thompson's pals or associates. That's if the personnel department had rung anybody in the first place.

He and Voyle strode into the railway station and stopped in the centre of the concourse, looking up at the departures board. The next train due to leave was in fifteen minutes to Westport. They made their way across the concourse towards the toilets, situated in a corner beside a walkway between the concourse and the ticket hall. During the day, the railway station was a focal point for homeless people, who whiled away the time there until the night shelters reopened. Some were more obvious than others. Brody spotted a number of faces he recognised. They quickly looked away and shuffled off. News would rapidly spread along the bush wire all the way into the city centre. Within minutes his presence would be known. So they needed to be quick.

A couple of security guards employed by the railway company – typically hard men types, pumped biceps, shaved heads, dark paramilitary type overalls – were manhandling a group of street drinkers off the premises. Brody led the way into the men's toilets, sliding over the turnstile as everyone else was doing too. A cleaner was mopping the narrow walkway between the urinals and the toilet cubicles. The place stank of disinfectant and God knows what else, the men standing at the urinals mostly staring ahead at the tiled wall in front of them. The place was dank and grim. The men at the urinals zipped up and walked away...except for one. A small skinny man in tight jeans, with a pink sweater covered in black love hearts, dirty blond hair and tanned leathery skin.

'Hello, boys.'

'Ross,' Brody said, 'how's it goin'?'

'Nowhere since you two showed up. What's a girl to do?'

Brody nodded to the door. 'Don't you have a train to catch?'

'No, darling, heaven forbid I'd come to a railway station like this to catch a train.' He pulled up his fly slowly and paused, his fingers on the zipper, looking at Brody.

Brody pointed to the door, and Ross smiled, displaying a few yellow teeth in an otherwise empty mouth. He walked to the turnstile, called, 'See you, boys,' slid over it with practised ease and traipsed off like he'd just come offstage at the famed Gaiety Theatre Christmas panto.

Now Brody knew that if Thompson was in here, then he knew he was here too. There was no one left in the jacks, only those behind the closed doors of three cubicles.

Was Matt Thompson one of them?

Brody indicated for Voyle to stand at one end of the row of cubicles, while he stood at the other, the one closest to the exit. He mimed the words *We wait*, and Voyle nodded in understanding. A toilet flushed, and a cubicle door opened. An old boy emerged, looked at them both, then at the sinks, like he was making his mind up on whether to wash his hands or not. He didn't, and walked away, stopping briefly to squirt some gel onto his hands from a wall dispenser by the door. Two to go. A minute passed; another cubicle door opened. No toilet flush. A young man emerged, wearing a shirt with the tails outside his trousers, slightly wrinkled and with fresh press lines, like he'd just bought it and taken it from its wrapper. Which he probably had. Brody made the assumption he was preparing for a job interview. The lad was holding a rucksack in one hand, clothes, presumably his old clothes, hanging out of it. He didn't wait around either, and legged it.

One closed cubicle door remained.

In the silence of the jacks, with nothing but the sound of dripping taps and gurgling pipes to be heard, Brody began to doubt himself. What if Thompson was in there, in that cubicle, and he *was* armed? Well, if that were the case, he'd played this wrong, very wrong. If Thompson was in there and he was armed, then he was up the creek without a paddle, they both were. Simple as.

The toilet flushed.

Brody tensed. The sound seemed much louder than it actually was, closer to that of a waterfall. He glanced to Voyle, who glanced to him at the same time. Their eyes met, then returned to the door.

Waiting...

What happened next shouldn't have taken Brody by surprise. But it did. A man rushed from a cubicle. But not the cubicle with its door closed. No. The man exploded out of the cubicle next to it, the one with its door open. Brody hadn't expected that. In fact, it was the last thing he'd expected. But it shouldn't have been. Because, if he'd thought about it beforehand, he'd have known that Thompson was fit and slim, so it would be easy for him to slide beneath the cubicle walls, cut half a foot or so short of the floor, and take Brody by surprise. Which he was doing right now. Thompson's feet scrambled on the damp floor as he swung left, gaining traction, and bolted ahead.

But it didn't make any difference. Because Brody was waiting.

'Come here, Houdini,' he said, reaching out a long, powerful arm and folding its hand firmly around the back of the escape artist's neck, pushing on it as Houdini tried to rush by him, sending Houdini crashing face first onto the floor.

Voyle already had the cuffs out; he ran down and snapped them on. They pulled him to his feet.

'This time,' Brody said, 'we're not going to leave you until we see the custody sergeant himself turn the key in your cell door. But first, how about a coffee? Maybe a sandwich? What do you say? You must be hungry.'

Thompson's mouth dropped open, his turn now to be surprised.

'Are you for real? Coffee and a sandwich?'

'Sure,' Brody said, 'this way.'

BRODY GOT an egg mayonnaise sandwich and three coffees. They sat in the unmarked, Voyle in the back seat next to Thompson, Brody sideways in the driver's seat, his back to the door, looking at them.

Thompson was hungry. Two bites had already taken care of one half of the sandwich. He kept his head bowed, munching away, like a hungry animal at a fresh kill. Brody waited for him to finish. It didn't take long. Thompson took a slurp of coffee and finally looked up at them.

'Thanks, man, I was starving, haven't eaten anything since…you know, I had to leg it yesterday.'

'You can return the favour,' Brody said, cutting straight to the chase. 'Possession of a firearm, ring a bell?'

'Possession of a what?' Then realisation seemed to dawn. 'Aw, you mean that yoke. Sure, that was years ago. Possession of a firearm, me granny. It didn't even have a firing pin. Bet you didn't know that? And I paid…' But his voice trailed off.

'Yes,' Brody said, 'you paid what?'

'Eighteen months, that's what. Eighteen months I paid for having that yoke, down in the Midlands Prison.'

'No justice in this world,' Brody said, 'is there, Matty?'

'Matty, is it? All palsy. You're taking the piss now, mister, big time.'

'No sign of you going on the straight and narrow, is there?' It was Voyle. 'You had a nice job at the Herbert. You went and fucked that up.'

'It was a nice job until you showed up.' He gave Brody a knowing look.

'My colleague didn't mean it like that,' Brody said. 'He meant a regular wage, career advancement, all that. His idea of a nice job and yours are two different things. Anyway, a firearm is a firearm. And that yoke, as you call it, pin or no pin, was a Beretta. It could have been modified to fire. Maybe you went and got yourself another one. Did you?'

'What kind of question is that. Why're you asking me that for?'

'The body found in room five three two…' Voyle said.

'Whoo.' Thompson's hands swung up into the air.

'Easy,' Steve said, taking them down again.

'What about the woman in five three two? That had nothing to do with me. Jesus, don't go there now.'

'How do we know that, Matty boy?' Brody said. 'Because you would say that, wouldn't you? I don't know if you killed her. Maybe you did. A Beretta, kind of shines a light on you, you must agree.'

'Fuck off, okay.' He paused, biting his lower lip. 'You're stretching it big time.'

'Maybe,' Brody said, knocking back the dregs of his coffee and turning round, fumbling with the keys in the ignition. 'Snap the cuffs on him again, Steve; we don't want to take any chances.'

'What,' Thompson squealed, 'where're we going?'

'Store Street,' Voyle said. 'Where you think we're going? Look on the bright side, you might get another sandwich.'

6

It had taken only a short time for Considine to discover where she could find Jeff Leech, ex-husband of the murder victim Sabina Happy. His ex-wife had reverted to her maiden name following their divorce. Considine knew by now, too, that the victim had been a successful businesswoman, owning her own beauty salon in Athlone town centre, Happy Days. She was known to the mules in Athlone, who described her as successful, yes, but her failed marriage had taken its toll, she'd been beaten down by the whole experience – and maybe literally, too, behind the closed doors of her home. No one could be completely certain.

Considine took a young uniform she'd come across wandering about the place with her. 'Rory,' she said as they got into the unmarked, 'that's your name, isn't it?'

He nodded.

'Thanks for coming, Rory, not a good idea to do this job in ones, and there was no one else around.'

'Aw, thanks.'

She laughed. Rory looked out the window like a petulant teenager.

There was no way Jeff Leech could have known his ex-wife was dead. Not yet. Not unless he'd killed her, that is. And, in cases like this, it usually was a spouse or partner. The 212 Xpress bus drew into the yard of Conyngham Road bus depot, and she and young Rory, sitting in the unmarked parked outside, got out and walked in. Jeff Leech was a bus driver, and as he stepped out of the bus, overweight, bald and sweating, Considine thought he looked to be mid-forties, but guessed he was younger.

'Mr Leech, a word, please,' she said as she and Rory approached.

Leech took in the lad's uniform.

'Guards. What's this about? Has that bitch gone and said something behind my back again. Has she? It's all lies. Anyway, we're not married anymore.'

Off to a good start, Considine thought.

'No, Mr Leech, your ex-wife hasn't done that. Your ex-wife is dead.'

She thought maybe she could have been a bit more subtle about it, but he'd set the tone. She studied his face carefully, his expression like someone had just boarded his bus without buying a ticket.

'What're you talking about?'

She was about to repeat it, but he spoke.

'Seriously, Sabina's dead.' The tone softer, cocking his head to one side, curious, perplexed even. 'What? How? Where?'

'Can we go somewhere a little more private to answer those questions?' Considine asked.

'Naw, I'm alright. You can tell me right here.'

She did, and his chin went down onto his chest, and his shoulders drooped. He stayed like that for a moment and looked up, took a breath and blew it out in a steady stream. *Christ*, Considine wanted to say, *it's okay. I just told you your ex-wife's been murdered; you can show it.* She reached out and rested a hand gently on his shoulder, but he shook it away.

'No, don't touch me. You crowd didn't help either, coming round to the house every time she called over every little thing.'

Considine had checked. Patrols had frequently visited their marital address, either in response to calls from Sabina herself, or from concerned neighbours. None had resulted in any official complaint from her, but nothing unusual in that; it was the same in the majority of domestic abuse cases.

'Who did this to her? She didn't deserve it. I loved that girl, you know.'

You had a funny way of showing it, Considine thought.

'Well, we don't know,' she said. 'That's what we're trying to find out.'

Something passed behind his eyes. 'And what? You think I might have had something to do with it?'

Considine didn't answer. She'd allowed him to chew on that bone for a moment.

Leech was holding a small satchel in his hand, *Dublin Bus* stencilled along the side. He dropped it to the ground by his feet and rubbed his hands over his face.

'Everything alright there, Leechy,' a man dressed in oil-slicked overalls asked as he passed by.

Leech didn't answer. The man glanced over his shoulder a couple of times as he walked towards a maintenance garage.

'The problem was,' the bus driver said, 'Sabi and me

married too young. I didn't look like this back then. I worked out. I had hair. I had prospects...'

I coulda been a contender, Considine thought. So far, Leech seemed sorry only for himself.

'...we drifted apart,' he went on. 'And then she started that business. Jesus, I hated that. It became her baby. We didn't have any, you know, babies, that is. We tried, but it just didn't happen. She wanted me to go get checked, like come on, there's nothing wrong with me. She replaced me with that fucking salon.' He looked away. 'I don't want to talk anymore. Can I go?'

He was jealous, was what he was saying, of his wife's success in business and her good looks. She had wanted him to get checked, which meant she probably had. So likely the reason they hadn't any babies rested with him. That wouldn't make him jealous, that would make him mad. Some men couldn't handle that, and Considine guessed he was one of them. More than anything, what men like Leech here couldn't handle was not being in control. But he did have control, and from now on would have to be happy with it being over a fifteen-tonne bus.

'Where were you last night?'

'What? Where was I last night? I was home of course. I'd work in the morning.'

'Where's home?'

'A shitty flat near the East Wall.'

'Anyone vouch for that?'

'Yeah, well...' His voice drifted off. Then, 'But she didn't deserve it, you know. No way.' He shook his head. 'To die like that. Sabi, poor Sabi. God.'

'You were saying, Mr Leech, anyone vouch for you being at home last night?'

He looked at her. 'Yes, yes, of course someone can vouch for me. I, um, sublet; the landlord doesn't know about it. I have to. I can't afford what he's charging for that kip on my own. So, yes, I have somebody with me. The fella who just passed by a minute ago, Kenny, he's a mechanic. Kenny's separated like me, but he's got three kids. Makes it easier – for both of us.'

'Wait here,' Considine said. 'Rory, stay with him.'

Considine went to the maintenance garage, found Kenny, verified the story. It was exactly like Leech had said.

'I'm sorry for your loss, Mr Leech,' she said when she got back. 'You can go. We know where to find you if we need you again.'

He bent down and picked up his satchel. 'You'll get the bastard, yeah? Who did this to her? Won't you?'

Considine thought it a shame that Leech couldn't have displayed this level of care for his ex-wife while she was still alive.

'Yes, Mr Leech,' she said, 'we'll get him.'

As he walked away, she thought, *I hope*.

7

Marty Sheahan sat with his phone pressed against his ear, listening as Inspector Pierre Jousten of the Belgian Police based at Interpol HQ in Lyon, France, the world's largest international police organisation, flicked a lighter a couple of times, and the sound of a deep draw followed as he brought a cigarette to life. Jousten was mid-fifties, and on the two occasions that Marty had met him, always wore a dark trench coat with a trilby hat and had an untipped Gauloises Brunes on the go. Old school. For a man who smoked two packs a day and ate very little, he was fresh faced and possessed boundless energy. Marty had already searched Pulse and found nothing similar to what had happened in room 532 of the Herbert Park Platinum on there. He wasn't surprised; he would have heard about it if there had been anything similar. Still, had to check. But with Interpol, having 195 police forces under its charter, it would be a different matter.

'Thank you for returning my call, Inspector,' Marty said.

'And for speaking English too. As you know, my French isn't very good.'

In fact, it was non-existent.

'As is the case with most Anglophones,' Jousten said haughtily. 'Is a good job, then, I can speak English, no?'

So up your own arse, Marty thought, yet not quite certain either if old Jousten here wasn't merely taking the piss.

'Yes, it is a good job,' Marty agreed, not bothering to get into the subtleties of the definition of Anglophone, him being Irish and all. He also remembered a conversation with a Canadian he'd had one time who'd insisted that he knew better, that Ireland was still a part of the UK.

'It didn't take long,' Jousten said.

'Well, what did you find?'

'What I was looking for. Similar MOs, of course.'

'You did.' Marty's voice rose an octave. It had been just over an hour since he'd contacted Jousten's office. He hadn't expected a result this quick.

'In fact,' Jousten said, 'in the last ten years we have recorded almost seventy thousand deaths by semi-automatic handguns throughout Europe, EU and non-EU nations combined. Strip out the suicides and those we determine to have not been the victims of organised crime, and you're not left with a lot, less than one thousand, the majority female, and these are mostly domestics.'

'And within those,' Marty said, 'any recurring MOs?'

'It's hard to decipher an MO; a person is shot dead, they are shot dead, no. For example, two people were murdered on a metro bus in Hamburg, killed by two different people using semi-automatic handguns. Would you call that an MO? Yet no connection was discerned between either.'

Marty wondered where this was going. Didn't he just say he'd found recurring MOs?

'So, no MOs,' he said, tetchy. 'Is that what you mean?'

'I didn't say that,' Jousten replied.

'Well, I thought...'

There was that hollow sound as the Belgian policeman took a long draw on his cigarette again.

'I was about to say,' he said, 'that a number of deaths have been recorded and marked as indeed having similarities.'

'How many deaths?'

'There are five.'

'Over what time frame?'

'Five years. Five for five.'

'What are the similarities?'

'All shot by semi-automatic handgun...'

Well, I know that, Marty wanted to scream.

'...and all female, aged between twenty-three and thirty-nine, all post-coital, all found in hotel rooms and...'

'Let me guess,' Marty said, 'all shot once in the head and once in the chest.'

'Correct.'

Shit!

But he didn't say that. What he said was, 'Wow.'

'And I'm not finished,' Jousten added.

'You're not? There's more?'

'Yes. The scene of each killing was clean. There was nothing of evidential value left by the killer. Like a ghost, no?'

'Hm,' Marty said. 'And?'

'Yes, and...'

'There's something else?'

'Oh yes, there is something else...' the Belgian answered, his voice trailing off.

Jesus. Marty threw his eyes to heaven and waited for Jousten to tell him what that *something else* was.

'And it is this, my friend,' Jousten said, 'a robbery, no, in the same city as the murder. But not on the same day, a day or maybe two after. And not *un petit* robbery, no, *un grand cambriolage*. A big bank robbery. In fact, five robberies, five cities, Nice, London, Milan, Antwerp, and Valencia.'

'Wow,' Marty said again.

'And all of them...well, in fact, we are not correct in calling them that, robberies. If we are correct, we must call them burglaries, no, and not, what you say, aggravated burglaries, because no one was injured and no weapons were used, that we know of, that is. In these...burglaries. It doesn't sound the same, does it? A robbery sounds much better, no? Anyway, these took place in banks close to a river, and each bank was entered via a sewer tunnel running off that river either directly beneath that bank or very close to it. Entry was made through the floor into the vault in all cases. These bad men are very good, no? They made off with a lot of money, altogether maybe twenty-two million euro, but no one is completely certain.'

'Wow,' a third time. 'What? In cash, bonds, jewels?'

'Cash. Some bonds, yes. Some jewels. But mainly cash. Old cash. Taken out of circulation, before it was brought to the incinerator, no, to be burned. They seem to have a preference for old cash. Virtually untraceable. Now, would you mind, Martin? But please don't mention that word again, "wow". You will do that for me, no?'

Marty was just about to say it again, but he stopped himself in time.

'We commissioned a profiler,' Jousten said, 'to help us catch this ghost killer. We didn't know if the robberies were connected then, but we are pretty certain they are now. Pascal Dórea, you know him?'

'Yes, I know him. He assisted us in a case some time ago. He is very good.'

'You think so? But not all a bit, what you say? Wishy-washy, no?'

Marty laughed. 'You surprise me, Pierre. I would have thought you'd be on board, a man such as yourself.'

'On board. What's this mean? On board?'

'A figure of speech, that's all, meaning you would be open-minded, supportive of a profiler, that's all.'

'And I am, no...but he is just so...just so right all the time. Does that not, how you say, bother you? Someone who is always right. It is good, yes, but still...'

Aha, Marty thought, that green-eyed monster again.

'What did he say?' he asked, moving things along and not getting into it.

'I will email you, no?'

'Yes. Good. Thank you. Now, question, why was the cash not brought straight to the incinerator? Why would they hold it in a bank vault first?'

'Oh, because the cash came from all over, from an entire country. They needed a safe place to store it beforehand. The incinerator was usually in an industrial compound out of town, and the cash would be taken there under armed guard.'

'Five robberies,' Marty said, 'or burglaries, whatever. And five murders, in five different cities, over five years.'

'Yes, that is correct.'

'That's a lot of fives, Pierre.'

'Maybe it's about to become six, no?'

THE PROFILE PIERRE emailed over was succinct and to the point. Marty read it quickly on the computer screen first, then printed out a copy, placed it on his desk, and went over it a second time, more carefully on this occasion. It read:

The killing of victims found at the hotels Créte d'or – Nice; Premie – Antwerp; Scaglia – Milan; Brillo – Valencia; Royal Embankment – London, display a clinical efficiency devoid of gratuitous violence. In all cases, victims were post-coital, female, young (or relatively so), attractive, and taken by surprise. They did not know their killer before their encounter with him. He is likely to be in his early thirties, attractive, charming, displaying a false sense of sophistication. Females will be drawn to him. The victims share a commonality in that all had recently emerged from relationships: two had just divorced, one separated, one had broken up with a boyfriend following a three-year relationship, and one, her boyfriend was deceased. I infer through this that all victims were emotionally vulnerable and open to seeking validation by gaining the attention and affirmation of a man displaying the traits as outlined. The females engaged in consensual casual sex as a means of (temporarily) achieving this validation.

The killer I deem to be extremely astute in observing subtleties in human behaviour, more particularly, in spotting the vulnerability traits that he seeks out. He is pursuing in this the familiar, in particular, mirroring the relationship he had with his mother. The killer is engaged in role-playing, regressing to a point in his life dominated by confused anger and sexual deviancy expressed in the encounters with his victims through a preponderance for rough sex. It is probable he engaged in a sexual relationship with his mother while a teenager and possibly even earlier. It is also probable, but by no means certain, that he may share an underlying psychosis or mental disorder with her, one that is undiagnosed with a resulting internalisation of confusion and violent fantasies. His emotions centring around love and intimacy are skewed. This man will not be married or in a stable relationship; he is unable to maintain either. He finds meaning and understanding in casual, anonymous sexual encounters with women who meet the criteria he desires. However, not all encounters result in the killing of the woman.

I consider there is a link with the level of violence exerted through rough sex that, if satisfied, avoids the emergence of deadly tendencies and the subsequent compulsion to kill. Or perhaps his urges increase exponentially at times of stress – a bank robbery would fit this criterion of extra stress. The killings do not follow any set pattern, the dates are random, and always two shots, one to the head and one to the chest, symbolising the clinical nature of the act of murder in the first (removed through the use of a handgun), and the sentimentality in the second, the chest symbolising the heart. Each time, I believe he believes he is killing his mother.

This person I deem to have received an education in engineering, probably one that is partial because he will not have graduated. He prefers the life of a career criminal, operating outside the norms of a society to which he feels he does not belong. However, his extracurricular activities will be kept secret from the other members of the criminal enterprise to which he belongs. They will not have sanctioned these, because they will bring attention on them, as they are currently doing so now. The discovery of his activities will have grave consequences for him.

I believe he is an internationalist, possibly American or Canadian, bi- or multilingual (possibly French Canadian), aged in his mid to late thirties.

MARTY SAT BACK and pondered what he'd just read. How did Pascal Dórea do it? Science or witchcraft? A combination of both? Either way, he was usually spot on. While the profile gave him an understanding of the person they were looking for, it did not bring them any closer to catching this person. He still remained exactly what Jousten had called him, a ghost.

8

Khabib was pissed off. With him. Big time. He knew it. They all knew it. More pissed off than even the last time. And that was saying something. That last time when he'd promised Khabib he wouldn't do it again. Yet he just had. But Khabib didn't know that, not for certain. So he couldn't condemn him. Even the cruellest of pirates did not condemn one of their own unless completely certain of their guilt. So there was nothing for it. Black was white, and white was black. He would lie. He had to. Big time. He would lie, lie, lie, lie. Otherwise, he knew, once this job was over, so too would be his existence on this God's green earth. It's not like Khabib hadn't warned him. He had.

'Believe me, Khabib, I had nothing to do with it. Nothing. Do you hear me? *Pleaaase*, you must believe me. I would never lie to you. Never. Christ, Khabib, you must believe me. Come on now, we know each other too well, don't we?'

'Do we? And don't say Christ Khabib to me. I'm a

Muslim. Don't fuck with me, just don't. I'm warning you. I *have* warned you.'

'I'm not fucking with you. It's the truth. Anyway, I don't even have the piece anymore. I got rid of it in Athens, just like you told me to.'

And after this job, he definitely would be getting rid of it – if he survived, that is.

Khabib held his mobile phone up, shoved it into his face, the headline from a BBC newsfeed filling the screen:

Female Found Shot Dead in Dublin Hotel Room

And beneath, a subheading:

Killed by automatic handgun favoured by terrorists and gangsters.

Khabib pulled the phone away and shoved it into a pocket, his hand emerging clutching a pack of full-strength Camels. He sparked a lighter to life and fired up a cigarette, took a long draw. They were the only two in the room. The apartment was a large Airbnb near the airport. Clyde and Lisbeth had left. Tyler took this as a sign Khabib might be thinking of doing him here. But he wouldn't, would he? Surely not? He couldn't. Not here? That would create problems. And Khabib needed him. For now, he needed him. Surely, they hadn't come this far just to walk away. But shit, when the job was over, what then? Would Khabib do him then? Did a bear shite in the woods? Yes, he would. For definite. Call it intuition. All he could do was lie his ass off. Nothing else for it. Maybe if he lied enough, just maybe, Khabib might believe it long enough that he might...Well, what exactly? He was fucked, that was the bottom line. Jeez, why couldn't he just have strangled the bitch. There wouldn't be any of these problems if he had. But no, he had to go and use the fucking artillery. What was wrong with him?

That nine-millimetre devil, that was what was wrong with him. The fact that something so small could be so lethal fascinated him. Always had. A bunch of bikers with metal chains, knives and knuckle dusters couldn't do in half an hour what that little piece could do in two seconds. It gave him his sense of who he was, of *what* he was. It was his friend, his protector, his vengeance. It had saved his life more than once and, in a sense, given him life too. His father had had it first. It wasn't so much handed down to him as taken from the old man's dying fist. When he was eleven years old, Tyler had shot the motherfucker in the very centre of his forehead. His favourite shot. Then as now. It was enough. It was always enough. The second shot delivered out of mere habit. After that it was just him and Momma. The day he'd shot his father, she took him to Mr Sundae's and bought him a whipped toasted caramel – his favourite – and as many chocolate mousse cakes as he could eat. He'd gotten sick that evening, but he'd never felt as good. His mother got rid of the body. He didn't know how. And no one came looking for him. That was the kind of man his father was; no one seemed to notice. Still, Tyler was his father's son. He was that kind of man too.

Pouf, pouf, just like that.

'You're grinning, you motherfucker,' Khabib spat, and literally too, spittle falling from the corners of his mouth.

He hadn't realised that he was grinning.

And then he was flying backwards across the room, his

jaw erupting in pain. Khabib knew how to punch. He crashed against something as Khabib advanced. All he could do was cover himself as best he could and take it. But Papa had trained him well; he knew how to do that.

LATER, when the others had returned and they were all sitting around the living room, he was convinced they were looking at him funny. You could tell a lot from a look. Last time he'd gotten a look like that was during his one and only stretch in prison. Three and a half years he'd served in a Mexican shithole. He didn't want to do time again. No way.

No one spoke. They just looked. At him. But when Khabib left the room, Clyde said, 'You din her in, din ya?' He was from Glasgow, hence the name, short and powerfully built, used for the heavy work. But it wasn't his real name. And Lisbeth, who supposedly was Swedish, and it wasn't her real name either, because she always went along with whatever Clyde said, said, 'Yeah, course you did. You've gone too far this time, dude. You know that, don't you?'

No, definitely not Swedish. Though she might look like a member of an Abba tribute band, her accent was northeastern US. If he'd had to guess, he'd say Massachusetts, not Boston, it didn't have that distinctiveness, but Massachusetts somewhere. An explosives expert, so Tyler pinned her as being ex-military, definitely. And himself? Well, that was a little ironic. They all assumed him to be American, and he was happy to go along with it. Told them he was from Yonkers, New York. But in reality, he was from Ontario, Canada. And no, Tyler wasn't his real name either. It was Abraham, even if he'd left that behind him many years ago.

No one knew anyone else's real name. And that was the way Khabib liked it. That was the way they all liked it. Khabib himself said he was Lebanese, but Tyler didn't believe him. He thought he was actually British. Normally, though he spoke with an Arabic accent, there often was a definite British intonation, like he was playing up the Arabic to try to conceal the British, adding another layer to help hide his identity. If Tyler was to guess, he'd say London. He didn't think he was Muslim either. He didn't even have a beard. As for the one they called God? Who gave out the jobs for a fifteen percent cut. No one knew jack shite about him – or her – not even, he guessed, Khabib.

'Whatever,' Tyler said, 'but I didn't kill that woman.'

'Ach, you did, dinnae ye, ya mad bastard.'

Lisbeth grinned. 'Oh, you did, didn't you, ya mad bastard?'

Still, business was business, and they needed him. Nothing would happen while they needed him.

But what about when they didn't need him, when this business was done? What then? An image of a parking meter came to mind, the old-fashioned type, a red banner popping up because the money had run out, *Out of Time*, it said. Yeah, that would be about right.

THE NATIONAL & Provincial Bank on the corner of Essex and Wellington Street was an imposing three-storey limestone structure with stucco-framed windows and a colonnaded porch front. It resembled more a hotel than a bank. In fact, it had previously been a hotel, called the Hibernian, which had been converted into a bank in 1935, with a section of the old kitchens in the basement converted into a single large vault, and the old staff quarters, beneath the kitchens, the sub-basement, bricked up, and beneath this again a section of Victorian-era brick-walled sewer, part of a network that one time had sent Dublin's waste through its maze of tunnels into the River Liffey and on out into the sea.

The old sewer system plans had recently been digitised from the original architectural maps, dating back to the nineteenth century, and uploaded to the Office of Public Works website, the government agency responsible for its maintenance.

Still, in real life, looking down at a wrought-iron grille on an entrance to a tunnel, rusty and grimy, with moss and slime clinging to its brickwork, with the murky waters of the Liffey lapping through its grating, was stark compared against the clinical, clean, straight and perfect lines of a Victorian draughtsman's hand.

Khabib was impressed. The grille was almost 150 years old, after all. And yet, there it was, the same grille, on the same tunnel. Everything the same. Try to find workmanship like that nowadays. It would not be so easy.

He was leaning casually on the wall. He looked up and across the river illuminated in the streetlights and those of the bars and restaurants lining both sides of its banks. He was alone. He liked being alone. Especially at times like this. It gave him time to think. He knew that success lay in the small details. Get these right, and everything else would follow.

He thought of Tyler. He would not be coming out of those tunnels again. Alive, that is. Maybe in a hundred years' time, they'd find his bones somewhere down there. It might make a news item; they would wonder whose bones they were. Call it Tyler's moment of fame.

Khabib didn't care about any of that. He only cared about the here and the now. Still, he knew Tyler represented more than a small detail. Tyler was one of the best torch blowers and cutters out there – in this line of business, that is. He'd be hard to replace. Khabib wasn't superstitious, but he had a bad feeling about this job. Maybe when it was over, he'd consider retiring, to some place in southeast Asia. He'd like that. Or would he? He didn't need the money. It was the buzz. He loved the buzz; it was like a drug. Could he live without that? Maybe.

He turned and walked away, pulling up the collar of his coat against the Dublin evening chill.

AT MIDNIGHT, Khabib told everyone to turn in. It was then he told them the news they had been waiting for.

'We'll do the bank in forty-eight hours. But we go in tomorrow. Everyone knows the drill. Now give me your phones.'

With that announcement, Tyler knew he had forty-eight hours to work out what to do when this job was over. How he could walk away from it with his life, before his meter ran out, before the banner popped up *Out of Time.*

9

Brody was on the way out of his office when his computer pinged an incoming email alert. The computer didn't used to always do that. But since a technician had visited to give it a security sweep, it had, as well as a screensaver appearing with the legend:

> *Nothing messes up your Friday like finding out that it's only Tuesday.*

Brody remembered the technician had been a bit of a joker alright.

He paused in the doorway and checked the time. He had just under ten minutes to make it to the Northside Boxing Club, just a stone's throw from HQ, where he was due to coach kids from the tough corporation flats just off the North Circular Road. He'd promised the bulldog, Jimmy Nugent, reformed drug addict and onetime small-time criminal, now on a quest to save the kids from the area from going down the same path he'd gone down, he'd do it. It seemed to be working; referrals to the juvenile liaison scheme had dropped by almost fifty percent in the postcode since Jimmy began his work.

Brody returned to his desk, leaned over the computer and opened up the email. It was from the Herbert Park and said:

Sergeant Brody, please find attached CCTV for the time period specified. The cameras cover the foyer of the hotel and the corridor leading to room 532. Anything else, let me know. Regards, Chris Glynn.

Brody experienced that familiar feeling, like an invisible elbow nudging him into his belly. He sat down and opened the video file. The boxing club would just have to wait. First, he'd have a quick scan through, then delegate someone to do it properly later. Brody knew what he was looking for, footage of the person he'd seen leaving through the employee door, and he scrolled through until he reached it. He froze the image, the person striding out into the foyer. It looked like they were goose-stepping. The image was fuzzy, so Brody went into settings, knowing there was something there to help make it sharper. The techie had told him about it, a scraper or something it was called. He found it, Auto-Focus the name of the app underneath, clicked into it and imported the image. Immediately it was transformed into something a short-sighted person might see once they'd put their glasses on. It was sharp and in focus, and revealed a male about five-ten tall, Brody reckoned. This male was wearing a blue puffer jacket, with a baseball cap pulled down low over his eyes. Brody leaned in close, looking at the trousers and shoes he had on. They didn't fit with the casual puffer jacket and cap, instead, he could tell they were black formal wear, and the black shoes were dress shoes. Had he a uniform on underneath? Was he a waiter or one of the management team? What? The image was small to scale. Brody zoomed in, but it was like the short-sighted person had just taken their glasses off again. He tried it once more, but this time the scraper didn't work; it was only effective in scale. Still, this was good, this was very good. Brody made a mental note to check the clocking-off times of all staff on that date. He glanced to the top of the screen, where there was a digital imprint of the time. It read 22:03.

Of course, this person might be completely innocent, might have nothing to do with anything, just a bona fide member of staff going home at the end of a long shift. Speaking of which, Brody checked his watch again. If he left now, and got lucky and the lights were green all the way, he just might make it to the club in time. He closed out of his emails and hurried out of the office.

10

The changing rooms at Northside Boxing Club were nothing more than a couple of partitioned-off sections in opposite corners to each other, one for the kids and one for the adults. Brody got kitted out and was standing in the centre of the ring when he heard the muted sound of a telephone ringing. It was his phone, he knew, ringing from the bottom of his gym bag resting on a bench along one wall. About him were a gaggle of skinny kids in an assortment of ill-fitting wear, everything from their mothers' summer shorts and fathers' Bermuda shorts to one kid in pyjama cut-offs. Footwear was everything from plimsolls to everyday cheap sneakers to the one in pyjama cut-offs wearing a pair of high-end Nikes. Brody could only guess at how he had come on those. The class was basic boxing skills. This was the third week, and Brody was pleased with the attendance. He wanted to answer the phone, but more than anything, for this short while, he wanted to be here for these kids. For some, he and Jimmy were the only male role models in their lives.

'You not goin' to answer that, mister?' one of them asked, sniffling and wiping a glove across his nose.

The lad's name was Jimmy Kinsella. Brody knew his father had walked out on them when the kid's mother had given birth to the latest of their five children, a baby girl. Little Jimmy was light on his feet but didn't punch very hard, and certainly not hard enough for the kids around here to take notice. Consequently, he kept getting pummelled in the ring. So Brody was reluctant to put him in it now. He felt sorry for the kid, though he tried not to, because feeling sorry for somebody didn't help.

'Call me Jack, why don't ya, Jimmy? You know me well enough by now.'

The lad rubbed his glove over his nose again and looked away, not answering. The lad might be physically present, but a part of him wasn't, never was, a part of him was cowering deep within himself, hidden, too scared to come out.

The phone was still ringing. Brody inwardly cursed and went and answered it. Marty was on the other end. When he told him what Pierre Jousten had said, Brody whistled softly and said, 'Wow.'

Marty laughed.

'What's so funny?'

'Nothing, boss, only you said what I said when I was told, that's all, *Wow*.'

'Right, can you get this circulated immediately? Intelligence for now, Marty.'

'Already done, boss. And I got word back from forensics. That print, on the shower handle, belongs to the victim.'

'Did you let the super know?'

'I did. She alerted the GNBCI.'

The Garda National Bureau of Criminal Investigation.

'Good again,' Brody said. 'I'd better talk to her. I'll ring her when I finish here.'

'Anything else, boss?'

'Yeah, go home and get a good night's rest. You'll need it. See you at the ranch in the morning.'

'You mean the HQ, boss, don't you?'

Jack laughed. 'Whatever,' he said, and hung up.

A chorus of excited young voices sounded behind him.

'What's going on?' he asked, looking over his shoulder just in time to see young Kinsella falling to the floor. Another lad was standing over him, fists held high, laughing.

Brody shoved the phone into his bag and strode over, pointed a finger. 'What'd you do that for? You're new here. What's your name?'

'Stephen Dempsey.'

'Right, Dempsey, why'd you push young Jimmy?'

''Cause he's a faggot, that's why. I don't like faggots.'

The rest of the boys laughed.

'That's enough,' Brody snapped, and they fell silent. 'Go home, Dempsey. I don't want you here. Come back when you've learned a bit of manners.'

'You can't send me home?'

'I just did.'

'Make me.'

'You're a cheeky little bollocks, aren't you, Dempsey?'

The lad gave him a twisted, well-practised snarly grin, one he probably used each day at school to intimidate his teacher, probably a young female recently out of teacher training college. In that moment Brody realised he was handling this all wrong. This wasn't a gouger, this was a kid.

'Okay, Dempsey. Listen up, everybody. Sparring partners.

And, Dempsey, you can stay, but you're with him...' Brody pointed. The lad he pointed to was Joshua Obianagha, one of the best boxers for his age in the club. And outside the ring, too, he wasn't one to be pushed around. The lad had to stand up for himself. Brody knew it wasn't easy being black in this part of town.

'Him,' Dempsey said, 'but he's...'

'He's what?'

'Black.'

'So? You have a problem with that?'

The lad didn't look so cocky any longer.

'No. I don't have a problem with nothing, me.'

'Tough guy, eh?'

'Yeah, tough guy. I'll show ya. He'll go down just like the faggot Kinsella went down. White is best. You'll see.'

'I don't believe you just said that.' Brody was beginning to think maybe he should have sent the lad home after all.

But Obianagha, fair dues to him, just laughed and waved a hand through the air. He'd heard it all before. Which, in some ways, Brody considered, was even worse, because it meant he was, or was becoming, immune to it. And maybe Dempsey was beyond saving. But still, Brody wanted to give it a go.

BRODY PUT little Jimmy Kinsella and another lad, Ray Clarke, in first. Three rounds of two minutes each. Both were similar, weak hitters afraid of their own shadows, products of dysfunctional home situations. Brody had seen it all before, next stop might be the discovery of smack, and then one more stop after that, forever chasing the dragon but never finding it. Jesus, if only he could save them. But he was a cop, not a social worker, although he knew cops increasingly had to be both. Anyway, by putting them in first, at least they could relax and not have to worry about it again.

Brody was impressed, though, all the lads were coming on, holding their guard up just like he'd shown them, countering with some thought and using the space in the ring to manoeuvre, or, if they needed, to retreat and give themselves time to recover. All of them had come to the club with a wildness about them, flailing arms and exhausting themselves until all they could do was fold over, breathless. He knew why they were doing this; it was because they were scared. Boxing was about expending violence, yes, and for most of them violence featured in their lives, and because they were kids, usually they were at the receiving end of it. But Brody wanted to show them that boxing was about so much more. It was about control, of your emotions, your energy, and ultimately, of yourself. It was about tact, resolve, intelligence, planning and calculated response. Learn to master these, and you gain control, and when you gain control, you can win. In every aspect of life these attributes could be utilised. They could change a life. And for kids like these, that change could save them.

'Okay,' Brody said, clapping his hands. The last two lads stepped out of the ring. It was now the turn of…'Dempsey and Obianagha,' Brody called, 'step up.' This was the last sparring bout. Both came into the ring and stood facing each other.

Brody could feel it from Dempsey, a raw – and misplaced – rage towards Obianagha. Brody was certain Dempsey didn't understand or question this rage. In his reality, it was acceptable, encouraged, especially when it was directed at someone like Obianagha.

'Touch gloves,' Brody said. Obianagha immediately raised his and brought them forward, but Dempsey didn't. 'I said touch gloves. Dempsey.' The gloves went up, half-heartedly, going through the motions only because he had to. Brody nudged both lads a little further apart, brought his arm up and then down between them, paused, and withdrew. 'Box,' he said.

The flurry was immediate and vicious from Dempsey. Brody had rarely seen such aggression in so young a lad. Obianagha was taken by surprise too. But he was immune to the blows, his guard up, his head bent, his shoulders forward. Dempsey couldn't get to him. Brody knew what was coming. Dempsey couldn't sustain the onslaught, and as soon as his momentum faltered, Obianagha sent in a cross. Dempsey had no guard up; his arms had fallen to his sides. He appeared to be so used to punching others without any thought of any blows being returned to him that he'd forgotten exactly where he was, or who he was up against.

The cross hit his nose straight on, and Dempsey wobbled, blood streaming from one nostril.

Brody stopped the fight immediately, and Dempsey screamed at him, 'Wha' ya do that for? That was a dirty shot; me hands were down. That bastard couldn't bait me, so he couldn't.'

'He just did,' Brody said. 'Go and get yourself cleaned up, Dempsey. I mean it. You can have a rematch, no problem.'

'I can?'

'You can.'

Dempsey wiped his hand across his nose and seemed

taken aback at the amount of blood on it. It was dripping onto the canvas.

'Right then,' he said, sounding a little relieved, 'but I want me rematch.'

Brody watched him leave the ring. The other lads were quiet, looking at Obianagha. What he saw on their faces was respect. Little Jimmy Kinsella seemed enthralled, as if he'd made a discovery, as if he'd found out the meaning of something both profound and simple at the same time, something that maybe could change his life.

But as Dempsey cursed loudly to himself in the partitioned-off changing area at the end of the gym, they knew this wasn't over. Not by a long chalk.

Brody nodded to Obianagha, who smiled that dazzling smile of his in return. All in my normal day, that smile said. Brody knew the other lads would be watching this rematch very closely, to see if it really was true, that the bully didn't always win.

'Right, lads,' he said, 'well done. Now go and get changed. See you all next week.'

11

Later, on the drive home from the boxing club, Brody flicked the Bluetooth on the steering wheel and rang Superintendent Ryan.

'You heard from Marty?' she asked before he had a chance to speak, dispensing with all pleasantries.

'About an hour ago, give or take.'

'Serious hitters.'

'Yes, serious hitters,' Brody agreed.

'Course, it could all be a coincidence.'

'You think?'

She didn't answer. Which didn't surprise him. Superintendent Ryan wasn't going to give an opinion either way – not yet.

In the background he could hear the sound of a TV; he guessed the evening news. He couldn't hear any other sounds, though, or voices. He realised he knew very little of the super's private life. No, that was incorrect. He knew nothing about it at all. He remembered what she'd said, that the murder would be an easy one to get to the bottom of. Did she feel the same way now? He doubted it. Nothing was turning out to be easy about any of this. That's what you get for tempting fate.

'We'll wait and see what ballistics throw up,' she said, 'that should give us a better indication. We get any word on that?'

She knew as well as he did that Marty was looking after it. If he had something, he would have mentioned it. Yet she was asking him. He supposed it was her way of appearing to be in charge, or maybe shifting responsibility to him. Well, he wasn't going to go along with it. He didn't answer the question either, told her of the CCTV footage he'd received instead, of his plan to request shift times for all staff on duty at the hotel on Tuesday evening.

'I think we need to at least make a plan to deal with the likelihood a bank has been targeted. That we might already be on countdown.'

'Don't be premature, Jack. Like I said, it may be all a complete coincidence.

Which Jack had already considered. But, he reminded himself, he didn't believe in coincidences.

'And if it's not?'

'Well,' she said, 'if it's not, then it's not. No way can we monitor every bank near a river in this city, if that's what you have in mind. And remember, they came up through the sewers.'

'I remember. If we wanted to, we could put a team into each bank that fits the criteria. It's possible.'

'That's a lot of manpower. We'd need a team of at least three to four, multiplied by, I don't know, at least fifteen banks. Seriously? Jeez, I don't see anyone sanctioning that.'

'It wouldn't be for long. Today is Wednesday. If this is going down, then it'll be at the weekend. Makes sense.'

'I'm attending a liaison meeting tomorrow, via Zoom, with the GNBCI.'

Liaison, as opposed to contact. A talking shop. Whatever.

'Even watching that many CCTV monitors will take a lot of manpower,' she added.

It sounded to Jack like she was talking herself out of it.

'CCTV monitors of what?' he asked.

'I dunno, manhole covers,' she said. 'How else can they get into the tunnels? It's obvious, it's the only way in.'

Jack had never really thought about it. But he immediately saw another route.

'They could come in from the river itself. Less chance of being spotted, I'd say. Those old sewer tunnels all end up in the Liffey.'

'There's no evidence they went in that way with the other jobs, is there? I don't like this. We're talking as if a robbery, a burglary, whatever, is imminent. It may very well not be. Let's not tempt fate, shall we.'

Jack wanted to laugh. *That's rich*, he thought.

'It may very well be about to kick off too,' he said.

'The situation will be monitored, Jack, okay?'

12

During an active investigation, the unit room was like a workshop. It needed a constant delivery of raw materials to maintain production. By next morning, raw materials had arrived in the form of further CCTV from the Herbert Park Platinum Hotel, and finally, the preliminary ballistics report from Forensics Services Ireland. And then, a hat trick, Mercedes at FSI was on the phone – which could only mean one thing.

'Mercedes,' Brody said, 'you've got something for me?'

The young Spaniard had both flattered and astonished Brody not so long ago by asking him out on a date. Brody had declined, told her he was old enough to be her father – which he was, just about. It hadn't created any awkwardness between the two of them afterwards. Jack admired her *cajones*.

'I have got a pubic hair for you, if you must know,' she said, and giggled, 'a single pubic hair.'

'Oh.' Brody's mind whirred.

'Yes,' she said, 'exactly two point one centimetres long.

He likes to shave down there, Jack.'

'Oh, he does, does he?'

'Kinky, *qué*?'

'Or maybe he doesn't want to leave behind any evidence.'

'Well, that did not work for him.'

'Didn't it?' Brody felt the invisible elbow into the belly again. 'That means you have a match?'

'*Sí*. Matches a DNA sample taken in 2001, from the body of a woman murdered in the town of Beaverton, Ontario, Canada. Scrapings from underneath the fingernails of the right hand, loose skin along with traces of dandruff, like she'd been running her hand through his hair. Weird or what? Anyway, the killer was chased from the scene. He ran into a forest. A vast forest, and he was never seen again.'

'Really? Never seen again?'

'This is not a fairy story, Jack, yes. He really ran into a forest and was never seen again. But...' She paused. 'If you want me to read you a fairy story sometime?'

'And what then?' he asked, ignoring that offer. 'You said they chased him. Who chased him?'

'I don't know. It was an information note attached to the DNA report. Sometimes we do that, to give context. They thought he may have been eaten by a bear – he wasn't.'

Brody tried to make sense of what he'd just heard, decided he needed to contact the Canadian police and get that report asap. A single particle of pubic hair turning up like that in Ireland, a DNA match to a murder victim in Ontario. No, Jack did not believe in coincidences.

'Where was it found exactly, Mercedes?'

'In her belly button.'

'Her belly button?'

'Yes, Jack, her belly button.'

'How could it get there?'

'You can use your imagination, Jack. Or maybe he planted it.'

Jack thought about that. Maybe the killer *did* plant it.

'Who's the suspect? In the Canadian case. And who's the victim? Does the note tell you that?'

'Yes, Jack, it does. Prepare yourself.'

'I'm prepared. Go on.'

'The suspect is Abraham Jackman.'

'Okay. And the victim?'

'Gloria Jackman.'

'Hm, are they related?'

'Yes. They are. It was his mother.'

'What?'

This was not enough information for her to have warned him to prepare himself. That didn't win any cigars. But what she said next did.

'He was just fourteen years old, Jack, when he killed her.'

Okay, that did. Jack took that in. 'Christ, that's young, very young.' He paused. 'Which would make him, what? I calculate about thirty-five. And never heard of again. No wonder they thought a bear ate him. Anything else?'

'Maybe. We're still doing tests. I'll let you know.'

'Thank you.'

'And Jack?'

'Yes.'

'Do you, you know…?'

'Do I what?'

'…shave down there?'

'I'll have to speak to *your* mother, Mercedes,' Brody said. 'Like seriously.' And he hung up.

Yes, that girl had *cajones*, crazy *cajones*.

13

Brody was impressed with the detail the Mounties had compiled on their subject. He read the six-page report their Interpol National Central Bureau had forwarded him, which was now freely available on the RCMP website. It had protected status once, but with the passage of time, the decision had been made to lift it. They'd nothing to lose now, after all.

Abraham Jackman was his name. He was the son of Samuel Jackman and his wife, Gloria. Samuel Jackman was an evangelical Christian, but Gloria didn't have much faith in anything – certainly not before she met Samuel, that is – apart from what she could shove into the tips pouch of her apron at the Rooster bar and diner, where she worked waitressing and bartending shifts. Indeed, Brody thought, opposites do attract.

The report told Brody that Abraham, or Aby for short, was an only child. His father, Samuel, was a distant and dour character, obsessed with the Bible, the wrath of God, and conspiracy theories, all in that order. He farmed a hundred-acre wheat and cattle farm and believed every bad harvest or burst pipe or cow with a lame leg was a sign of God's displeasure with him. While there was an occasional bad harvest, there was always a burst pipe or a lame cow, and his life was one of constant penance seeking the redemption of God. It was hard for Gloria and her young boy, Abe. But it drew them close, very close, it seemed, very, *very* close. The rumour was that Samuel had come home one day and found his wife and son in bed together, doing what mothers and sons should never do. He was not angry with either of them, however. Instead, who he was angry with was himself, taking it as yet another sign of God's displeasure with him. But some within his circle, religious zealots just more extreme, believed his wife to be bewitched. Brody blinked, like for real. And they believed the son to be her imp. At this point Brody did a quick Google search for the meaning of witch's imp, which told him they were *Attendants of the devil who assist witches in their evildoings.* The community began to give both mother and son a wide berth. As far as Brody was concerned, all that was missing from this tale was the Salem witch trials.

    Her body was found in an outhouse by Samuel one hot July afternoon. She had been stabbed once through the heart using a kitchen knife with a twelve-inch blade. The knife had been rammed into her chest up to the hilt. Responding constables found young Abraham himself cowering in a storm drain close by. He admitted to killing his mother, but the constables didn't quite believe him; they thought he was in shock. He was a kid, after all. They took their eyes off him for just a moment while they set about preserving the scene. That was enough. He took off. They went after him, but he was fast and knew the land a lot better than they did, like the back of his hand. He ran into the forest. It stretched for thousands of acres. He was never seen again. It was like he had disappeared off the face of the earth.

'Wow,' Brody muttered. How was that possible? Being eaten by a bear was the only logical conclusion. The Mounties thought so too. Until now, that is.

'WE'RE GETTING DISTRACTED,' Brody said. He was back in Superintendent Ryan's office again.

She was standing by the window, just like the Old Man used to do. Brody's old boss liked to gaze out in the hope of spotting some deer when he had something to mull over. Maybe she was doing the same.

'Take a seat, Jack,' she said and turned.

Superintendent Ryan looked tired, he thought. She sat behind her desk and looked at him. It was already almost lunchtime. Jack sat down.

'I've been giving it some thought,' she said. 'And I agree... I spoke with Chief Super Shanahan over in the GNBCI. He's open to suggestions on this.'

'With respect. We don't have time for suggestions. We need to make a plan. And implement it.'

Her narrow eyes narrowed even further, a hard sheen to them. She wouldn't like Jack telling her what to do.

'Really. Just like that?'

'Yes,' Jack said, 'just like that. And with everything we have. I have a friend, he's a baker, and he says you put everything in at the beginning because even if it's too much rather than too little, you can always adjust as you go on. But if you don't put enough in at the beginning, that's it, you can never make it up again; you can never recover. Put all the ingredients in now, whatever's available, that's what I say.'

'Can you speak in plain English? You've lost me.'

'It's just like I said. We put everything in now, extra patrols, extra traffic stops, extra everything, but, more than anything, a team into every bank on or near a sewerage tunnel anywhere in Dublin. And we do it now.'

'God, you're not asking for much.'

'Me? I'm not asking for anything. I'm just telling you what I'd do, that's all.'

'What *you'd* do, you mean. But what if *you're* calling this wrong?'

What if *you're* calling it wrong? Jack could almost hear the can of blowback repellent hiss as she pressed the cap.

She sat back and peered at him, her eyes calculating now.

'Okay, Jack, okay, so tell me, how do *you* propose to do this, *exactly*?'

14

Khabib was driving, Tyler in the passenger seat. Tyler noted he was never left on his own now. In the apartment someone was always around, someone always with him. The only thing he was allowed to do without anyone looking was take a dump. Even then he could swear someone was outside the bathroom door.

The vehicle was a Mitsubishi pickup with a removable hardtop cover over the cargo bay. Nothing that would stand out, but powerful and fast enough if they should need it. And, like everything else, it had just appeared. God, the great hidden maestro in the sky, not God *God*, but the one they called God, whatever, whoever, or wherever he was, had pulled a lever, and it just appeared. He was better than God. Because if you asked this God for something, he always delivered.

The Mitsubishi reminded Tyler of what his father used to drive, an old Subaru Outback. That was back in the day. Back when Tyler wasn't Tyler. No, when he was Abraham, or, as Momma used to call him, Aby Baby. Back then, before

THAT day. After THAT day, Abraham had never been seen again. They say he was eaten by a bear in the woods. Naughty bear. Lately, he'd been thinking. It wasn't fair. Why should Abraham have to die just so Tyler could live? He'd been thinking about it a lot, actually. No, it wasn't fair, because Abraham had never gone away, you know. He lived. That was why he'd left that teensy tiny reminder, because a part of him wanted to be noticed. Demanded it, in fact. Not that it would make any difference. They wouldn't find it. Because if there was one thing that was certain in this life, it was that cops were the stupidest, dumbest motherfuckers on the face of this green earth.

They drove through a gritty part of town, boarded-up shopfronts, a burnt-out warehouse of some description. Khabib swung a right at a junction, following the Mitsubishi's sat nav, swung a left and a little further along turned onto a rutted track that led them onto a flat expanse of waste ground. They drove past a hoarding that announced:

Comerford Downs

Homes for Modern living: Commencing this Spring!

Comerford Downs, Where Dreams Begin...

There were oases of barren waste ground like this in the central areas of every city; God was always able to sniff them out. The ring of security cameras high on steel poles all the way around had each been turned the other way. This God could command anything.

As the Mitsubishi pitched and rolled over the rough

ground, Tyler found himself starting to get a little nervous. He didn't normally do nervous; it was one of the reasons why he was so good at his job. But there was a first for everything. After all, you needed calm nerves to hold cutters and drills, the cutters heating to a thousand degrees at their tip, and, used in relays with the drills and other equipment, he could cut through the thickest concrete, steel, rock, whatever. You name it, he could cut through it. Or your money back. Guaranteed.

But not now; now he was a little nervous.

Khabib didn't speak. Nothing unusual in that, and Tyler thought: *He's goin' to do me. I know it. He's goin' to do me here.*

He didn't move, not a muscle, like that time when he was a kid and his father was driving the Subaru, playing the preacher Jim Bakker on the cassette deck, and he'd started shouting that the devil was everywhere, that he was just waiting for a chance to grab your soul when you weren't looking: *You're going to hell, boy, repent before it's too late and beg for your sins to be forgiven. If you don't, you're going to burn in hell for all eternity. All ETERNITY, boy. You have any idea what that's going to be like?* And, in that moment, young Abraham was convinced that he could see the devil in his father's eyes, and that the devil wanted to kill him. Still, old Pop was entitled to be a little angry; after all, he'd caught him in bed with dear Momma, that would be daddy's wife. *I mean, I would have killed me after that.* But he didn't kill him. In fact, after that blow-off, he'd started to cry, muttering that it was all his fault, that the devil was clever; it was he who was being taken along the road to eternal damnation. Pathetic, really.

Khabib reminded him of that now, reminded him of his father, even the way he drove, sitting slightly forward in the seat, slumped over the steering wheel, chewing on a dilemma. And the dilemma wasn't the devil or damnation. No, the dilemma was him.

He didn't move. There was nothing to do but wait.

But then Khabib said casually, 'Get ready; we're almost here,' and Tyler blinked, and he knew that Khabib *wasn't* going to do him after all. Knew by the way he'd said it, and also, *because* he'd said it. Like, for real, if he was going to kill him, he wouldn't tell him to get ready...or would he?

Ahead was a collection of semi-derelict sheds and outhouses, breeze-block walls and corrugated-iron roofs, the iron rusty and pockmarked by weathered holes.

He drove the four-wheel drive into the middle one, turned until it was facing back the way they'd just come, and cut the engine, got out. Tyler followed. What they'd come for was resting against the end wall behind the truck. Four of them, same as last time, same as every time, canvas satchels, heavy, but not so heavy they couldn't take one each and hoist it into the rear of the Mitsubishi. Two would contain the tools of their trade; these were the latest, pioneering, cutting-edge cutting, mining and drilling equipment: ten years ago, the contents of those two satchels alone would have required a small box truck to transport. The other two satchels had in them military-grade wet suits along with the other paraphernalia they'd require.

They worked quickly and silently. It didn't take long. Less than five minutes and they were climbing back into the Mitsubishi, their load secured on the flat bed. Khabib rammed the Mitsubishi into gear and spun the wheels as he moved off again. They'd gone just a short distance when he braked hard. Tyler hadn't had time to put on his seat belt, and he was sent flying forward, thinking, *I got this wrong; this is the end; he is going to do me.*

As he fumbled against the dash, he braced himself for the partial explosion that he expected to hear as the gun's pin hit the charge at the bottom of the round, releasing it through the barrel and into his head. A partial explosion only. Because he wouldn't have time to hear the end; he'd be dead.

But instead, there was...nothing. He turned his eyes to the side, expecting to see a muzzle pressing against his temple. Then, after that, the shot would come. Surely, then it would come? But there was no shot. And there was no muzzle. Instead, what he saw was Khabib open the door and jump out of the SUV. Tyler flopped back into his seat. Christ, he'd been certain this was it, *certain*. The end. But it wasn't...not yet.

He scrambled out of the Mitsubishi too, thinking something had to give; this couldn't go on. He almost wanted Khabib to shoot him in the head. Get it over with. Crazy or what? He looked ahead and...froze.

A motorbike was heading towards them, white with yellow stripes, a blue light at the back – turned off – fixed to the top of a metal pole, the rider clad in black leather.

A police motorbike.

Shit!

The bike kicked up a cloud of gravel and dust as it approached. Tyler stood still, Khabib ahead of him, hands held loose by his sides. They both waited. The bike was almost upon them. At the last minute it swung across in front of them and came to a stop. The cop swung a leg lazily over the machine, kicked the bike stand down with the heel of his boot as he did so, and stood before them, flicking up the visor of his helmet, his hands on his waist. He didn't speak, his eyes flicking from one to the other.

'Yes, officer?' Khabib said. 'Can I help you?'

'Did I speak? No, I don't think I did. So shut up.'

Tyler stiffened. He could see Khabib do the same. This cop was up to no good.

As if reading his mind, the cop smiled. 'Got everything you need there, did you, boys?'

What the fuck? Tyler thought.

The cop stepped up to Khabib. He was taller, and he peered down at him, like a storm trooper dressed in that helmet and leathers of his. Then he stepped around him and moved to the Mitsubishi. They both turned and watched him as he paused by the bonnet, touched it with a finger, ran it along the side as he moved to the back, where he clenched his hand and tapped it gently onto the hardtop canopy a couple of times.

'I saw you turn off the road out there,' he said, standing back and pointing. 'I was waiting for you, see. You took your time.'

Tyler wondered that if God really was God, then was this one of his angels? And, if this were the case, then why had he chosen to appear here, especially now?

Tyler didn't like it, didn't like it at all. His brain jumped a notch back into the groove of thinking Khabib might, after all, be going to do him. This was getting boring already. Maybe this was part of it. But for the second time Khabib said something that told him this wasn't the case.

Khabib said, 'What you talking about?'

'What am I talking about? Don't you know?' The cop swung his arms in an expansive gesture. 'I'm talking about how all this shite got here. You ever think about that? Well? I mean, you just show up like rock stars, the stage all set up for you, lights and everything, the roadies already done all the work.' He stabbed a finger against his chest. 'Hello. It was me. I brought all this shite in. Alone. Now you know. It just didn't appear out of a clear blue sky. Maybe when all this is over, you'll remember my contribution, okay? That's all I'm saying.'

'And how would I do that?' Khabib asked. Tyler could hear the change of tone. Khabib was dangerous when he had a tone like that.

'Let me tell you,' the cop said. 'It's not complicated. You just…'

'I just?'

'Drop a little, that's all. You won't even miss it. Just a little…keep me happy for the next time. You need me, remember.'

'Oh, I think I get it now,' Khabib said, like he was stupid and the lightbulb had just come on.

But Khabib wasn't stupid. He wasn't stupid at all. The one who was stupid was the cop.

Khabib shook his head.

'So,' he said, 'you thought you'd just come in here and ask for a contribution, is that it? In the middle of all' – it was Khabib's turn to open his arms in an expansive gesture – 'this. Like we have nothing better to do. You thought that would be a good idea. Really?'

The cop shrugged. 'Why not?'

Which all went to reinforce Tyler's low opinion of cops.

'And he knows about this, does he?'

The cop's eyes narrowed inside that white helmet of his. 'He? Who's he?'

'God,' Khabib said.

'What the fuck you talking about?' the cop spat.

Tyler couldn't help but smile. The cop was on a contract, someone as far down the food chain as Japan was from the moon. He knew they were dumb, but he never thought one could be *this* dumb.

'Could I make my contribution now?' Khabib said. 'Will that get you off my back? Call it a one-off payment?'

Although his mouth was partially hidden, Tyler could tell the cop was beginning to smile. The dumb, *dumb* fuck.

'Course,' he said, and laughed. 'But no credit card, mind.'

Yes, Tyler thought, *you're fucking hilarious.*

'One minute,' Khabib said and turned, went to the truck and opened the driver's door. 'This. If it's not enough, I don't know. But it's the best I can do right now. Come here and have a look.'

The cop sauntered over.

'There,' Khabib said and pointed, taking a step back. 'You can have that, right there.'

The cop moved closer, starting to lean into the cab, as Khabib came from behind. Khabib grabbed the sides of his helmet with both hands, yanked it back and viciously rammed it forward again against the roof of the Mitsubishi, twice. He released it and looked about, stepped over and picked up a rock that was lying there, stepped back again. The cop was still on his feet, swaying, making a low moaning sound. Khabib swung the rock in a wide arc and propelled it forward, passing it through the gap in the helmet where the visor went, crashing it right into the centre of the cop's face. There was a dull plopping sound, and a geyser of red erupted. The cop began to howl as Khabib quickly followed up, swinging the rock again, *plop*. The cop stumbled back against the Mitsubishi, the howling changing to a loud rasping, gurgling sound, coming from where his nose had been, a piece of crushed bone protruding from the ripped and torn flesh like a hook in its place. Blood foamed from between his lips and bubbled down the chin guard of his helmet. He staggered forward, then back, then sideways, turning as he did so, and Khabib kicked him in the back, collapsing him onto his knees. Khabib stood over him, raised his leg, and stomped down onto the back of his head, flattening him against the ground, then stomped again and again into the back of his head, *plop, plop*. When he stopped, the cop was completely still and silent. Tyler knew he was dead. Had to be.

'Take an arm,' Khabib called, and he didn't hesitate, went over and bent down, grabbed one. Khabib took the other, and together they dragged the cop into the shed.

'Shit,' Khabib said, dropping him, 'that's all we need.' He stood panting, looking down at the body.

Tyler was about to ask, *What now?* But stopped himself. Khabib wouldn't have liked that.

Khabib looked outside and pointed. 'That bike. Bring it in here. Now.'

Tyler brought the bike in and pulled it onto its stand.

'Help me get him on it.'

They pulled the body onto the bike, where it flopped forward over the fuel tank, the head lolling to one side. Khabib reached under the body. Tyler could hear him unscrewing the cap from the fuel tank.

'You got a match?'

'No.'

'Then go and look in the fucking truck.'

Tyler found an old lighter in the glove compartment. He checked it. It worked, just about.

He handed it to Khabib, who had a crumpled tissue in his other hand.

'Lift him up so I can get my hand under.'

He watched Khabib flick the lighter a couple of times, sparking a weak flame that crawled out of the burner. 'Get a move on,' he barked, and Tyler pressed his hands beneath the cop's chest, hoisted the dead weight just enough for Khabib to pass the burning tissue under. 'Fire in the hole,' he said, and dropped the flame into the tank. Tyler took his hands away and ran.

Maybe there wasn't much fuel in the tank, maybe it was because there was a body lying on top of it, but the explosion was muted. They turned. Black smoke seeped out from beneath the body, but nothing appeared to be burning, then...

Swoosh.

It all went up, a blue, yellow and orange fireball engulfing the bike, the flames dancing wildly, the smoke thick and black, funnelling up into a miniature mushroom cloud. Tyler could see the cop's leathers start to melt, long sinewy blobs falling to the ground, the air fizzing and crackling, a fireworks display taking hold in the centre of the inferno as the electrics went up. The body began to slide from the bike, the momentum taking the machine with it, both toppling to the ground, man and machine, indistinguishable, fusing together into one macabre, melting, metallic, rubber, flesh stew.

Without a word, they got into the Mitsubishi and drove away.

15

They sat in the conference room at the Phoenix Park around the big old rosewood table, five of the most senior gardai in the country: three males, two females, along with the head of the Central Bank, Desmond Long, and a senior official from the Department of Finance, Philip Gates, as well as Jack and Superintendent Ryan.

Assistant Commissioner Padraic Kelly held a laser pointer in his hands, staring up at the huge screen that took up almost the entire wall at the top of the room. On it was a street map of central Dublin, stretching from the Sean Heuston Bridge in the west, to the Ringsend Bridge in the east, and inward for five hundred metres on either side.

He glanced to Superintendent Ryan.

'Banks,' the assistant commissioner said, 'your information is for banks, not any other types of financial institutions, is that correct?'

'The information is for banks, sir; yes, that is correct.'

The assistant commissioner looked from Superintendent Ryan to Brody, a *look*.

'Okay then, Superintendent Ryan, let's follow the trail.'

'Sir?'

'The information you received. Why we're all gathered here at such short notice. Can you spell it out in greater detail?'

All heads turned to take in Ryan.

'Well,' she began, 'it's not, um, information as such. It's...' Her voice trailed off, and she looked to the bankers, both dressed in dark pinstriped suits, their grey hair combed back. 'What I mean is, it is information, but we came upon it as the result of a separate investigation into...' Again she looked to the bankers.

'It's okay,' the deputy commissioner said, 'you can say it.'

'...the murder of a female at the Herbert Park Platinum Hotel, sir.'

'We all know about that, Superintendent. No secret.'

'Yes,' she said tentatively, 'but other details have not been released...we held them back, sir.'

Brody realised that Kelly seemed to be enjoying Superintendent Ryan's discomfort. Even now, at a time like this, the spaghetti hats were playing their little power games. They were so long off the streets, he considered, dealing with budgets and spreadsheets and whatever else they dealt with, they had morphed from police officers into bureaucrats. Brody hated that.

'Ladies and gentlemen,' Kelly said, 'what Superintendent Ryan is trying to say is that our investigation has led us onto some very important discoveries. Run us through it, please, Superintendent Ryan.'

Superintendent Ryan got up and went to the top of the room.

The AC pressed a button on the bottom corner of the

display screen, and the image changed to one showing the façade of a building. He pressed the laser pointer to life, and a green dot appeared on it and swept across. He handed the pointer to her.

'Our IT section compiled this very hastily in the last hour,' she said. 'It should provide a good overview.'

Brody had only heard about it just before the meeting, in an email briefing. But no matter, this was good.

She held the pointer steady on the façade of ornate stone, in front of which were a couple of trees at the side of a street, a perimeter crime scene tape extending between the two and down towards the building to form a rectangle. Over the open door of the building in Germanic script were the words *Zomat Bank.*

'Seven point five million euro in used notes was taken from the Valencia branch of the Zomat Bank right in the heart of the Spanish city in March 2019,' she began. 'The raiders came up through a sewer pipe and into the vault. It happened on the weekend and was not discovered until Monday at start of business. Initially it was thought to have been connected to the Russian mob; the Spanish police went down that investigative rabbit hole for a time. Back then there was quite the Russian presence in the city, your ordinary common or garden tourist mainly, but the Russian mob was beginning to make an appearance. By the time Russia invaded Ukraine in spring 2022, the mob had built up quite a presence throughout eastern and southern regions of the country. The Guardia Civil has now ruled out the Russian mob. Who, by the way, have virtually disappeared. The Guardia Civil also discounted them for another reason, because something else happened in Valencia at about the same time as the bank hit. Specifically, forty-eight hours beforehand...'

Superintendent Ryan fumbled with the TV, pressed a button on the bottom corner of the screen, and the image changed once more, this time to one of a woman: an attractive woman with olive skin, gazing out at them with large brown eyes, a dazzling smile, and short black hair. Actually, a striking-looking woman. The green dot settled on her right cheek. 'This is María Théresa Gomez, thirty-five years old, mother of two, pharmacist working in a senior executive role with an international drugs company based in Barcelona. She was attending the company's annual conference at the upmarket Brillo hotel in Valencia at the time. Her husband had died just the year before from cancer. She was found shot to death, lying naked across her hotel bed, by housekeeping staff two days later. As you can see from the briefing notes that I emailed you all, five banks were hit in the past five years, and before each one, in the same city, a female was murdered, shot to death in a hotel room.'

Chief Superintendent Walter Shanahan of the National Bureau of Criminal Investigation sat forward. 'Why in God's name did it take two days to discover the body? Can anyone answer me that?'

Brody knew the answer to that before Superintendent Ryan gave it. And anything she did know was only because Marty had dug deep into the Interpol report and found it. Otherwise, she would have known nothing. No credit to Marty given, of course, or expected. As you were.

'A Do Not Disturb card had been placed on the door,' she said, 'that's why. With the conference and everything, I suppose,' she added with a shrug, 'they just, well, forgot all about it. Anyway, I can't account for why they did or they didn't. But it was. And that's why.'

The GNBCI chief, apparently happy with this answer and his contribution, sat back, knitted his hands together across his ample chest and nodded once.

'So,' she said, 'we may have a problem, and we don't have very long to deal with it.'

Correct, Brody thought, *we do not have very long to deal with it, and what time we do have you're eating into right now.*

Assistant Commissioner Kelly gestured towards the bankers.

'Mr Long, Mr Gates, the reason why I asked you both to attend here today at such short notice, and thank you for obliging me too, by the way, is because there is also another interesting aspect to all this. The amounts taken from each bank were primarily in used banknotes. This seems to be the main focus for the raiders. I'd like to explore it...'

Brody inwardly groaned. *Explore it.* For some reason, a Pac-Man came to mind, munching its way through rows of yellow dots in an arcade machine. Brody grabbed the edge of his seat to stop himself from screaming, *We don't have time to play fucking* Pac-Man.

The assistant commissioner nodded to Ryan, and she went and resumed her seat, placing the pointer on the table before her.

'Can you tell me about these?' she asked the bankers. 'How is this old money collected? And how is it stored? Also, where is it stored? And do you have an operation at the moment for nationwide collection and incineration?'

Brody sat up. Assistant Commissioner Kelly had finally gotten round to the rub of this...

'And do you have an operation at the moment for nationwide collection and incineration?'

'We don't really know,' the head of the Central Bank said in his flat, unhurried monotone. 'For security reasons, the operation to deal with the collection and disposal of used notes is coordinated separately by the Central Bank security section. Also, I believe, each bank manager is informed only the evening before that the money is to be collected from his branch, that is. The notes will have been removed from circulation by each individual bank over the previous month. Oh, and it is not a nationwide operation. We do it province by province, on a rotating basis.'

'Oh, okay. And what? The money is taken directly from the bank to the incinerator, then, is that it?'

'Oh, no, no. It's not,' the head of the Central Bank said. 'That would not make any sense at all.'

The AC shifted in his seat and scowled, seemingly unhappy with his comment being dismissed like that.

'No, the money is collected from each bank by security truck in a province-wide operation. It is quite a complex operation, carefully coordinated, making sure each bank is ready when the truck calls, that there are no delays. Then it is taken to a designated bank here in the city. That bank will then hold the used notes overnight. The next day it is all brought to the incinerator. And the bank manager of that city branch will not know anything about it until literally the truck arrives at his door. He is given no warning whatsoever. Anyway, it's not a major issue for him. It simply goes into the vault. But not knowing anything about it helps protect him from the possibility of a tiger kidnapping or anything of that nature.'

'And who decides, then?' Kelly asked. 'I mean, who

makes the final decision as to which bank stores the cash overnight before it's incinerated?'

The banker pursed his lips.

'Well, I really don't know. No one does. It's randomly selected by a computer algorithm. We like to think it a failsafe method. We designed it ourselves. It's always worked. And I have full faith it will work this time too.'

'You mean no one knows,' Kelly spluttered, 'but a bloody computer.'

'Well, yes, we think it's quite clever. I mean, don't you? But what I can tell you is that on previous occasions it's been a bank somewhere in the city centre, or close to it.'

'Well, that's something, I suppose,' Kelly said sarcastically.

Brody raised a hand, and Kelly glared at him. Brody kept his hand up.

'Yes? Brody, isn't it? *Sergeant?* What is it?'

Brody knew bloody well Kelly knew who he was.

'Yes,' Brody said, going along with it. 'Brody, that's right.'

'What is it, Brody?'

'Exactly,' Brody said, taking his hand down, 'what is it? With respect, we don't need to know how the money gets to where it gets to. Just that it does. We need to move things along.'

Kelly's bottom lip folded up over his upper. Brody guessed he'd done this since a boy, an automatic reflex. He could imagine him in a playground, pouting like that and wanting to cry. Except he couldn't cry now. Brody didn't have time for sentimentality or for politeness. This wasn't a polite chat in the senior officers' mess, after all.

Brody could feel all eyes on him, a heretic in a chamber of zealous puritans. He had a problem with management, he was the first to admit it, and they had done little to mitigate his opinion of them. To him they were all administrators, risk averse, afraid of making mistakes, culturally conditioned to pass the buck, all reaching for their can of blowback repellent as a first line of defence.

'We need to decide how to counter this,' Brody said. 'And we need to decide immediately, as in right now, this minute.'

Kelly glared at him, but then smiled.

'I like that, a forthright approach.'

Brody knew he didn't, but what else could he say?

He still hadn't moved anything along.

'I was going to get to that,' Kelly said.

Yeah, Brody thought, *but when?*

The assistant commissioner pointed to the chief of the Central Bank. 'How many banks are there in the Central Dublin area, Mr Lyons?'

'A lot.'

'Do you know the exact number?'

'Not exactly, no.'

'Rough, then?'

'Fortyish, I'd say.'

'Hm, that many.' Kelly seemed to think about that. He looked to the other senior ranks, all conspicuously quiet. 'Maybe we get some of our people into them overnight?'

'In where, exactly?' Lyons asked.

'Well, the banks of course,' Kelly snapped.

'Yes, I know that. But do you mean into the vaults?'

'Oh, yes, of course, the vaults. We could lie in wait. Sound the alert when we hear them breaking through.' He smiled. 'Be waiting for them when they arrive.'

'That would be risky,' the banker said.

'Well, of course, it carries a certain level of risk. We don't know who we're dealing with, after all.'

'No,' Lyons said. 'That's not what I meant. I mean oxygen. The vault is airtight. You'd need oxygen and masks, wouldn't you? That sort of thing.'

'Hm...' Kelly said. Brody could tell he'd never thought of that. 'Couldn't we leave the doors open?'

The banker laughed aloud, and Kelly's lower lip folded over his upper again.

'They're on a time lock. That's the whole point of having a vault.'

'Let's open this to the floor,' Kelly said, trying to recover his authority, like he was the one who knew what to do, and opening it to the floor was something a good senior officer would always do. 'Brody, what about you? You seem to have a lot to say. Have you any ideas?'

Superintendent Ryan glanced over at Brody, her eyes contracting, becoming smaller, darker, like she was in the schoolyard too, and the girl she usually hung around with had just started playing with someone else.

'Yes,' Brody said, 'as it happens, I do. Trouble is, no one wants to hear about it.'

'I WAS JUST ABOUT to pick up the phone and call you,' the voice on the other end of the line said. A young voice, an eager voice. Marty guessed the voice belonged to one of the batch of new interns. They usually hit the labs at Forensic Services Ireland around about this time of year.

'I got there first,' he said. 'What's your name, lad?'

'Shaun Foley, with a *u*.'

'Okay, Shaun. What you got for me? You have got something, don't you? Otherwise, you wouldn't be ringing.'

'I'd ring you anyway; communication is important.'

Yes, Marty thought, *young and eager alright.*

'Fire away,' Marty said.

The young lad laughed.

'What's so funny?'

'Nothing...' he said, 'well, you just said fire away. Like, as in fire away. Get it? As in...'

Marty laughed too. 'Alright, yeah, yeah. I get it.'

'Okay,' he said, and there was the clicking sound of fingers on a keyboard, 'let me go through this with you.'

'Why not just email it over, and I can go through it myself. If anything needs clarifying, I can get back to you. Saves time.'

'You will be getting back to me. So why not save us both the hassle and I'll do it now?'

Sure of yourself, lad, aren't you? Marty thought. But he liked that.

'Shoot,' Marty said. 'That's not a joke, by the way.'

The lad didn't laugh this time. 'Okay,' he said, serious. 'First off, the rounds used in the shooting dead of the victim at the Herbert Park Platinum Hotel are .40 hollow points, from a semi-automatic handgun, something like a Glock. But it could be any one of a number. This is only my second time coming across this particular type of round, however.'

Marty wanted to ask him what type of round he was referring to, but he held his tongue. Something told him this lad had everything covered.

'That's what I meant,' the lad said, 'about why you'd be ringing me. Because I can't be specific, about the exact type of round, that is. Just a hollow point. And a hollow point is designed to do just one thing, and one thing only, clean entry with a devastating impact on the inside, literally disintegrating any bodily organs it comes into contact with, and bouncing around the way it does, that's nearly everything. Impossible to survive. The last time I saw one, and the first time too, was in New York, on an exchange programme with Fordham College in the Bronx. The NYPD have a specialised technical unit based at the college. I went out with them on a couple of jobs. Hollow points, even in New York, are hard to come by. You have to know people, the right type of wrong people, if you get me? Also, we have an international register of specific ammunition types used in unsolved homicides. I matched it against this register…oh, and a silencer was used.'

A silencer. Marty pondered that.

'The barrel rifling on the spent rounds, as you know, are just like fingerprints, unique. The weapon that fired the rounds was used in five other murders. These were in…'

'I know,' Marty said. 'Nice, Antwerp, London, Milan and Valencia. We can skip that part.'

'Oh, you've been doing your homework. That's good, that's very good.'

Thank you, Marty thought. This lad was starting to irritate him.

'Those are the takeaways from this case,' he said.

The takeaways. He'd probably picked that up in New York.

'I'll email you over the full report,' he added.

'Thank you, Shaun with a *u*…and…'

'Yes?'

'Good work.'

Marty pressed down on the hook switch of the desk phone, released it again, and dialled Brody's mobile.

BRODY SAID the same when Marty told him of the ballistics report.

'Good work,' and added, 'so it's the same person, no doubt.'

Also, now that he'd said it aloud, it being the same person, this added more resonance to the statement. He thought of that, the *same* person. Here. In Dublin. Right now. No doubt.

'Thanks, Marty.'

Brody shoved the phone back into his pocket and set off back down the corridor he'd just come along to the conference room he'd just left in order to take the call. To be honest, he'd been grateful to get the call, any excuse to leave before he really said something he'd regret. As far as he could see, the top brass were being deliberately as vague as footprints in a bog, impossible to follow. A bureaucratic outcome. Designed to cover arses. Everyone was happy – except for Brody, that is.

This would change things.

He stormed into the conference room and took them all by complete surprise. They were milling around, Superintendent Ryan and the bankers included, drinking steaming drinks from porcelain cups on porcelain saucers, a plate of biscuits and a jug of milk on a side table. Well, at least they got their priorities right. Very cosy.

They fell silent, staring at him.

'Well, what brings you back, Brody?' It was…well, what was the fella's name exactly? Brody couldn't remember. No surprise there, because the fella hadn't said one word throughout the entire meeting, sitting so still Brody had wondered for a moment if he wasn't dead. And now he'd suddenly come to life and found his tongue. Well, hooray for that.

'Ballistics have confirmed,' Brody announced, 'the same weapon used in the Herbert Platinum murder was used in the five other murders. Which means, beyond doubt, he's here. In Dublin. Have you heard me? Therefore, I propose, like I said, if we can't get into the vaults, then we get into the sewers. We can at least do that. A bank is going to be hit.'

'Sergeant, Sergeant...' It was what's-his-name who'd just discovered what his tongue was for again. 'That won't be possible, getting into the sewers. Not right away, it won't.'

'Won't it? Why?'

'Well, *Sergeant*, we can't have personnel going into sewers just like that. Not on their ownsome, we can't. The rules state members of the Water Unit must be with them. And they need to be informed in advance. I can tell by your expression you're dubious, but health and safety must take priority. Officers have lost their lives on just this sort of operation in the past. The Water Unit at the moment is involved in a job down in west Limerick. It will take time.'

'And who the hell are you?'

'Hm, Brody, have to say, I don't like your tone. Chief Superintendent Owen Gallagher, if you must know, Fraud Squad.'

'This isn't a fraud case?'

'Well, I know that. Now I do. And before you ask, I previously headed the Rules and Procedures Committee on the update of the working manual back in '08. That's how I know about the Water Unit. Okay?' He laughed and looked about. 'You know, gentlemen, this sounds a bit like a job interview, what?' Gallagher raised an eyebrow. 'I propose you grab yourself a cup, Brody. And we'll talk about this a little more.'

The Mad Hatter's Tea Party, Brody thought, *that's what this is.*

He turned and stormed back out of the room.

16

Voyle and Considine were rushing to the scene on blues and twos, and somehow they had ended up in the lead of a convey of two marked and three unmarked squad cars, screaming and weaving their way through Dublin city traffic. Considine, acting as the observer in the passenger seat, had her window open and her hand poised to flag back any traffic threatening to impede their progress.

They arrived at Delancy Street in just under five minutes.

Gaggles of uniforms and detectives, not just the local Pearse Street mules but from Store Street and even Irishtown station in Ringsend, had responded, some abandoning their cars on the road outside, forcing traffic to tail back and snake their way around. As the tailback grew, drivers further down who couldn't see what was happening began leaning on their horns. It sounded like someone was playing random notes on an out-of-tune keyboard.

Voyle pulled the unmarked onto the pavement by the road in front of the crime scene. They got out, crossed and went under the crime scene tape onto the patch of waste ground on the other side, heading towards a collection of low, semi-derelict sheds and outhouses directly in front of them. The stench of burnt flesh, oil, rubber and leather grew more pervasive with each step. A figure emerged from an outhouse, started towards them, dressed in operational uniform, cargo pants, fleece jacket and baseball hat.

'Well, look who's flown in on their magic carpet,' the figure said when they reached him.

'Duddy.' It was Voyle. 'How's she cuttin'?'

'Inspector Duddy to you, me boy.' He tapped his right shoulder epaulette. 'Not bad, eh Steve? Not bad at all. I'd begun to give up on ever getting this baby.'

Duddy's eyes swivelled to take in Considine, looked her up and down; he said nothing, returned to Steve. She and Duddy had history.

'We're waiting on SOC,' Duddy said. 'Why're they always the last to arrive, huh? And...' Sweeping a hand through the air. 'Look. They're falling over each other here' – and jerking a thumb over his shoulder – 'a bunch of them were in there plodding around too. So I don't want you two going traipsing in there making things any worse either. Clear?' He looked off to the side at a uniform who was standing there. 'Hey, Rafferty, go down and sort that out, for fuck's sake.' He pointed with a stabbing motion. 'Look, over there, for Christ's sake. Those gawkers. Ask them if they saw anything; shoo them along if they haven't.'

The uniform nodded sheepishly and started off towards a gate in the perimeter where a bunch of people, joggers and dog walkers it seemed like, were milling about, rubbernecking.

Duddy glanced to Voyle again. 'This whole place could

be a crime scene, for all I know. A motorcycle mule. Back in there.' He jerked his thumb over his shoulder again. 'Poor bastard.'

A little way inside the building that he'd indicated lay a smouldering, blackened heap.

'When the fire brigade got here, it had more or less burned itself out,' he said. 'And no one reported it, typical for around here. A mobile patrol saw the smoke and had a look. That's how it was discovered. Too late to do anything. The poor bastard's head fried inside his helmet; the rest of him mostly melted away, including his leathers. Here, I thought those things were supposed to be fire resistant. Well, the ones he was wearing weren't.' Duddy scratched the bridge of his nose. 'Never came across anything like it before, have to say. What about you, Voyle?' He was still studiously ignoring Considine.

Steve shook his head. 'No, can't say that I have either.'

Considine took out her phone from a pocket of her windbreaker.

'I'll try Brody again. It says he's out of coverage; maybe his phone is dead.'

She walked away, stepping around Duddy, heading towards the building with the blackened heap inside it.

'No, you're not, Considine,' he called after her. 'You're not going in there. D'ya hear me, Considine? Get back here. Now.'

'Kiss my arse,' she called back, and walked on.

BRODY DIDN'T NEED Considine to tell him anything. As he left the operations building at Garda HQ in the Phoenix Park to head back to his office in a separate annexe, he knew instantly that something was up. It was in the air, like an electrical charge: when it's one of your own, it's always the way. Even the way people walked was different, like they had a train to catch. He saw one of the civilian press officers emerge from a building and head away in the opposite direction. He called out and ran over, was told the news, of a motorcycle cop found burned to death in a building on waste ground near Dublin Port.

He rang Considine.

'Boss, I tried ringing you,' she said.

'It's my phone; it keeps losing charge. I need a new one. I've just heard the news. You know who it is yet?'

'Unofficially, yes, the local mules are naming him as Declan Sinnott. It's his bike, the reg can still be just about made out, and GPS had him turning into the location. Twenty-five years' service, last ten on bikes. Due to retire in six months' time.'

Aha. Sinnott. Brody knew him, or knew of him, to be more precise. Deci, as he was known, an awkward character, prickly as a hedgehog, rumoured to be on the take, but nothing could ever be found on him. The brass were now simply counting down the days until he retired and they could be rid of him.

Brody finished the call and stood with his hands on his hips, thinking things through. The murder at the Herbert Park Platinum was one thing, now this murder – brutally – of a cop with a dubious reputation, and an imminent major bank heist. Any one of those was a major deal, but all three together? *Nah*, Brody thought, *not coincidences, they're all connected*. It was like he could actually smell something, could hear it, but just couldn't see it – not yet.

'I've been trying to ring you.'

Superintendent Ryan was standing at the bottom of the stairs leading to the third floor, where her own office was situated. Brody realised she must have been watching from her window and had seen him entering the building. Brody walked along the corridor. His own office was at the end. He could hear her following. He went in, took off his jacket and sat behind his desk, indicated to one of the two empty chairs on the other side of it.

'I'm fine,' she said. 'I'll stand, thanks.'

He told her of what Nicola had just told him. 'Horrible, yes,' she said, 'but we haven't been called in on that yet.'

'It ticks all the boxes for why we should be.'

'Maybe...'

Her non-committal response added to Brody's impression that lately the MCIU was being sidelined on jobs – again. This went against everything he'd been told by the commissioner himself, who'd lauded the unit for being the most effective within the organisation, having the highest solved-case rate, relatively speaking, of any other section. The commissioner had said, too, that the old boy nod and a wink backslapping cronyism culture would no longer be tolerated. To which Brody had said to himself he would adopt a wait and see attitude. And now that he had waited, he was seeing that those words appeared to be nothing more than thermal updrafts over the equator, all hot air.

He was disappointed, yes, but not surprised. Then again, even a commissioner trying to change the direction of an organisation such as An Gárda Síochana was like trying to turn a forty-tonne juggernaut from a standing start without the aid of power steering. The very success of the MCIU might stir resentment in some, the bureaucrats and administrators, those obsessed with controlling their fiefdoms and plotting the takeover of others. An organisation structured on rank and outcomes was always going to be one of constant power plays. Which could have benefits, bringing out the competitive best in people, but it also could have the opposite effect, and bring out the worst.

'Jack, this bank job you think is going to happen.'

'Think? I thought we'd gone beyond that; all agreed it *was* going to happen.'

'Anyway, we decided on a stand off and observe approach.'

'A what?'

'We can't get into the vaults, and we won't be going into the sewers. The most prudent approach is to stand off and observe. We agreed. It's an effective strategy that's worked in the past.'

Brody shook his head. 'We agreed? Who agreed? And where was this agreed?'

'The meeting.'

'The meeting. You mean, when I wasn't there? After I'd left. That meeting?'

'After you'd stormed out, you mean.'

'The meeting had ended when I stormed out, remember.'

She had nothing to say to that.

'And how's this stand off and observe supposed to work in this case?'

'Um, Superintendent Cleary's organising it.'

'I don't remember any Superintendent Cleary at that meeting.'

'That's because he wasn't. He's based at Anglesea Street down in Cork. But he's the most experienced at this sort of thing. The assistant commissioner is going to speak to him.'

'He's going to speak to him, is he? I'm convinced a bank is going to be hit. And when it is, will you still be speaking about it?'

'Convinced, are you. Really? God, it must be great to be so self-righteous.'

'We've already been through this.'

'You're overreacting, Jack.'

'Someone needs to.'

'I've told you. It's in hand. Trust me, it's been looked after. Don't worry about it. Now, the murder at the Herbert Park Platinum? That's more tangible. How're we getting on with that?'

Her look said it all, *Move on, Jack.*

He shook his head. She didn't get it. She simply didn't get it. None of them did. The bank raid – oh yes, that was going to happen, he was certain – and the murder of that woman in room five three two of the Herbert Park Platinum were one and the same, intrinsically linked. And now the murder of Deci Sinnott. He couldn't prove it. How did you prove instinct?

'Fiona,' he said, and Superintendent Ryan blinked. He thought that might get her attention, because he'd never referred to her by her first name before. 'This time, you're going to have to break the rules.'

She opened her mouth, but nothing came out of it. Brody saw something pass behind those small, dark eyes of hers. She closed her mouth again. Listening. Waiting.

Brody spoke. 'We have to get somebody into those sewers. I don't care how you work it, but that's what needs to happen. If you don't do this...' He let that hang in the air.

She took the bait.

'If I don't do this, what...?'

'Well then, when this is all over, your neck will be the one on the line. Not anyone else's in that room. And not mine. I'm a sergeant, after all. But yours. Because I told you about this, and you told them. They'll say you didn't make a convincing enough case, but had you done, they would have acted. Believe me, they'll look after themselves. You'll be left to swing. It's the way they work.'

'Say I do, and nothing happens. How's *that* going to look, for *both* of us?'

'Think of what I'm saying. It's going to happen; the markers are there. Our profiler indicates, too, we're dealing with one sick puppy, by the way.'

'I know what you're doing,' she said slowly. 'The big bad boogeyman. Well, it won't work. I'm not frightened.'

'Fine, do what you want, then, but I did warn you. Now, anything else? I've things to do.'

She didn't answer, standing there, looking down at him. Then Superintendent Ryan sighed loudly, pulled over a chair and sat down.

'Okay,' she said, 'out of curiosity, what did you have in mind? Doesn't mean I'm going to do anything with it, of course.'

'Of course.'

'So. Tell me.'

ALONE IN HIS office after Superintendent Ryan had left, Jack opened a drawer in his desk, shifted through the contents, found what he was looking for, a phone charger, took it out and swivelled his chair around, plugged it into the wall. He reached back and took his phone from the jacket he'd just draped over the back of the chair, saw it was dead again, plugged the charger into it, and placed the phone carefully onto the ground. He swivelled back, and it was then he noticed the red light on his desk phone blinking. It had been hidden behind his desk lamp. Jack played the voice message, leaning forward in his chair:

'Hi, Jack Brody, this is Detective Wayne Henderson, Royal Canadian Mounted Police. I'm ringing in connection with a case you're working. If you ring me back within the next couple of hours, you should get me. Otherwise, I'll contact you again, maybe tomorrow. Thanks.'

Jack picked up his desk phone and punched in the number showing up on-screen, waited while it connected. Then, a voice on the other end: 'Ontario branch office, RCMP, Special Constable Wayne Henderson speaking, how can I help you?'

'Jack Brody here. You rang?'

'Jack Brody. Yes, I rang. Listen, I was just about to go out the door. You want to ring me back a little later on? I can give you more time then. I only got five minutes now.'

'How long will it take?'

'Five minutes if I get straight into it.'

'Can you get straight into it?'

'Yes. Will do. Here goes. Abraham Jackman. I'll assume you know the details of the case this end...'

'I do.'

'But what you don't know is that, despite the crap put out 'bout him having been eaten by a bear, we always believed him to be alive, out there doing his thing, not eaten by a bear, a bear has more taste, but just could never prove it either way, that's all.' Henderson allowed himself a little chuckle. 'But this match you just got on a pubic hair from your murder scene...'

'We're not releasing that.'

'Relax, neither are we; we don't want to give him any heads up, now do we? Anyway, now we know, it's confirmed, what we always guessed, that he's out there. The question to be asked now is, why? Why's he doin' it? And why's he doin' it now? He left that hair there for a reason, no doubt. I think the answer is he's fucking with us, me and you both, letting us know, that's all, and you know why? Because he thinks he's smarter than us, that's why...By the way, you may not want to hear this, but I don't think you can do a damn thing about what he's planning either; you don't have enough time. He knows that too.'

'The bank, you mean?'

'Of course the bank. Although he doesn't always hit banks.'

'He doesn't? I didn't know that.'

'That's only what you hear about because of the link drawn to the murders of those unfortunate women. He does other stuff too, fun stuff, for him, that is. Just like other people do surfing, he does his stuff.'

'What other kind of stuff?'

'We have an intelligence database, Jack. We follow his MO, as best we can, because the brass here liked to think he was dead; it wrapped things up neatly for them. They had their heads buried in the sand. You know what the brass are like?'

Brody smiled. 'Oh yes, I do.'

'Anyway, we followed his MO. He's got a certain way of doing things; you could call it his style. We follow it. Anything, anywhere, shows up with his scent on it, we log it.'

'Okay, and what is it?'

Jack thought this was going to take more than five minutes.

'I'll get to that. Currently he's left a trail behind him stretching from Belize to Florida to Montreal all the way up to Anchorage, Alaska. Like a vacation itinerary. Not bank jobs, no, he's on vacation. You know about the bank jobs already, you just said.'

'Yes.'

'Well done, good work on your part; not everyone makes the link straight away. Okay, to give you a flavour, take Florida. We believe he spent a week living with a woman down there, let's say of a certain vintage, in her mansion on Pinellas Drive. When no one heard from her after a week, they went to look. I mean they, her estate, whatever, had to pay someone to go and look, she didn't have any family of her own, and no one else could be bothered. Can you believe that? She had all the money in the world, and no one could be bothered to go take a look and see how she was. Anyway, they found her hanging from a chandelier. She'd been filleted, her entrails left lying in a heap on the floor, a gold-plated toilet brush shoved up her vagina. A seriously sick fucker, wouldn't you say?'

'And you think it's *him*?'

'I do, and so does everyone else here think it's him. He

called her Gloria mama, this woman, by the way. We played back messages he left on her answering machine. That's how we know.'

Brody took in the news. Yes, this fella was a lot sicker than he'd thought.

'You know who Gloria represents, right?' the Mountie asked.

'His mother.'

'Correct. Gee, you're ahead of the game.'

'But the brass...' Brody said, and his voice trailed off.

'I know, man, I feel for you, I really do.'

'And what you just said doesn't tally with what happened here in Dublin. That was a relatively clean killing. One shot to the head, one...'

'Yeah, I know, one shot to the chest. Same MO as the other killings tied with the bank jobs.'

'How do you explain such a radical departure?'

'I can't. Other than when he's on the bank thing, that's work, he's working, so maybe he reins himself in, yet he still can't help himself, only he tones it down. I don't know, to be honest. But what I do know is he's getting worse, that's all I can say. To me, it's like he's spiralling out of control. Florida happened three months ago, by the way.'

'What about forensic evidence? In Florida, I mean.'

'Nada, the place was virtually sterilised. Another reason to believe that if something is left behind anywhere, it's only because he's done it intentionally.'

'But it's not nada like you said, is it? Didn't you just say there were voice messages. You have his voice. You know what he sounds like.'

'His voice, on a recording machine, useless.'

'I go back to what I already said, how do you know it's him?'

'You sure you ain't gettin' like the brass yourself there, Jack? They say the same thing.'

'Do they? Oh, heaven forbid.'

'We just know it's him, okay. Call it an...'

Brody finished the sentence for him. 'An instinct.'

'You got it...Plus, there are other little details.'

'Such as?'

There was the sound of an intake of breath. 'I'm sorry, Jack, but I'm going to have to plead the fifth on that one. Nothing personal. I need to hold some things back.'

'Why? If it was him.'

'It *was* him, Jack. We have some sensitivity issues, let's just call it that, people who spoke to us, who are still speaking to us, extended family-type situation. We can't risk putting anything out there. And anyway, none of this is going to help you find him. Not right now it isn't.'

True, Brody thought.

'The victim in Florida,' Brody said. 'Was anything taken?'

'No, even though the house was stuffed with artwork, jewels and some cash. Still, nothing was taken.'

'But isn't this man a thief? Why? If it was just there for the taking?'

'For the hell of it, that's why. He got off on it, Jack. No other reason, he just got off on it. Which points to what I believe is a separation kind of thing, between what he *has* to do, like those bank jobs, and what he *likes* to do.'

The worst kind, Jack thought.

'You know anything about the bank team?' Brody asked. 'He can't be doing those jobs on his own.'

'Nah, and I'm not really interested in them. I'm interested in him. They've never done a job in Canada far as we know, or the US for that matter. Which is interesting in itself. Again, that separation thing. Maybe they fly in and do the jobs, fly out again, I don't know. Maybe they have a planner, a scout, that's how it usually works, someone who makes it all happen for a cut, but just doesn't get his hands dirty, a kind of criminal consultant. But, word to the wise.'

'Go on.'

'Banks aren't your real issue, if you value life over money, that is. He's your real issue. Now, gotta go. I'm way over my time. Hope I've been of some help.'

'Yes, you've been of help, thank you.'

The line went dead. Jack stared at the phone. How much help the Canadian had been, he wasn't sure of. Jack still was no closer to apprehending this person.

An image of the victim in room 532 flashed across his mind, the bullet wound to the centre of her forehead like a third eye. An undercurrent of anger trickled through him. He checked his mobile phone call log for the number he wanted, then used his desk phone to ring it.

AND LISTENED as it rang out six times. He was about to hang up when: 'Chris Glynn, hello.' The manager of the Herbert Park Platinum Hotel.

'Mr Glynn, you were supposed to ring me, remember? Detective Sergeant Jack Brody.'

'Oh, um, Detective Brody, yes…I'm so sorry. I forgot. I've a lot on my mind.'

Brody didn't answer right away. He paused for a couple of seconds so he wouldn't say anything he might regret.

'We all have a lot on our minds, Mr Glynn. This CCTV of the person leaving through the employee door I asked you about. Did you check the roster like you were supposed to? What did you find? I'll remind you this is a murder investigation. It's important.'

'I don't need you to remind me, Detective.'

Then why the fuck didn't you call me?

'Did you do it or not, Mr Glynn? Did you check?'

Brody prepared himself for the answer...*Oh, um, well, I was...you know...*

But Chris Glynn didn't say that. He said instead, 'Yes. I did. I said I would. And I did.'

'Oh.' Brody was surprised, but also relieved. 'And?'

'At that time, 23:10, nothing. The kitchen staff had finished; the night staff had arrived; all that was left were the bar, concierge and desk staff. All of those, with the exception of the bar staff, finished at midnight. I checked the time clocks too. The answer is no, a member of staff was not leaving through that door at that time. But that doesn't mean someone else wasn't, of course. The corridor leading to it can be accessed from a door at the end of the guest corridor. It's really only a partition wall separating the two, it allows the housekeeping staff to park their trolleys there, and the room service staff do the same. The door is not locked; there's no need; well, I used to think there wasn't...' His voice trailed off.

Brody considered that.

'I also,' Chris Glynn continued, 'had a look at the CCTV. Just in case a member of staff had stayed behind for some reason or other. Which they shouldn't have done; when they clock off, they should clock off and leave.'

'And?'

Brody realised he'd somewhat underestimated the hotel manager.

'The person in that clip doesn't seem familiar at all. The build, the gait...does not ring a bell. I know all my staff, Detective Brody, and that person isn't one of them.'

'You sure?'

'Yes. I am sure.'

Brody paused, again thinking over what he'd just been told.

'Thank you. I'll be in touch again if I need to. And thank you for your co-operation.'

'You're welcome. I want this person caught just as much as you do.'

'Yes, of course. I'll be in touch if there's anything. Thank you once again.'

Brody hung up and sat back. He was concerned the spaghetti hats weren't taking this as seriously as they should. He knew they'd be watching everything, and at the first hint that Brody was right, that what he had predicted was indeed about to or was happening, they'd be like the cavalry charging over the horizon, their horses running him over and galloping on to glory.

He thought of ringing Commissioner McKay. He had assured him on his last case, when Brody had met a similar level of apathy, that it wouldn't be tolerated in the future, that he was stamping out such shoddy practices.

Brody decided not to. More than anything, he wasn't a snitch. He was a sergeant, way down the food chain. But then again, McKay's enthusiasm for him to take promotion to inspector was both faith in Jack's abilities, but also a desire to shuffle the familiar playlist.

Was the fact that Jack was so far reluctant to take this promotion a sign that he too was part of the problem? He pushed the thought from his mind, instead imagined this case as a Rubik's Cube, and rotated one side, then another in the opposite direction, and another from the side. His mind jumped ahead to the different rotations required to line up a row in a single colour, any colour. He thought he could spot one. If everything fell into place, that is, if his predictions were correct, and for that, he needed his boss, Superintendent Ryan, on board.

His telephone rang. Jack snatched it up, almost forgetting it was still plugged into the wall. He avoided pulling the cord out just in time, seeing Ashling's name flashing across the screen.

He listened.

'Jack,' she said, 'where are you?'

'Ashling, lovely to hear from you. Where am I? At work of course...'

She was silent for a moment. Then, 'Fine, Jack. It happens. You didn't remember. Okay, that's fine too.' But he could tell by her tone that it was far from being fine.

'What is this, Ashling? I didn't think we...' And then he remembered. 'Oh, shit.' The other morning, yesterday morning in fact, as she was leaving his house, she'd said something about meeting him after work tomorrow – tomorrow, that would be today – in the what...what was it? The Old Shillelagh. That was it, a pub just off Capel Street. Yes, that was it, and maybe afterwards they'd go for a bite to eat.

Shit, shit, shit.

He'd completely forgotten.

'Ashling, jeez, I'm sorry. I-I...'

'I know, you forgot. Anyway, you're busy, I understand. I heard it on the news by the way, about the motorcycle guard and the poor woman in the hotel room. You have a lot on your hands. Look, I'm sorry...'

'Sorry? You don't need to be sorry. It's me who needs to be sorry.'

Again, she was silent. 'I didn't mean it like that. I meant... sorry, for getting this wrong. Us wrong. This may not be a good time to say it, okay, I know it's not, but when's a good time to say it? I'm sorry, that's all, it's not working out, between us I mean, because I need someone in my life who's more available. Is that selfish? Possibly. But that's what I need. I have to be true to myself. I'm sorry, this is not a good time, I know, I feel bad, that poor motorcycle man and everything, but Jack, it's me, I'm the one who always rings, I'm the one who always arranges. If I didn't, I'd never get to see you. I mean, right now, you just...what? Forgot?'

Jack froze, feeling like he'd been blindsided by something, a truck, a wrecking ball, whatever...no, this he hadn't seen coming.

'Ashling,' he said, 'I didn't mean...' He stopped. What didn't he mean? What was he trying to say? He didn't know. And that holiday he'd been thinking of. He'd never even gotten beyond the thinking part, had he?

He was still silent.

'Nothing to say, Jack?'

'Ashling, I've plenty to say.'

'Then say it.'

But Jack didn't. Because he *had* nothing to say. What *could* he say? In that moment he thought of Caoimhe, all the times she had arranged things too, all the times she had meals ready when he came in, all the times…she did everything, that's what she did, everything. Old school, looking after her man. Jack, her man. Shite, he didn't even know it, not back then and not now, not up until a moment ago. So, no, there was nothing he could say except…

'I'll make it up to you. Give me another chance.'

'Look, Jack, it's no big deal; we haven't been together that long. Let me just reverse out of this and move on. I think it would be best, for both of us. You're married to your job, Jack, simple as that, you always have been, and you always will be.'

There was the sound of a deep intake of breath from her end, released in one hurried, what Jack guessed to be resigned, gush, followed by a clicking sound, then nothing. It took him a moment to realise she had hung up. He took the phone from his ear and stared at it. Had that really just happened? Yes, was the answer, it had. And to think he had been contemplating organising a holiday for them both. He hadn't just misread the situation; it was like they'd both been watching a completely different movie.

For the rest of the day Jack was in a foul mood. He had to work closely with Superintendent Ryan, who seemed to sense something was up. But she didn't comment. In fact, they only spoke when they needed to, concentrating on what needed to be done, and they had a lot to do and got a lot done.

Jack didn't think of it at the time, but he would later, of just how well they did work together, just what they managed to get organised, as they turned his plan into action, ready for the following day.

And, for a little while, it stopped him thinking of Ashling Nolan.

The plan, because if they couldn't get to the sewers, maybe the sewers might come to them.

'Just to recap,' Superintendent Ryan said, 'you know someone in river rescue at Dublin Fire Brigade.'

'Yes, I do.'

'And this person knows someone in civil defence who's trained in listening equipment for use, primarily, in earthquake zones.'

'Yes, I do.'

'But we don't have earthquakes.'

'Thank God for that,' Brody said. 'But other countries do, and they send out a team when requested to search under rubble, situations like that. Seemingly the unit can go where other nations' units have difficulty, because we don't have any political baggage.'

'Being neutral, militarily, you mean?'

'Yes,' Brody said.

'And in this case, they can place listening devices into the sewage system and what...just sit back and listen?'

'Something like that. I don't know the full ins and outs of it. I think they can even route it to a mobile phone.'

Superintendent Ryan raised her eyebrows. 'Intriguing. You'd better get on with it, then.'

GERALD BRENNAN, third officer at Dublin Fire Brigade, was silent as Brody told him of what he had in mind. Though

Brody was selective in his words. If this were a stew, it would be one without meat.

'I don't see any problem,' he said, 'I'll contact TT. And he'll ring you back, yes?'

'TT?'

'Tony Tennant, TT for short, a volunteer officer up at Park Gate. Works as a sound engineer, so they've utilised his skills perfectly.'

'Yes, seems like they have. Right then, Gerry, we must meet up for a pint when this is all over, have a catch-up.'

'Yes, Jack, I'll look forward to that. Hold you to it, okay?'

'Yes, you take care, and thanks again.'

Brody hung up and waited for Tony Tennant's call.

'I'M GOING to need verification from your commanding officer,' TT said when he did call about half an hour later.

'Of course,' Brody said, 'Superintendent Ryan will give you that.'

'Superintendent Ryan, that's his name?'

'She.'

'Oh, right, whatever...wait a minute, am I right, it said on the message something about sewers, is that correct?'

'It is.'

'What's this to do with exactly?' Tennant spoke fast, and his tone was sharp, and Brody had an image of a small man who did everything fast, the human equivalent of a Jack Russell terrier.

Brody had been hoping he wouldn't ask that question, that he'd just get on with it. But the little Jack Russell was having none of it. They were curious by nature.

'There may be a bank that's about to be held up,' he said, laying it out straight and raw, 'and we believe they may come in through the sewers. We want to hear about if and when they do.'

Tennant was silent, sniffing at that, Brody imagined.

'Aw, right,' Tennant said, 'and when's this going down?'

'I believe over the course of the weekend, this weekend.'

'That soon,' Tennant said. 'I'd better get a move on, wouldn't I? I need to think how to do this. Any particular part of the sewers?'

Brody was impressed. The man, unlike the senior police officers he'd been dealing with, was thinking how to get it done right off the bat, not the reasons for him not to.

'No,' Brody said, 'we should have more precise information later, but we need to have something set up by then.'

Jack was thinking of a call from a bank manager confirming he or she had received a message they'd be storing cash – if that's what it was – in their branch over the weekend prior to incineration.

A moment of self-doubt struck him. *What if I'm wrong. And what if the spaghetti hats are right?*

'Are you still there, buddy...?'

'Yeah,' Brody said, 'I'm still here. We're guessing it'll be the city centre somewhere. But we don't know.'

'And how am I going to insert mics down there...I've never even been down there. Unless...'

'Yes, unless.'

'You've got to give me a margin here, Brody, because I'm just thinking aloud. I can hang mics from beneath the access points, the manhole covers, the way they hang a water pump, same principle.'

'If you say so.'

'Look, let me scribble out a few details, and I'll get back to you, okay?'

'Okay.'

Tennant hung up. *Yes*, Brody thought, *TT got things done.* He found a way. Brody supposed that dealing with life and death, earthquakes and other calamities, would do that. Certainly, they would.

17

It was 8 p.m. when Jack left his office. For better or worse, he – okay, *they*, himself and Superintendent Ryan – had a plan. It felt strange that they should be working together on essentially a clandestine operation, both flying beneath the radar. He reckoned it was a first for her. As he drove along the North Circular Road, he realised something wasn't sitting well with him about Ashling Nolan. It was this: if she was willing to give up on their burgeoning relationship that quickly, then maybe he was better off. Without her, that is. He didn't want to do the bitter remorse thing – and being the one who was dumped, that would be too easy – but still, maybe there was a reason why she lived alone in that one-bedroom apartment of hers. I mean, she didn't even have a cat.

Neither do you, he thought, *and you live on your own too.*

Okay, he was doing the bitter remorse thing: *Watch it, Jack.*

As he tried his best not to ruminate about this – which wasn't easy, as his mind kept slipping a cog back into thoughts of her – he became aware of a car in his rear-view mirror that he was convinced he'd spotted a couple of times already. An orange Renault Clio, popular yes, but not that popular that it would keep popping up like that, hanging back a couple of car lengths. Either it was a – that word again – coincidence, or he was being followed. Jack, not being sold on coincidences, was leaning towards the second option. He went through Hanlon's Corner and swung a left at Grainger's pub onto the Old Cabra Road, drove slowly along there, watching in the rear-view as the Clio swung a left too. It was now just one car length behind. Jack tried to catch a look at the driver, but it was dark outside, and all he could see was a silhouette. A Lidl supermarket came up on his right, and at the last minute he turned into it, moving along the parking lane by the side of the building before turning into the car park at the end. Just as he did, he glimpsed the Clio move from the road outside and along the parking lane just as he had done. This surprised him. His abrupt turn off from the road should have given the Clio driver an indication they'd been rumbled.

Which made him think, just maybe, that he wasn't being followed at all, that it actually had been one of those rare occurrences, a coincidence. These did happen, after all, let's not forget – occasionally, that is. Anyway, while he was here, he needed to buy some groceries. Jack reversed into a space and killed the engine. A moment later the Clio moved past along the parking lane and pulled in two rows behind. Now Brody watched in his rear-view mirror. The driver wasn't moving. *To hell with this*, he thought.

Brody got out of his car quickly and stooped so that he remained below the roof line of the other vehicles. He made his way between the rows of motors towards the Clio, seeing the outline of the person behind the wheel as he emerged onto the parking lane where it was facing him in a space opposite. He straightened and crossed. As he reached it, the driver looked up. Brody smiled, feeling immediately reassured. Because this had been no coincidence. He grabbed the door handle and pulled it open.

'Well, well, Mandy Joyce, in all the car parks in all the world...'

'Jack,' said with false surprise, 'I was just thinking the same thing myself.'

'I bet you were. What's up?'

'Well, I'm all out of cheese...and milk too. You?'

'Very funny.'

'What? I'm not being funny. Jack, it's a supermarket, come on, and last time I checked, this was a free country.'

'So you weren't following me?'

She laughed, but Jack could tell she was nervous. 'God, no. You mean...what? You thought I was following you? Like, dream on. You're not so important.'

'You sure?'

She looked away, back again, said nothing for a moment. Then, 'Okay, okay. I was following you. Um, can we go someplace for a minute and talk?'

'Talk. About what?'

'Please...?'

'Why should I?'

'I'm sorry, the remark earlier, a bit tasteless, the girl being fifteen, I was jiving.'

'Some things you don't jive about.'

'I know. I'm sorry. I owe my life to you. I'd never do anything to upset you, not really.'

It was true. A year before, he'd saved her from a crazed killer.

'I know you don't have to talk to me,' she said, 'but I'm asking, please.'

He looked at his watch. 'I'll sit in with you.' He went round, opened the passenger door and got in. 'What's this rigmarole?' he asked. 'You following me like that? If you wanted to talk to me, you have my phone number.' He looked around the interior of the car. 'And didn't you used to be fussy about what wheels you drove?'

'I still am. But necessity is the great leveller, isn't it? I heard this car described as an automotive phallic symbol, which is why women like it. It's true too; it does a bit, doesn't it? Not why women buy it, though. For me, I couldn't afford anything else. I'd much prefer a Lexus. Remember my UX 200? Smooth. When I'm back in the game, I'm thinking maybe a Range Rover next time.'

Jack couldn't help but laugh.

'It didn't last, did it? Your journey into the wilds of Leitrim and your inner soul.'

'My inner soul? I never said I was going on a journey into my inner soul.'

'I'm in a hurry, Mandy. I'll ask again, why were you following me?'

'Following you? Putting it like that makes it sound, I don't know...dramatic. I wasn't really following you. It's not like I'm working for a foreign government or anything.'

'No?'

'The Russians, Jack? That who you mean? Or the Chinese?'

'If there was a story in it.'

'Jesus, you have a low opinion of me.'

'In a professional capacity, yes, that's quite possible.'

'Okay, I'll tell you. You know I'm trying to get back in the game. And that's not easy. Once you're gone, you're gone, and all that. It's like you never even existed; you're erased. I'm erased. The next crop of young ones coming out of journalism school are in the field, half of them working for free just to get their leg in the door. That's what I'm up against. You think I'm bad, they'd sell their own mothers to get a story.'

'So would you, Mandy, one time.'

'One time is the operative word. I'm not getting any younger, you know.'

'Don't give me that,' Jack scoffed. 'What are you? Mid-thirties? If even that? That's not old. Come on now.'

'It's all relative. I'm old for this game.'

'Then change games. I thought you had.'

'So did I. The whole Leitrim thing. I tried, I really did, but I miss it too much. Jesus, I want to get back in front of the camera so bad, it's almost like a physical ache, just like the good old days, the star on top of the tree. It's where I belong. Look at me now, driving this yoke, dressed the way I am.' Jack couldn't see how she was dressed. 'I want to be back under the bright lights, Jack, wearing freebie designer dresses and...driving a Range Rover. I mean, is it too much for a girl to ask?'

'Maybe,' Brody said, 'but you still didn't answer my question. Why were you following me?'

She sighed. 'I don't really know myself. But I was thinking that if I followed you for long enough, you might lead me to something.'

'Did you now? Well, tonight, the only place I would have led you to was Drumcondra; that'd be a wasted journey.'

'Yeah,' Mandy agreed, 'it would.'

He watched her as she stared out the windscreen. Mandy Joyce, the onetime nation's highest-paid and favourite TV news reporter, driving a phallic symbol of a car, only in her thirties, but feeling washed up and too old for the game. What was the world coming to? He couldn't help feeling sorry for her.

She turned and looked at him. 'Can you give us a hand, like? I need a story, Jack. A story that'll blow every other story out of the water. A great big, big...*story*. Help me get back in the game, Jack. That's all I need.'

'Help you get back in the game? You're not asking for much, are you? How can I help get you back in the game? Why the hell do you think I can rescue your career?'

'Don't give me that. Something's up, Jack, I know it. What happened to that poor unfortunate cop and the woman in the hotel room? I have a feeling about this, call it an...'

'I know, an intuition,' Jack finished the sentence for her. 'You should have been a mule, Mandy, you really should.'

And Jack meant it. As far as he was concerned, she had more intuition in her little finger than Assistant Commissioner Padraic Kelly and all the spaghetti hats Brody had been dealing with lately put together.

'We haven't found any link between either murder,' Jack said. 'Intuition and facts are two different things. Don't go getting them mixed up now.'

'Hm,' she said, 'so, hand on heart, you can tell me that both killings are not linked.'

'I don't have to tell you anything, Mandy.'

'No, Jack, that's right, you don't.'

'I'll tell you what, though...' he said, thinking.

'Yes, you'll tell me what?'

'When I know, I'll let you know.'
'Know what?'
'I can't say. Not yet.'
'So something's up. I was right. Come on, Jack, throw me a bone.'
'Right. I can throw you a bone, but one that the meat's long been chewed off of, so no surprises. But no one else will know about it, not this side of the Atlantic anyway.'
'Jack, what the hell's that supposed to mean? What are you talking about?'
'Canada, Mandy. Abraham Jackman. Look up the RCMP website. That's all I can say. Work it out. That's no problem for you.'

She reached for her phone in the driver's door well, her face illuminating in the light of its screen. As Jack opened the door, she hardly noticed, her thumbs working a flurry as she jumped into a hot spot and surfed the web.

THAT NIGHT, as Jack lay in bed, he thought of Ashling Nolan. He thought about what she'd said, about how he was married to his job. Was that fair? He thought of Caoimhe too. She'd never mentioned any of this to him, about him being married to his job, not once. But then, Jack suddenly realised, he had thrown himself completely into his work only after she had died. Still, you don't cut the boat loose in a storm, you tie it tighter to the jetty.

But Ashling Nolan had cut him loose.

Eventually, that helped him to drift off, thinking of boats bobbing about in a harbour as the storm clouds gathered. He wondered why their owners had left them like that, out on the water, at the mercy of what was to come.

What was to come...

The storm.

That's what was to come.

18

It was 6 a.m. At this hour, with only a light breeze blowing in off the river, the smell of roasting hops from the Guinness brewery was heavy in the air. At other times it was lost to the smells of a busy city, to its traffic, industry, its people, its food, everything. But at this hour, with all still relatively quiet and the air relatively clean, Dublin reached back in time, carrying a fragrance that was centuries old, like an elusive and rare bird, witnessed only at certain moments. This area of the Quays, close to Heuston station, where Brody had earlier arrested Matt Thompson, and next to the Seán Heuston Bridge, opposite the Guinness brewery, was a moment caught in time. A horse and carriage could as easily be imagined passing as a car, the cityscape the same as it was in the eighteenth century, and, at this hour, the smells carried on the air the same too.

Khabib knew none of this, of course. Nor would he care if he had. He parked the Mitsubishi along a cobblestone side street. He'd been debating whether or not he needed to get rid of the pickup, unsure whether it had been captured on

CCTV somewhere and right now someone was joining up the dots. But then he decided he didn't need to. If it had been captured on CCTV, so what? There would be no link to that motorcycle cop. And right now, that was all that mattered. The cameras on that patch of waste ground had been turned the other way. In fact, to get rid of the pickup now might, instead of deflecting attention, turn it onto them.

'Wait,' he said to the others. They had all just gotten out of the Mitsubishi, Tyler losing concentration for a split second and banging the door shut.

'Motherfucker,' Khabib hissed, raising his hand, about to swing his open palm through the air against Tyler's cheek, but stopping himself just in time. 'Get your shit together. Now. Before we go in. You hear me?'

Tyler nodded. 'Sorry,' he whispered, 'my hand slipped, sorry.'

'You motherfucker, now you're lying, aren't you? I'll deal with you later, make no mistake.'

Khabib looked around. On one side of the street there was a high stone wall, weeds sprouting from out of the grout between the stonework in places, opposite a row of low, two-storey houses, most looking like they hadn't been lived in in years, but a couple still looked occupied. On one window was a flower box with what appeared to be fresh flowers in it.

'Wait here,' he said and went up the street, at the top emerging onto the street running next to the road running into the city centre by the river. He waited until the traffic released from a traffic light up ahead had passed, then ran across the road and leaned over the wall, looking down into the water. The tide, as expected, was out, the banks of the river a ribbon of dirty, grey soft silt like piles of bakers' dough.

He looked both ways along the wall, spotted the metal rungs fixed to it off to his left. He also checked a CCTV camera fixed to an electricity pole behind him. You really had to look hard to notice that the lens had been smashed.

He smiled. Perfect, everything seemed perfect, just like it always was, just like God had made sure it always was.

And then he thought of Tyler...well, almost perfect. That asshole's meter was running out. And would be out. Right after this job. For certain.

He ran back across the road. Khabib made sure to leave the Mitsubishi unlocked with the keys in the ignition, a bait too good to ignore for any teenage joyriding junkie or someone needing it for a certain type of job – just as he had needed it.

Clyde went down first. The satchels containing the equipment were sent down after him, and the Scottish ex-miner had to leave them balanced at the end of their ropes while he took the laser cutter from one satchel and set about removing the access grille over the tunnel. It left them exposed, for a very short time, but there was no other way around it. They all had high-vis vests on, so passing traffic would assume they were city workers, especially at this hour.

The soft, dough-like silt along the edges of the river stretched into the sewer tunnel, but the movement of the raw sewerage that one time ran through here, and the overflow water that still did at critical times, had created a cylindric effect. Swinging from the rungs into the cylindric area was the hard part. Fall into the silt and in no time a person would be sucked down to waist level at the least, maybe higher. It would take a four-wheel drive with a winch to haul them back out again. If they weren't taken out in time, they would drown beneath the incoming tide.

They all made it from the rung over the silt and in, Lisbeth the last and the lightest person to do it. Still, Khabib grabbed her round the waist, not that he needed to, he didn't, nor did he need to grip her so low.

Tyler caught the look Clyde sent Khabib as he did. It was the same on the last job too. In the apartment there'd been none of that, only on the job, and only lately too. Weird. Khabib was building up to something with Lisbeth, Tyler felt certain. Now, that would be interesting.

The silt along the sides of the tunnel wasn't in place for long. About ten metres in, it was gone completely. It grew steadily darker as they moved in until it was almost pitch. That was when they stopped and turned on their head torches. It was almost completely silent too, nothing but the drip, drip sound of water from the brickwork into the shallow dirty water below, and the occasional scurrying sound and squeaking of rats. The beams of their torch lights lit up the tunnel for maybe twenty metres ahead before becoming lost to the blackness. Khabib consulted his sat nav, a small, powerful piece of specialist equipment with the ability to operate underground and only available to elite special forces – and people like him. God could provide anything, after all. He led them ahead in single file, beneath the streets of Dublin, moving with determined, practised ease. With each step into this subterranean world they took, he forgot more and more about the world above. He was entering the *zone*. All that existed was this moment and what he had come to do. Everything else faded and was forgotten, just what lay ahead. Khabib led them on.

19

Jack turned the shower heat regulator all the way into the blue zone, the explosion of frigid water against his skin igniting every nerve, shocking him into uber consciousness. It was what he needed right now. He hadn't slept well, and he felt like he'd spent the night at an airport. As he dressed, the feeling returned, something gnawing at him. It wasn't just Ashling Nolan, although what had happened with her weighed heavily. It was more. Images of his dream flashed across his mind, of the dark storm clouds, the boats bobbing about in the water. His sense of foreboding became sharper. The storm, he felt, was almost upon them.

In his office he sat heavily behind his desk, eyed the free-standing punch bag in the corner. Jack turned on his computer and, while he waited for it to boot up, stood again and stepped over to the heavy.

He needed that gnawing feeling inside him gone; he needed his head cleared; he needed to be able to think straight. He lifted the pair of gloves from their hook on the wall next to the bag. He'd give it five minutes, that's all, five minutes. He put on his gloves and started, concentrating on landing each shot, of transferring every piece of energy up through his right leg and into his arm, then into his fist, crashing it into the heavy, before switching, doing the same with the other leg, as the anchor loop on the heavy holding the bag jiggered about, coming perilously close to bouncing free more than once. When he finished, Brody stepped back, panting, his forehead coated in sweat.

'You're going to need another shower, boss.'

Marty stepped into the office and looked at him.

'Clearing the head, is it?' he asked.

'Nothing that can't be sorted with a bit of help from my friend,' Brody answered, nodding to the punch bag. 'Anyway, perfect timing. I want you to go and get everybody into my office in, say, ten minutes, will you do that, please?'

'Your office?'

'Yes, my office, Marty.'

'You don't usually...you usually go down to the unit room, don't you?'

'I do. But this time it's a bit more...you know.' Brody tapped the side of his nose a couple of times.

'Oh, I get it,' Marty said, and nodded. 'The walls have ears and all that. By the way, I finally got him...'

'Got who?'

'The concierge at the Herbert Park Platinum. You told me to have a talk with him, remember.'

'Oh yes, good man, Marty.'

'His name's Walter Valtez.'

'Is that Maltese?'

'Close.' Marty grinned. 'Miltown Malbay in west Clare, actually. Seemingly, the name's common down there.'

'Well, you learn something new every day.'

'He's only a young fella, a student at TCD, psychology, fits his studies in around his job.'

'Okay, and what'd he have to say for himself?'

'It's what he didn't say, boss. Definitely in on it, if you ask me, but from a distance. I think he was a spotter; in his role he could identify the ones he thought offered the most potential. But proving it's going to be a different matter.'

'Hm,' Brody said, 'impossible I'd say, not unless one of the others gives him up, and so far they haven't even mentioned his name. Of course, they may not have known he was involved.'

'He has no history on the system either. Although he tried to hide it, he seemed shook up by it all. Got in a little too deep, if you ask me. An earner on the side, something tells me he won't be doing that again.'

'Harmless, eh? You really think it's a one-off for him?'

'Well, you can never be sure...but yeah, I do. I created intelligence on him. If he gets up to anything again, we'll know.'

'Good work. It's Store Street's baby now. I don't think they'll want him getting away with this, not just like that. They can deal with it.' Brody checked the time, 8:10 a.m. 'Go down and get them, Marty, will you?'

'Will do,' Marty said, and left the office.

CONSIDINE AND MARTY sat on the other side of Brody's desk, while Voyle leaned back against the side wall, beside the heavy, ankles crossed and arms folded. Brody thought he looked strangely like a wood carving. It also struck Brody –

again – that the unit had not grown since its formation over a year ago. With the success rate it had already achieved, it should have. But as yet, it hadn't. '*Shenanigans that could not be tolerated*' were the words the commissioner himself had used in describing the behaviour of some senior officers during a recent case. The proof was in the pudding. And this pudding had stayed the same.

Brody realised he was staring at a spot on the wall.

'Right,' he said, coming back into the moment, 'myself and Superintendent Ryan have had a chat.' He briefly went over the dilemma again, of neither being able to get into the vault, nor into the sewers.

'The first person who'll know of where the money's to be stored, these used banknotes, is the branch manager. If that's what's going to happen. He will receive a text message minutes before the money arrives. Every manager has been instructed by their head office to notify us immediately using a special number we've set up, should this happen. And when the message is received, we'll know where the money is. In theory, this will be the bank we also think is going to be hit. That's what they call the hypothesis model... of course, no one really knows if anything's going to happen, as yet. This process is out of human hands. If the raiders know, it means they've hacked the computer system some-how, and they'll be one step ahead of us.'

'We wait, boss, is that it?' Considine asked.

Brody shrugged.

'Well, yes and no. I want each of you to make yourselves available at a moment's notice for the next thirty-six hours. Any plans you have, scrap them.'

Marty made a low groaning noise.

'That a problem?' Brody asked, looking at him.

'No, boss, it's not. Nothing that can't be changed, anyway. No, I'm on board.'

'Good. And Nicola, Steve?'

'Of course,' Considine said.

Voyle nodded.

'Because I have a feeling,' Brody said, 'a storm is coming.'

20

The first time he went into the sewers had scared him. More than anything in his whole life before. But he couldn't show it. He'd frozen, just for a second, but that would be enough if Khabib had known. Khabib demanded perfection; it was what made the team so good at what they did, like the movement in a Swiss watch, smooth and tight – on time every time.

Tyler did not fear the sewers now. He no longer considered them the first stop on the path down into hell. He no longer saw the faces of his parents in the dark recesses, watching him, spectres, their reflections visible, shimmering on the rancid water.

In fact, he got to like the sewers in a way; he felt safe there, hidden in the darkness of a world within a world and yet outside a world, all at the same time. He fantasised about living in the sewers sometimes, emerging only at night like a vampire to satisfy his cravings. But he knew, too, that he never would. He never could. He'd gotten used to a certain level of comfort; Egyptian cotton sheets, he liked the way his victims lay on top of them, staring at the ceiling. They too deserved a level of comfort and respect. Didn't they? It was his way of making up for the fact he had never given his mother any in the way he'd killed her.

Dear Mother, I'm so sorry.

Tyler liked all that, cotton sheets and luxurious hotel rooms. No, he could never give up on them. Even now, it was giving him a hard-on, thinking of the next one he would fuck and kill. It made his life worthwhile.

They'd been sloshing through the shallow water for over thirty minutes now, Khabib at the lead, following his special forces GPS. No one else had any way of knowing where they were, so they were completely dependent on Khabib if they wanted to find their way out again alive. Just in case anyone got ideas. And only Khabib knew the passcode to operate that GPS. Sneaky.

When the sewers had been built, the old Victorian engineers had been forward thinkers. They'd built them wide and high, knowing that cities and populations only ever did one thing – increased in size. And whatever the future held, everything could only be bigger, faster, wider, greater than what had gone before. In an age when people strove to find answers, they were the first to admit that they didn't have them. Science did. The results were edifices to scientific engineering such as sewers like the ones they were in, great metal ships, and buildings that reached to the sky. Also, what they called a dry recess had been built into the wall of the sewer every so often, quite spacious, where work crews could take shelter when required, have meal breaks and, as sometimes happened, spend the night if they needed to.

This was where Khabib led them now, perfect as a staging post from where the team could work their way into the vault. Khabib stopped and pointed. Lisbeth was the first, climbing up the tunnel wall, foot grips hollowed out of the brickwork for this purpose. The old Victorians had thought of everything.

AT A LITTLE AFTER 3 p.m. a couple of white Land Rovers, with blue and red chevrons along the sides and the words Dublin Civil Defence printed above, pulled onto the central pathway of the four-carriage roadway running through the middle of O'Connell Street, the heart of Dublin city. TT and a volunteer got out of one Land Rover, wearing Civil Defence high-vis jackets and trousers. They went to the back door and pulled it open. TT reached in and began rolling out a length of electrical cord on a reel and cutting it into six sections. Another volunteer began doing the same at the back of the other Land Rover. With the lengths cut, TT's companion, a volunteer electrical engineer, began fixing a listening device to the end of each one, threading the copper wiring into the connections and screwing them tight and wrapping these in waterproof tape. Each listening device looked just like a small tea strainer.

It was easier to walk from this central position on O'Connell Street to their selected maintenance access points, remove the manhole covers and hang the listening devices from the undersides, rather than drive to each through the heavy traffic.

By 5 p.m. they were all done, their network of listening devices in place and fully covering the central Dublin area. However, their combined range could stretch to a distance of more than a kilometre, though at such an extremity anything picked up would be extremely faint.

'Great work,' Jack said when TT rang him to say the job was complete and he and his team were on their way back to the Civil Defence base on Wolfe Tone Quay.

'This is not something I'd usually say after I put in place listening devices,' TT added, 'but I hope you don't hear anything, not beyond anything you'd expect to hear down there, anyway. If you get me.'

'I get you,' Jack said, 'I get you,' and he thanked the Civil Defence volunteer again and disconnected the call.

21

The bank manager of the National & Provincial branch on Essex Quay, Joseph MacDowell, was in his office, looking out from behind his desk through the open door to one of the clerks as she slid off her stool behind the counter, watching as her skirt rode up her thigh, revealing a flash of white flesh. He watched as she walked to a filing cabinet in a far corner and opened a drawer. He knew that printed forms – increasingly becoming relics in a paperless world – were stored there, favoured by the bank's cohort of elderly customers. The teller took one from a top drawer and, he was delighted to see, bent down to open the bottom drawer. He held his breath, hearing in the background his phone sounding an incoming text alert, as he stared at the shapely outline encased in the tight navy skirt...he swallowed, then coughed hoarsely as he noticed the thin knicker outline pushing through the fabric. Christ. He turned away, unable to take anymore, a respectable man such as himself, reduced to this, a quivering wreck. *You dirty old man,* a voice in his head admonished him. *You don't have to look*, he told himself, something he always did, *after* he had looked.

He remembered the text alert and reached for his phone just as the teller began walking back to her station, or shimmying, as he decided she was doing in that tight dress of hers. He couldn't help but look again. The girl had a perfect hourglass figure, that's what she had. She resumed her stool, but there was no flash of thigh this time, her back was turned to him. He brought up the message on his phone and looked at it; it was brief and to the point, five words: Imminent Arrival of Security Cargo. So the latest consignment of used banknotes was coming to him, was it? Very good. And hadn't he read somewhere something about informing the head office about it? He went into his emails to check. Yes, there it was, a special number for him to ring. Joseph MacDowell kept the screen open as he lifted his desk phone, about to dial.

'Mr MacDowell.'

He looked up. It was her, the hourglass-figured clerk he'd just been perving a moment ago. *Yes, Joe* – he hated being called Joe, his name was Joseph, for God's sake, but that voice in his head called him this when it was displeased – *yes, Joe, you perv, you dirty little old man you*. He felt himself blush. Was she new to the branch? He couldn't remember having seen her before. God, she was beautiful. She was everything he'd want in a woman – if he were thirty years younger, that is. But he wasn't. She was young enough to be his granddaughter.

He realised her lips were moving.

Was she speaking?

Yes, she was – to him.

'Sorry, what was that again?' he said, glancing away, as if he had other things on his mind.

'A man, at the counter. He asked to see you.'

'Me. Why? If he wants to see me, he needs to make an appointment. Can you tell him that, please? What is your name, by the way?'

She smiled, her beautiful face lighting up as she displayed two rows of perfect white teeth.

'My name is Wendy. But Mr MacDowell, he says he has an appointment. His name's Trevor Hook.'

'Oh, you should have said, still, you weren't to know, were you? Trevor, yes, of course, the builder. Tell my assistant, Mr Cruise, there's a cargo coming for the vault. Can you do that for me, Wendy?'

'Yes, Mr MacDowell, of course, will do.'

'And tell him it's imminent, will you do that too?'

She nodded. 'Yes, of course, I will.'

Like there was nothing she wouldn't do. He felt his cheeks glow. *Oh yes, you dirty old man.*

'Very good,' he said. 'Yes, Trevor. Send Mr Hook in now, Wendy, thank you.'

She smiled again and nodded as MacDowell pushed his phone to the side, forgetting all about the text message, and with it the requirement to notify head office of the arrival of the 'cargo'.

22

'I've sent you a link,' Tommy Tennant told Brody. 'If you open it, you'll have access to the audio from the mikes. I'd recommend you wear headphones. If it seems like there's nothing to hear, give it a little time, you'll hear something anyway. It'll take a bit to get used to.'

'I'll hear something even if there's nothing. What do you mean?'

'See, the microphones are super sensitive, they have to be, but we can't make them so sensitive they'll blow your ears off. Tell you what, are you near a computer?'

'I am, a laptop.'

'Bring up the link on that. I'll stay on the line...'

Brody did. 'I have it here, the link.'

'Good, now click on it.'

Brody did that too.

'Now, what have you got?'

'I've got two rows of little boxes, six boxes in each row, with a line through each and looping both rows together. And each box is numbered. It looks like a simple outline.'

'Good, that's the whole idea,' TT said. 'It is simple. Simple enough that a shepherd in the mountains somewhere in the Middle East or Asia or wherever can use it. Click on a box, any box at all.'

Like a game show, Brody thought, to reveal the prize.

He clicked on the middle box in the top row. The box altered to become a series of numbers with a small circle above.

'Is that a GPS?' Brody asked.

'Yes,' TT said, 'it is. It identifies the location of the microphone. It's fixed to the underside of the manhole cover. Click on that number.'

Brody did.

'Hear anything?'

'No,' Brody said, '...oh, wait a minute. I do...I think.'

Brody turned his head to the side and leaned in closer to the computer. From it he could hear what sounded like low breathing. He went into volume settings and turned it up. The breathing sound increased, uncannily like someone with bronchial problems was on the other end and had their mouth pressed against the microphone.

'What the feck's that?' Brody asked.

'It's the air, cold air rising from the bottom of the tunnels, in a perpetual process, wafting against the relatively warmer air at ceiling level, expanding outward, breathing, just like it sounds...'

'Fuck,' Brody said, and immediately apologised. It didn't seem right to swear into the ear of someone whom you hardly knew.

'Click on another one,' TT said.

Brody did. This sound was different. A swirling noise, like water down a plug hole. It grated against his ears, right down into his eardrum. He winced and quickly turned the volume down.

'Water?' Brody asked.

'Yes, water.'

Brody realised he'd need someone on this twenty-four seven, for the next couple of days at least. He thanked TT for his help again and hung up, went to the door of his office and called the one person he knew had the stamina and concentration for this job. 'Considine,' he called, 'can you come up here a minute?'

Brody explained what he needed her to do, then left her to it and went down to the unit room. He sat at Considine's desk and made a phone call to the Central Bank to ascertain if word had been received from anyone having taken delivery of a consignment of used banknotes. He was told that no message had been received. He hung up, thinking that maybe it wasn't going to happen. It was late on a Friday. If it was going to happen, surely it would have happened by now?

THERE SEEMED a general air of calm in the unit room. Voyle had his feet up on his desk. Marty had just filled a paper cup with water from the cooler in the corner and was taking it back to his desk. It had been two days since the discovery of the body in room 532 of the Herbert Park Platinum Hotel, and one day since the murder of the motorcycle cop. The golden forty-eight hours had run out on the first case, and now they – Store Street – were midway through it on the second.

But neither was like a normal investigation. The links

weren't there, the investigative avenues not so much blocked as non-existent. It was like an alien entity had swooped down from on high, carried out the vile deeds, and flown off again.

Something was not right, yet Brody could feel the storm clouds, heavy and leaden, about to break.

A pubic hair, a single pubic hair, that was all that had been discovered. But from that, Brody had learned much, just not enough. The killer had scented his own trail. Why?

It was almost half four, a time when the working day, the working week, for most people was almost over. And still no word received of any consignment of used banknotes having been received. Brody still had a feeling. But could he have gotten this all wrong?

23

Trevor Hook stayed in the bank manager's office for over an hour. MacDowell rarely entertained anyone for such a length of time; this was almost one-eighth of the working day, after all, for God's sake. But Hook was an exception, a one-off, an inner-city boy who rose out of poverty and made good. The press loved him. And Mr MacDowell was fascinated by the man. Hook had done it completely legit too, built his fortune on a foundation of hard work and within a framework of savvy investments along with a dollop of good luck. He was now one of the wealthiest property developers in the city. And wealthy people like him rarely used their own money for their projects, everyone knew that. They used other people's, that of shareholders, the banks. And Mr MacDowell was happy to oblige, although for a loan of €8.4 million he had to get approval from head office first, of course.

Still, when Trevor Hook left his office, and by the time MacDowell had signed some important legal documents in relation to other business, and *then*, by the time he'd approved two mortgage loan applications, and then, after he'd sat back and watched Wendy for a bit, he realised he'd forgotten something, but just couldn't remember what. This made him restless. He checked the time on his office clock, a quarter to five. Just over an hour from now and the staff would all have left, and he'd be locking up.

What in goodness' name was it he was forgetting?

He glanced out his office door, could see customers queuing up on the floor of the bank, but not for tellers – there was only a handful of these now – but for machines. Soon, he imagined all the tellers would be gone. Who knows, sometime in the not-too-distant future the bank might be completely automated too. Maybe he'd be replaced by a robot? He almost grinned as Wendy suddenly swivelled on her stool, reached forward for something on the counter, her blouse pulling against her ample bosom. Then it struck him.

The delivery!

Of course. He'd received a text message telling him of an imminent delivery of used notes. He'd been given a number to ring…goodness. Still, no panic. He'd do it right away. A little late maybe, but it was a Friday, after all. And a Friday was always a particularly busy time.

He reached for his desk phone, checking his computer or the number he had to ring.

24

Brody was studying the still CCTV images of the person leaving through the employee door at the Herbert Platinum the night he rumbled the honey scam team. He was thinking he would have to organise relief for Considine in a couple of hours. He knew that concentrating on listening the way she was was as physically draining as digging a ditch. He would also have to have the CCTV images forwarded to the Mounties. They'd know what this Abraham Jackman character looked like as a kid. He zoomed in as close as he could, before the image pixelated and became impossible to discern. Jack guessed the man in the photograph was about five eleven tall, of good build. Probably worked out. His hair was short and black, and his skin looked tanned, but that might just be the light in the photograph. From what he could make out, the man seemed to fit the profile. Something about him, yes, he looked the part, he looked like a player.

Brody checked Pulse for an update on the murder of the motorcycle garda. There was nothing but forensics and pathology additions. Seemingly Deci Sinnott was suffering from cirrhosis of the liver, but he probably didn't even know it.

Brody saw that an Inspector Duddy had been added – likely by himself – to the case as investigating officer. Which was fine, but he didn't think that would make any difference. In fact, if the wheels continued to spin in the mud the way they were, he might come to regret it.

Brody's mobile phone rang. He snatched it up. 'Yeah, Brody.'

He listened, jumped to his feet.

'What's up, boss?' Voyle asked. 'You look like you just got your finger stuck in an electrical socket.'

Brody pulled the phone from his ear.

'It's about to break, that's what.'

'What's about to break?'

'The storm, Steve, the fucking storm, that's what's about to break. The money, the used banknotes, they've arrived.'

ASSISTANT COMMISSIONER PADRAIC KELLY was sitting in his favourite pub, enjoying a Friday after-work couple of pints of Guinness, the way he always did at the end of the week, when Brody called. In fact, he debated whether or not to take the call. If he didn't, it would then be passed along to the duty inspector to look after. Assistant Commissioner Kelly liked to keep a healthy work-life balance, after all. But in the end, he answered, pressing the phone to his ear with a sigh and placing a finger against his other ear in an attempt to drown out the background noise as best he could. 'Yes, Sergeant Brody,' he said haughtily, 'how can I help you?'

Before Brody had even finished speaking, Kelly was already leaving the pub, offering a muttered excuse to his pals that they couldn't hear anyway, and leaving a half-finished pint of the black stuff behind him on the counter and the pub door swinging in the breeze.

THE ALERT BRODY issued on Pulse drew response cars from both the Dublin Central and South Central districts. Just in time he'd sent an addition to his alert, which was that all cars on the final approach should turn off their sirens and travel on blues only. And after this he sent an addition to the addition. This was the recall of all cars. Brody had become alarmed by the radio chatter and realised that every available car in the city centre was racing to the scene. Not what was needed. That would only serve to snarl up traffic and create a scene. Everything he didn't want.

No, no, no. This called for subtlety. He had them called off. If anyone had a problem with that, they could talk to him about it later.

As it happened, only two cars arrived at the scene – and discreetly, taking up parking spaces with paid-up parking tickets on their dashes, too. Brody and Voyle were in the first car, and they arrived a couple of minutes ahead of Assistant Commissioner Kelly. The AC, with a pint and half of porter inside him, had determined he was okay to drive. That might have ended badly if he'd been pulled over. But he hadn't.

Brody and Voyle were going through the bank's front door when they heard a voice. 'Wait up.'

They turned.

The AC was dressed in sneakers, jeans and hoodie. It felt

strange for Brody to see him out of uniform; in street clothes, he appeared to have sliced a decade off his age. In fact, Brody thought the AC looked more like a street dealer who'd just wandered up from his patch on the boardwalk.

'Where's Superintendent Ryan?' Kelly asked.

Brody shrugged. 'She wasn't in her office. I left a message. And I tried ringing you, too, but got no answer.'

'I was driving. I didn't hear it ringing.'

Brody was about to ask if he had Bluetooth. Because if he had, the chances are he would have. But he didn't comment, not on that.

Instead, he said, 'Our first priority is to make sure we have this vault emptied. We know if they're going to hit anywhere, it's here. What do you say? We get everything taken out.'

The AC stopped. He didn't look very impressed with that, probably because it wasn't him who had said it. 'Let's see what's what first, shall we?' He stepped through Brody and Voyle and into the doorway. 'Right, follow me.'

Brody glanced at Voyle, who clenched his right hand into a fist at groin level, motioning as if he were tossing a dice...or something else.

25

Joseph MacDowell looked up from his desk to see three men striding into his bank. For a moment he wondered if they'd come to rob the place, but he knew they hadn't. If they had, they'd have covered their faces at least. He thought the one in the hoodie and jeans looked particularly suspicious. It was right on closing time, and the tellers had started to cash up, and the porter was closing the door behind them. But he paused, looking back at the three men. MacDowell nodded, and he closed the door. The manager had sent his assistant along with a junior clerk into the vault to check the metal cases containing the used banknotes. They were surprisingly small cases, because, depending on the denomination, each one could hold up to three million euro. And each case had to be opened and visually inspected. Of course, if anyone was tempted to stuff some notes down his or her underwear or in his socks, it was no use. The junior was watching the assistant manager, and the assistant manager was watching the junior. And if the two of them were still somehow in on it, well, still it wouldn't be any good. Because the rules stated that the police would have to be called. And when they arrived, they'd search both of them anyway. Such a scenario had never come to pass, however, not once, ever, in the entire history of the bank – or any other bank in the country, for that matter.

Mr MacDowell didn't know what all the fuss was about. The three men introduced themselves by displaying their garda identification. Turned out the one in the hoodie was the most senior of them all, an assistant commissioner no less.

Mr MacDowell brought them into his office and closed the door. The one in the hoodie, his name was Kelly, said: 'The consignment of used banknotes you received.'

'Yes.'

Kelly paused and glanced to his colleague, the one who said he was a sergeant, then back again. 'Yes, well, we don't want you to place that in the vault...'

'You don't, but...'

'Hear me out,' Kelly said. 'We need you to empty that vault, in fact. Because we have reason to believe someone might be planning to steal the contents.'

'You do? W-what, are you serious?'

'Well, of course I'm serious. Do I look like I'm not serious? This isn't candid camera...what's your name, MacDowell, is it?'

'Yes, that's right. And that's impossible, to empty the vault.'

'It may be difficult, I'll grant you, but come on now, nothing is impossible.'

'Well, that is, because they've just locked the bloody door on it.'

'Can't you open it again?' Kelly twisted the drawstring of his hoodie around his index finger. 'How hard can it be?'

'No, I can't. That's the whole point. It's on a time lock. Impossible.'

'Oh.' But this Kelly character didn't progress any further from that one word.

'In that case,' it was the other one, Brody, the sergeant, 'we will probably need to maintain a presence here tonight, all night, in the bank.'

'You will?' MacDowell couldn't hide his complete surprise. 'Why?'

He caught the look between the sergeant and Kelly.

'We just do,' Kelly said, 'and I expect you not to discuss anything outside this room...You are aware of the Official Secrets Act, aren't you?'

'Well, no, why would I be? I'm a bank manager.'

'Suffice to say, if you divulge anything about this, you could be prosecuted, and, if deemed appropriate, a custodial sentence could be imposed. That's what it means.'

'You mean I'll be sent to prison?'

'Possibly.'

'Possibly,' MacDowell said, pushing himself up from his chair. 'Right then, I've heard enough. I'm calling the regional manager. He can deal with this. I'm not standing for being threatened with a prison sentence when I've done nothing wrong. And in my own office too. I mean, with respect, who do you think you are? Waltzing in here like this...'

'Mr MacDowell.' It was the sergeant again, Brody.

'Yes.'

'We have no wish to cause you upset. Sorry. But in the interests of saving time, I'd ask you just to go along with this.

We will be clearing it with the chairman of the bank very shortly.'

'You will? The chairman?'

'Certainly.'

He didn't think this Brody fella sounded too certain about that. But it was good enough for him, just to have him say it.

'Fine then,' MacDowell said. 'In that case, what is it you want me to do?'

26

They worked in silence. This was not a direction or an order, it just was. No one spoke, not unless they absolutely had to. Tyler liked this silence. In fact, now, he felt he needed it. They were in the recess of the sewerage tunnel, but where exactly this was, only Khabib knew. And he hadn't told them anything about it, or anything else for that matter, not yet. They would only know what the target was when they moved to cut through the wall into the vault. They prepared by setting up the sodium rechargeable lights and switched off their battery head torches, conserving the juice. They each checked their equipment and made sure everything was ready to go.

Then, again, they waited. For Khabib to give them their final instructions. There was nothing else to do. Time seemed to lose all its relevance down here, all context evaporating, then gone. In that there lay a certain freedom.

If Tyler hadn't caught the furtive look from Khabib, he might have thought that everything was as it always was, that it was business as usual. But he caught the look, and in that look got clear confirmation that no, nothing was as before. This time it was different. Very different.

27

Considine took off her headphones and sat back in her chair, rubbed her face briskly with both hands.

Marty raised a finger. He had offered to help her, and she had accepted. Two sets of ears were better than one, after all.

'You just missed it,' he said. 'I think I can hear something. But I'm not certain.'

She put her headphones back on again quickly and leaned forward. They both listened. Marty closed his eyes; he found this helped. There was the now familiar – even in the mere hour they'd been doing this it had become familiar – hollow in and out breathing-like sound. There was something different about it on this occasion. Or was there?

Marty squeezed his eyes tighter shut still...what exactly was different about it? Maybe it was his imagination, but he'd definitely thought he'd heard something. Tighter still he squeezed them shut. What was it? Perhaps he'd been too hasty in telling Considine. But then, in the background, so low he could just about hear it, coming through that sound of silence, a soft tapping, like a ballpoint pen on a piece of paper, *bip, bip, bip.*

He opened his eyes, saw that Nicola was looking at him.

'What is...?' she began, but Marty sliced a hand through the air in a motion for her to be quiet.

As they both listened, concentrating on nothing else.

28

They hadn't stayed in the recess for long and were now on the move again, climbing down into the tunnel, Khabib leading them further in. Their equipment was on their backs, and it made a soft tinkling noise as they moved, the light from their head torches bobbing about across the tunnel walls.

For a brief moment, Tyler thought he saw something. He looked to the side, and what appeared to be a tiny light, similar to a flickering candle, seemed to shimmer and jump just ahead of his vision, finally disappearing into the darkness behind him. He glanced over his shoulder and for a fleeting moment thought he glimpsed it again, within that washed space between the edge of torchlight and the inky darkness.

It reminded him. Of the first time he'd gone into the sewers. He'd seen it then. Not that he knew what it was. He didn't. Not back then. But he did now. He froze, stared into the darkness behind him. He knew it was there, somewhere. And then the spectre revealed itself, wafting across his vision a short distance away, the ephemeral translucent image of Gloria, his dear momma.

He watched, fear beginning to wrap itself around him like a cloak, as Mama beckoned to him with a long, bony finger. He felt someone push him roughly in the centre of his back. It was Clyde, who hissed, 'Keep fuckin' movin' on, will ya.'

Tyler stumbled, his feet sloshing through the water before he regained his balance and looked ahead again. Khabib had stopped, was looking at him. He couldn't see Khabib's face; the light from his torch was right in his eyes. Tyler used his hand to shade them against the glare, feeling a cold sense of maliciousness cutting through the stagnant air and passing right through him.

Khabib said nothing, but turned again and continued on. They followed.

29

'Steps,' Considine whispered, 'someone walking through water. What d'you think?'

Marty listened some more and then nodded slowly.

Bip, bip, bip.

Not like normal footsteps, both distorted and muted at the same time, sounding distant too. People were down there, and whoever they were, they were on the move.

'Will you keep listening?' he asked, whipping off his headphones. 'I need to ring the boss.'

Considine nodded.

'I'll save you the trouble, Marty.'

It was Superintendent Ryan. She walked into Brody's office and crossed to his desk, behind which they were both sitting.

'Jack was looking for you earlier, by the way,' he said.

'Yes, I'd say he was. I was called away. Nothing you need to worry about.'

'They're in the tunnels, the sewers; we can hear them. I need to ring Jack.'

'Haven't you forgotten? I'm the unit commander. You need to tell me.'

'And I just have, haven't I?' Not for nothing was he going to be a hot shot barrister down in the Four Courts one day.

Ryan's small hard eyes blinked. She reminded Marty of a cobra about to strike. But then she smiled. What a transformation, like flowers blooming on a thorny hedgerow.

'Yes, of course you have. I'll ring him myself if that's alright. How many are down there, do you think?'

'Hard to tell, a handful, three or four, maybe five.'

'Did they speak, say anything?'

'No, not that I could hear. Nothing.'

'And you're sure that's what it is; there's someone down there, moving about. Couldn't be anything else?'

'Maybe. I don't know for certain. You can listen yourself, but you'll just be wasting time. I'd take my chances that's what it is; they're down there.'

She looked uncertain, but then nodded, turning away. 'I'll ring Jack.' She paused. 'And anything else, you let me know first. Got that?'

They nodded, and she walked out of the unit room.

30

They moved ahead, following a long gentle curve in the tunnel and one on a gentle incline, the water dissipating until there was hardly anything at all, the sloshing sound of footsteps replaced by the hollow thump of rubber soles on stone. Khabib turned, as if into the wall, but his torch illuminated a side tunnel. They followed him. The roof here was not curved as before, but square, and much narrower. Tyler could feel the walls begin to brush against him, and with it came a sensation like he was being devoured by a monster. He felt his heartbeat quicken as the cloak of fear fell about him again and tightened. But he knew he could not show it. That he must not show it. The sound of their footsteps within the confined space grew louder, like a drumbeat.

Tyler swallowed, wiping the back of a hand across his forehead. They said that not far from Beaverton, just over the border into northern Pennsylvania, that at one time they burned witches. It was said they would take them, chained at the ankles, to a great pyre, where they would burn them alive, the procession led by young boys beating drums made from the hollowed-out stumps of oak trees. As he listened to the drumbeat of their feet, he could feel her presence. She was here, everywhere but nowhere. Watching. He knew it.

'What the fuck was that?'

They stopped.

Tyler realised he was laughing. He stopped. The one who had spoken was Khabib. He stormed down to him, pushed his face right up against his. Tyler forgot about Gloria, his dear old momma. The cloak of fear began to squeeze tighter than ever. There was only one person in this world who could do this to him – and that person had his face right up to his now. He could smell the sweetness of Khabib's breath, could almost taste those Medjool dates he liked to eat.

Khabib turned his head to the side, like he was trying to make sense of something, something intriguing to him. The light of his torch angled over Tyler's head, so that he could see Khabib's brown eyes, normally soft like golden syrup, but burning now with the intensity of a pyre in northern Pennsylvania as they burned a witch to death.

'Something up?' Khabib asked, his voice low and ugly.

'No, Khabib. Why would there be? Just...thought of something, that's all.'

Khabib did something then that he did not expect. He smiled.

'Sure now?'

He nodded with grave certainty. 'Yes, Khabib. I'm sure. Very sure. Course.'

'Good. Okay. Now let's get a move on. We're almost there. Not long now.'

Khabib went and resumed his place at the head of his

small group. Tyler knew it was all a false niceness. Khabib needed him now. Because Khabib's eyes had never changed. In them the pyre still burned.

'Wait...' Marty said.

Considine had just walked over to the window, was leaning onto the sill, looking out, a headache beginning to take hold.

'...they're talking. I can hear voices.'

'You can?'

She went back to the desk and put her headphones on again.

They both listened...

Voices!

'...*sure now?...Yes, Khabib. I'm sure. Very sure. Course...Good. Okay. Now let's get a move on. We're almost there. Not long now.*'

Considine and Marty stared at one another. They looked like contestants on a reality paranormal show after they'd just heard something weird. They listened once more, but didn't hear voices again.

Marty pulled his headphone from one ear. 'Did he say "Khabib"?'

'Sounded like it,' she said, keeping her headphones in place.

'That's what I thought too,' he said, removing his completely and standing up. 'Right, will I let her know? Superintendent Ryan, I mean. She said to tell her before anyone else.'

Considine didn't answer; her eyes were closed, listening to her headphones.

31

The four uniforms looked at Brody like he'd just told them a flying saucer had landed on the roof of the GPO.

'What?' one said, his name was Hanlon, a tall lanky fella who had pitted skin, a residue of teenage acne, Brody guessed – which wouldn't have been too long ago either. 'We're spending the night in here? Am I hearing right?' He looked from Brody to the door, where the AC was standing. The door was closed, and the AC seemed to be making sure it was locked. 'And what...' But his voice trailed off, like he was intimidated by the presence of such a senior officer.

'...is he doing here?' Brody finished the sentence for him. 'Is that it?'

'Yes.' It was another member of the group, a female, small of stature, very small. It wouldn't have been so long ago she wouldn't have made the minimum height requirement. But there was no height requirement anymore.

'I told you. We believe this bank is going to be entered

during the night, through…' He pointed towards the vault, a huge slab of metal set into the wall at the end. 'The vault.'

'And how are they going to do that?' she asked.

Hanlon answered for her. 'Through the floor, how else, isn't that right?'

'Good lad, Hanlon,' Brody said. 'That is right. Through the floor.'

'Well, fuck me,' she said.

Hanlon gave her a look, raised one eyebrow.

She looked like she was about to kick him.

'Can we stay focused, please,' Brody said. 'We'll organise refreshments, coffees and stuff, but we're making this up as we go along, to be honest. Tonight, here is where you're going to be. The situation is fluid. I'll come and go myself. We'll take it as it comes, okay. Everyone clear?'

'As mud,' Hanlon said, louder than he'd intended.

Brody ignored him, because at that moment his phone rang.

It was Superintendent Ryan, whom he hadn't heard from in a while. He listened to what she had to say, feeling that familiar invisible elbow nudge him in his stomach the way it did when an investigation started to gain traction.

It was happening; there *were* people in the tunnels. Now he was certain of it; this bank was going to be hit. He also had a name.

Brody spelled it back to Ryan; the name Marty had given her as mentioned in the tunnels. 'Khabib, yes?'

'Well, I don't know how to spell it,' Ryan said. 'Sounds right.'

'I'm going to see if I can get anything on that. I'll let you know if I do. You planning on coming down here?'

'Yes.'

'The AC, Padraic Kelly, is here.'

'I know, I spoke with him.'

'You did?' Brody said.

'Yes. Something I had to sort out.'

Brody had the feeling she wasn't telling him everything. But he wasn't going to get into it – not now.

'Like I say, I'll keep you informed.'

'Do that.'

He hung up.

'Is that a surname?' the operator asked when Brody rang the Pulse operations centre in Castlebar, an around-the-clock, twenty-four-seven garda support call centre when he asked her to check the system for anyone by the name of Khabib.

'I don't know,' he said. 'It could be, could be anything.'

'Really, could be anything, could it? Right, let me see if I can find anything on it.' He heard the sound of fingers clicking across a keyboard. 'There's a few Khabibs alright. Want to narrow it down a bit. Any MO you can give me?'

'Try bank robber.'

'Bank robber it is.' Then, a moment later, 'Sorry, the only Khabib with an MO that comes close is one who was an injured party in a robbery of a takeaway.'

'Hm, nothing else...thank you, it was a long shot anyway, as they say.'

'We have a new search facility...you read about it?'

Brody didn't feel like doing quizzes.

'No,' he said, a little shorter than he meant to, ready to hang up.

'With your permission, I can look in it. They trace individuals against an international databank.'

Brody doubted *they* – whoever they were – traced anything.

'Who?' he asked, curiosity getting the better of him. 'Who traces it?'

'That means no,' she said, 'you didn't read about it. The FBI, the facility is in their jurisdiction, available to trusted global partners, also with a separate link to Afripol…can you give me your shoulder number again? I need to input it a second time.'

Brody did, and she inputted it. 'Won't take a second.'

Brody waited. It took a little longer than a second, but not much.

'With the MO you gave me,' she said, 'which I broadened, because a bank robbery can also…'

'I know,' Brody interrupted, feeling like this girl was practising for her specialist subject on *Mastermind*, 'burglary or aggravated burglary, either or if they break into a building.'

'Yes, that's it.'

'I know.'

'Good for you.'

'Thanks.'

'Okay,' the operator said, 'it appears this is a first name. It's native to Dagestan; that's in the Russian Federation…'

'How do you know? Is that in this *facility* too?'

The operator laughed.

'Um…nooo. I opened another screen, Google. Anyway, I have a fella here who looks interesting.'

'You do? Go on.'

'Khabib Uzerbeke is his name, a history of both robbery and burglary. But not banks.'

Brody thought he could spend all day talking to this operator about the Khabibs of this world. The facility was global, after all.

'Not of banks,' he said, distracted, thinking ahead, wondering why the AC had ordered mules to stay in the bank overnight. Because while yes, the intruders might be in the vault, which was within the bank, they weren't going to break out into the bank. Or were they? Brody supposed, on the off chance that they might, it probably was prudent to have members waiting. Just in case. He almost missed what the operator said.

'Whoo, what was that?'

'Hotel rooms. He specialised in breaking into hotel rooms. There were a lot of them, all over Europe. He'd been working as a barman.'

Another invisible nudge went into Brody's belly, only harder this time.

'Had he now? A barman?'

'Yes.'

Brody thought of Matt Thompson. Coincidence? Too far a stretch?

'And some hotels in Ireland were hit too,' she said.

No, not a coincidence.

'The Connaught Castle. You heard of it?'

Was she taking the piss? Of course he'd heard of it.

'Consistently voted in the top five in the world by *Premium Hotel Traveller* magazine. That the one?'

'You don't need to ring a friend, then,' she said. 'That's the one.'

'What was the outcome?'

'He got six months in the Midlands Prison.'

'I was longer on a message,' Brody said.

'Sorry, what was that?'

'Nothing. When was this? When was he in prison?'

'That was back in 2014, February to July; he was released at the end of May.'

Served half his sentence, Brody calculated. The revolving prison door system. It wasn't called that for nothing.

'And nothing since?'

'Not according to this.'

'Can you give me the Pulse number of that incident, please?'

She did, and Brody jotted it down. He checked the time, 6:30 p.m. He thanked the operator and finished the call.

The AC seemed surprised when he told him he and Voyle were leaving.

'Who's going to keep an eye on them?' he said, nodding towards the four young mules. 'Because I'm leaving too. I haven't even been home yet. I changed in my office.'

'This could be important,' Brody said.

'Tell me about it, then.'

'Later, if that's okay, I need to get a move on.'

'Let me ring Ryan, then,' the AC said, taking his phone from his pocket. 'I haven't seen much of that lady all day.'

'How do we get out of here?' Brody asked.

'Let me.' It was MacDowell's voice. Brody had forgotten about the bank manager, and he was surprised to see him still here.

'What?' MacDowell said, noting his expression. 'You think I'd gone home, did you? Not on your nelly. This is my bank. You coming back again?'

'Of course, just can't tell you when, that's all.'

The bank manager took a large, old-fashioned key from his pocket and used it to unlock the heavy wooden door.

'Is that it?' Brody said. 'That's what you use to lock the door?'

'Good as anything else. Yes.'

'Suppose,' Brody said as he and Voyle stepped out onto the night-time city street. It was raining, and a stiff breeze blew in off the river.

The storm, Brody thought, *is rolling in.*

32

They sat in the unmarked. First up, Brody needed to find Matt Thompson. He rang the operations centre in Castlebar again. It wasn't hard to do, as it turned out. The operator told Brody that he was being held on remand at Mountjoy Prison. Silly boy, if he hadn't run that time, he'd be out by now. The others were. His bail application had been turned down because, officially, he was considered a flight risk. And the court date was not for some weeks yet. He asked the operator to check Thompson's Pulse catalogue. No surprises when he was told Thompson had been in prison for a time in 2014, too, around about the same time as Khabib had been in prison. And what prison? The Midlands. *My, my*, Brody thought, *aren't the coincidences stacking up?* He obtained the phone number for the relevant section at Mountjoy Prison, thanked the operator, and hung up. Next, he rang the prison and was put through to an officer on the landing.

'I'll get him,' he told Brody. And Brody waited. A couple

of minutes passed, then, 'Prisoner coming to the phone now.'

'Thanks.'

'What?'

'I said thanks.'

'Oh yeah, thanks. You're welcome.'

Brody supposed it was easy to forget about the everyday common courtesies in a place like a prison.

There was a crackling sound as the phone was picked up, followed by...nothing.

'Matt, you there? Matt, I can hear you breathing.'

Silence continued, but briefly. Then Thompson spoke, his voice sounding weighted, like it was a struggle to lift up each word and then to push it out of his mouth and into the phone. 'Tell me something to keep me on the line, or I'm hanging up, Mr Policeman. And tell me right now.'

Thompson wasn't in a good mood, understandably, which would naturally incline him not to be of any help to Brody. Which meant that Brody had to think real fast of something that would make him interested.

'How would you feel if you were to get bail?' It was the first thought that came into his head. He'd worry about the details later.

'How'd I feel if I was to get what...? Are you for real? Orgasmic, man, that's how I'd feel.' In that instant Thompson's words were no longer weighted, but sounded like rubber balls bouncing across a floor. 'You can get me bail, yeah? Is that what you're saying? Why, Mr Policeman? Why would you do that? Tell me.'

'I didn't say I could get you bail, Matt; what I mean is *maybe* I could help get you bail, that's all. There's a difference.'

'*Maybe*, oh right, yeah, there's a difference. Out of the goodness of your heart, is it? I asked ya, out of the goodness of your heart, is it? Why would you do that? What you after, Mr Policeman?'

'A fella called Khabib, that's what I'm after.'

Thompson didn't say anything for a moment. 'Khabib?' he repeated. 'That what you said?'

'Yes, it is, Khabib. A fella of that name was in prison the same time as you.'

'When was this?'

'Two thousand and fourteen.'

'That's, like, centuries ago, man; how can I remember that far back? Come on.'

'Doesn't ring a bell, then?'

'Ah, didn't say that, did I? Why'd you want to know about him for?'

'Does it ring a bell or doesn't it?'

'Maybe. Why'd you want to know about him? I keep askin'.'

Brody had nothing to lose.

'Because I think he's about to rob a bank, that's why. I believe he's part of a gang who're planning to come up through the sewers and clean out the vault.'

Brody pulled the phone from his ear as Thompson whistled, put it back just in time to hear him add, 'Yo, my man, Khabib, way to go.'

'I gather you approve,' Brody said. 'At your age, which is not so long ago I'll have you know, it was sportspeople who did it for me, principally boxers, not bank robbers. Those were the people who were my heroes. By the way, he was a barman too, this Khabib. Question, he put you onto the honeypot scam thing, did he?'

'Oh, nice one. Thought you'd slip that in there, did you? Catch me sleepin' at the wheel? No chance. Now you listen, Mr Policeman, back up to what you said about how I'd feel about getting bail.'

'What about it?'

'What about it? What the fuck about it? Exactly. That's what I want to talk about.'

'I was thinking,' Brody said, 'that there'd be nothing to stop your lawyer from making a fresh application, now would there?'

'No, there wouldn't, and you know it. Why would I have him do that? Something'd have to be different. Very different. What you really gettin' at, Mr Policeman?'

'You're right, something would have to be different. Depends on what's different, doesn't it? This Khabib. Tell me how I can find him.'

Thompson laughed.

'Oh, is that it. I didn't say I even knew him, Mr Policeman. And now you're askin' me how you can find him. You're making a lot of assumptions there.'

'I don't have time, Matty boy. I really don't. I told you. There's a bank about to be done over. Probably as we speak. I thought you might be able to give me something. Whether you can or you can't, I don't have time to try to discuss it or convince you about it. Sorry for wasting your time, Matty boy. Goodbye.'

Brody remained with the phone pressed to his ear, hoping that as far as Thompson was concerned, he'd think he really was saying goodbye.

One, two, three...

'Okay, okay, I knew him. How's this goin' to help me, Mr Policeman?'

'You know how. This is how it helps you. I speak to your solicitor, he speaks to the judge...The judges all like me, by the way.'

'Do they, Mr Policeman. I have only one thing to say about that though, don't I? A pig lying through his teeth is the same as a dog licking its balls, just can't help it.'

'Tut-tut, that's nasty, Matty, have to say, very nasty. Anyway, whatever, but if I were you, I'd take my chances; it's a helluva lot better than anything else you have going for you right now.'

Thompson didn't say anything to that. Brody waited.

'Okay, okay, Mr Policeman, but you'd better put a word in for me. Like a good, good word, yeah? You get me out of this fucking zoo, yeah, or I swear, I'll put it out there that you're a lying, scheming pig who no one will ever believe ever again.'

Which was rich, Brody thought, considering who it was coming from.

'I'll do my best,' he said.

'It's just like you say, Mr Policeman, I don't have much else going for me, so, yeah, like, fuck it. But don't get your hopes up when I say I knew him. I didn't know *know* him. It was prison, not a summer camp; you don't exactly get to know anyone; you make sure you don't get to know anyone.'

'What can you tell me? I'm against the clock here, Matty.'

'He's a bright spark, I can tell you that. He told me he wasn't going to get caught again, that he had something in the works, something big. He said he was upping it a gear.'

'Upping it a gear, what's that mean?'

'He never told me. I think he regretted even telling me that. But I was more interested in finding out how he worked the hotels; that was a real smooth...'

Thompson fell silent. Too much information already. Brody got the feeling he regretted telling him that too.

'He put you onto the honeypot idea, didn't he?'

'Thought you were against the clock. Why you bringin' that up again? I'm saying nothing about it, okay.'

Brody felt certain; oh yes, he had.

'There was a moth used to come and see him. Real cracker she was. Oriental, all arse and tits, unusual that, usually it's one or the other.'

'Don't suppose you know her name? Did he tell you? Do you remember?'

It was a long shot, Brody knew, so was surprised – very surprised – when Matt answered.

'Yeah, I do. Choo Choo.'

'What?'

'Choo Choo. Her name. I mean, how could you forget that?'

'Choo Choo? As in a train?'

'Yeah, Sherlock. As in a train.'

'Anything else you can think of?'

'That was years ago, man. I can hardly remember what happened yesterday. But Choo Choo. I remember that.'

FOR A THIRD TIME, Brody was back onto the operations centre in Castlebar. After inputting a number of combinations, the operator found someone on the system with a name similar to Choo Choo: Chi Chu. Not as difficult a task as might be expected, because she was the only one on there.

'Unfortunately, it's listed as intelligence,' the operator

said, 'so I don't have access. You'll have to do it yourself, I'm afraid.'

'I see. Let me do that, then. Thank you. I'll get back if I need to.'

He finished the call.

'What now?' Voyle asked.

Brody took the state phone from its console on the dash.

'When we getting those in-car computers they keep talking about?'

'They're coming, boss, like the west Clare train.'

'The Percy French song?'

'The very one.'

'But the train never arrived, Voyle, did it?'

'Exactly, boss.'

'Hm.' Brody waited while the state phone connected to the internet, then waited while it connected to Pulse, then waited once he'd inputted the name Chi Chu for the intelligence file to appear, until finally, after he'd gone through the rigmarole of inputting his reg number, date of birth, and four-digit security code, this appeared:

Chi Chu, associate of Khabib Uzerbeke, suspected offender in theft from the person, burglary and criminal damage (see related incidents). Chi Chu believed to be an alias, identifiable marks: small tattoo of Chinese sword, a Longquan, on right wrist, also small mole by right eye. No photograph available. Research shows she possibly fits description of Biyu Liu, also and better known by the alias Susie Q. CAUTION: This unconfirmed. Chi Chu, aka Susie Q, present during arrest of Khabib Uzerbeke, but no reason to detain. Subsequent information confirms that Chi Chu, aka Susie Q, to be Biyu Liu, wanted by police forces in America and Europe. Believed to be associated with the Yellow Dragon triad, but the exact association unknown. The Yellow Dragon triad specialise in white-collar crime and international fraud.

Brody looked out the window.

'This case is bigger than I thought,' he said, 'much bigger. We need to pass on what we have to Interpol asap. Here, take a look.'

Brody passed the phone to Voyle, who read it, then whistled, just as Matt Thompson had done.

'Have we stumbled on something?'

'Looks like it. We've been caught blindsided, though; these are clever bastards. No use us sitting out here or' – with a nod towards the bank – 'in there. We need to get down and flush them out. Otherwise, we'll be the ones waiting on the platform for the west Clare train that's never going to arrive.'

Voyle grinned.

'What's so funny?'

'Is that what they call a euphemism, boss?'

'Maybe.'

'I like it.'

THEY WENT BACK INSIDE. Brody told the AC what he'd found, then pointed to the floor and added, 'That's where they are, and that's where we need to be.'

The senior officer gave an emphatic shake of his head.

'No.'

'No?'

'Yes,' he said. 'I mean no.' He sighed. 'Look, I know,

Brody. You want to get in there. But that's you all over. Part of what makes you such a good mule, I suppose. I know what you think, of us I mean, the brass, and yeah, between you and me, you're not half wrong, okay? But, just for a moment, think, Brody. If you, *we*, go down there, go down there *now*, not knowing what artillery they're carrying, what do you think is going to happen? The charge of the light brigade, that's what's going to happen.'

'You don't know that for certain? I mean, why would they take weapons down with them? They've no idea they've been rumbled. It's extra weight I don't think they'd want to carry.'

'I can't risk it.'

'The military. Can't we get them involved?'

Again, an emphatic shake of the head, even more so this time.

'No. That would be a complete mix of the civil and military authority, open up a whole can of worms. This is a matter for the civil authority, and that's us.'

Brody wasn't so certain that was the case. He felt AC Kelly didn't want to pass his authority on to anyone, that's what; he wanted to be able to look after this himself.

Still, he did have a point. Because what if they were carrying weapons down there? If that were the case, it could result in a bloodbath.

33

Tyler was disorientated. All of them were. It was the way on every job. It was the way Khabib wanted it, being the only one who knew exactly where they were, and where they were going, and how they'd get back out again. The ultimate form of control.

Tyler had a thought. What if Khabib were to leave him behind down here? Take the rest of the crew with him, his head torch too, and just leave. Then what? A slow, agonising death, that's what. And then, as the rats ate his carcass, would dear Momma and Papa return to take his soul? Because he knew they were down here too; oh yes, they were. He'd seen dear Momma flittering about in that twilight world between the light and the dark in those snatched images at the periphery of his vision. As for Papa, he just hadn't chosen to show himself yet, that's all. But they were here. He could feel them. What of the others? Were they down here too? Those sad, pathetic, desperate bitches he'd picked up and dispatched, whom he felt certain he'd done a favour for, too, and all. Were they here, biding their time, waiting to reveal themselves?

Tyler shook his head, trying to, needing to, clear it, dislodge those thoughts. He wanted to stop for a moment, but daren't; he did not want to come to the attention of Khabib again. That wouldn't be good. He took a breath, concentrating on this moment, nothing else, just that, telling himself, *Get off the bridge; don't worry about where you're going or where you've been. Think of where you are right now. Get off the bridge! This is it. Here! Now! Get off the bridge if you want to survive.*

That was what was important, to get through this, to survive.

They seemed to be walking for ages, but because time had no meaning down here, he never checked his watch. It might have been five minutes, it might have been an hour, it might have been two. All that Tyler really knew for certain was that the equipment he carried on his back was beginning to weigh heavy. Yet he was glad of this because it offered him distraction.

And then. They stopped.

Khabib pointed off to his right. They looked in that direction, their torches lighting up the tunnel walls. There was another recess next to them, much larger than the last one they'd been in, not so high from the tunnel floor. Khabib pulled off his backpack, stepped over and hoisted it up, then pulled himself into the recess after it. They followed. Once there, Khabib ordered Clyde to set up the sodium lights. With that done, this piece of subterranean world became transformed, like a cover had been taken off, allowing a radiant sun to stream in. Everything became stark within the arc of the powerful light, the centuries-old grout between the bricks, sheened with a green slime, the rivulets of water that kept the bricks clean and in their original colour like brush strokes of pale yellow against the grimy, dark backdrop. And the rats, moving along the edges of the tunnel, in groups of two or three or individually, were unhurried, stopping every so often to sniff the air, their whiskers quivering, big as cats some of them, completely ignoring the interlopers in their world...for now at least.

Tyler watched Khabib consult the GPS on his wrist, it looked like an oversized watch, and study it closely. Khabib had never told anyone it was a GPS, but Tyler guessed that was what it was. Khabib only revealed what he had to, strictly on a need-to-know basis. Khabib pointed it at the tunnel roof, and the familiar dot of green light appeared, spreading out from it a web of spindly lines, and another, thicker line wrapping itself around the edge to form a perfect circle. From his pocket Khabib took a piece of chalk, reached up and roughly marked over where the central dot was on the wall, then roughly marked the outline of the outer circle. He pressed a button on the GPS, and the green light disappeared.

'Clyde,' he barked, 'get to work.'

Now they knew they had arrived at where they were supposed to be. They were beneath the bank vault. This was it. Clyde set to work, prising the bricks from the roof of the tunnel, following the outline of the circle Khabib had drawn, but leaving in place the centre brick with the dot marked on it. When he'd finished, what was left was a jagged circular outline exposing the hard earth behind the wall, compacted over the course of centuries. The distance from here to the vault above was always the same, give or take a few centimetres, and that was three metres.

Next, Lisbeth took what looked to be an oversized metal enema from her bag. Tyler knew this was a perforated aluminium capsule, tapering to a point at one end, and containing a small explosive charge. She pulled a metal rod from a pouch on the side of the bag and screwed it into the end of the capsule, reached up and pressed the pointed end against the earth Clyde had just exposed. The Scotsman was waiting, in his hand a small lump hammer, which he used to tap the end of the rod gently but firmly into the soil until all that was visible was the threaded end of the section of rod. Lisbeth screwed in another section, and Clyde repeated the process. It took three sections, as was usually the case, to push the explosive capsule what she considered sufficiently far enough into the tunnel roof. When this was done, she used a nail file to pull out from within the exposed end section of rod a very thin wire. She attached it to a single flex junction box and pushed in a command wire at the other end. Then she jumped down from the recess, ran out the wire for maybe fifteen metres into the tunnel. Safe enough distance, just in case. She summoned the others, and they left the recess, followed her into the tunnel and gathered behind her.

Tyler knew the explosive charge was large enough only to loosen the soil so that it would flush out under its own momentum. It needed to be just right, the charge, so the result would be a perfect cylindrical shape once the soil had dislodged itself. As it always had been before.

Lisbeth glanced behind her to Clyde, but it was Khabib who spoke.

'Do it,' he said.

But Lisbeth didn't do it. Not right away. Her eyes lingered on Clyde, and only when he nodded did she turn away and look down at the detonation button in her hands, glowing green within its metal casing. In fact, if you didn't know better, you could easily mistake it for a kid's toy.

Tyler wondered again what it was between these two, Lisbeth and Clyde? Were they fucking? Not that he would fuck her; she looked too much like a boy for him, even with those blonde curls of hers. Maybe that was what Clyde liked. Maybe. But there was something. Not that he cared, he cared about nothing except getting out of this tunnel alive. But he knew Khabib cared, he'd caught the look, that hooded hard look, not directed at him this time, but at Lisbeth for not acting immediately on his orders to press the detonator button. Maybe, he thought, this team had run its course. Five years was a long time, after all. Maybe it was time to change the line-up and start anew. In this business, changing a line-up might mean ending it.

Lisbeth pressed, and what sounded like a muted cough followed, but the muted cough of a giant that is, and with it a rumbling sound, all within the tight confines of the tunnel, amplified and of perfect acoustic clarity. An eerie silence followed. They waited. There was the tinkling of fine particles of earth falling to earth, and silence again. The seconds dripped by. They waited. Maybe this time it wasn't going to be perfect? Maybe this time it wasn't going to work? Then it came, another rumble, deeper and longer than before, and finally a *whoosh*, as the giant cleared its throat, sending a thick piece of compacted dark earth falling from the hole, bouncing once and toppling over the side of the recess onto the floor of the tunnel, where it broke up. Another thick portion followed; then a shower of fine clay particles fell and formed a pile on the recess floor like the ashes from a giant's fireplace.

Khabib led the way back into the recess. They gathered round and looked up.

It was a good job; it was a perfect job, the hole a cylindrical shape as if carved out by a large drill bit. It never ceased to amaze him, the wonders of engineering science, the fundamentals handed down from ancient Greece and Rome. And against such wonders, what was the value of a mere mortal's life? He knew that the velocity of the dislodged clay had revolved in a spherical shape, subject to the powers of the bigger sphere they were all on, spinning at this very moment, the earth.

Above them, at the top of this perfect cylindrical shape, like a silver sun, they glimpsed the vault floor.

This sight always excited Tyler. He guessed it excited all of them. From the corner of his eye, he saw Lisbeth lean into Clyde, rubbing her head against his cheek.

The glimpse of vault floor, that silver sun, was of pristine, gleaming brushed steel.

It was impossible to know what reinforced it, but something did, concrete maybe, or rods of twisted iron, or, Tyler had heard of these but never yet come across them, tungsten. He didn't think it was, not here. Maybe at a branch of the Swiss national bank. But not here.

He stepped forward. Usually, Khabib might nod his head to him or say something like, 'Up you go, Tyler.'

But not this time.

This time it was different.

This time Khabib didn't even look at him.

Maybe because this time Khabib knew that Tyler could see in his eyes those pyres burning bright.

34

'What the fuck? You hear that?'

'I didn't just hear it,' Brody said. 'I felt it.'

He and Voyle jumped from the car and ran to the bank. Brody banged on the door. And banged again. It opened, and MacDowell was standing there, pale as a ghostly apparition. Maybe it wasn't such a good idea to have him here, Brody considered. Either way, too late now. They went in, the young mules standing about, tense and uncertain. AC Kelly appeared from the shadows.

'My God,' he said, 'it *is* happening.'

'What did you think? I told you.'

'Yes, you told me, Brody. But, Christ, I get told a lot of things.'

'The meter is running. What're we going to do?'

'What are we going to do?' the senior officer repeated, taking his phone from his pocket and swiping a finger across the screen, like that might provide the answer.

There was loud banging at the door, a banging that didn't stop.

MacDowell went and looked through the peephole, pulled it open. Superintendent Ryan came in; with her were Marty and Considine.

'We were on our way,' she began. 'We hea...?'

Voyle finished the sentence for her.

'We heard it too. The bank is being robbed.'

Ryan came and stood next to him.

'I've been missing in action, Jack. We'll talk about that later. Right now, we need to deal with this. What you think?'

Brody nodded towards AC Kelly. 'Shouldn't you be asking him?'

'Right now, I'm asking you.'

'If you have rats in your house,' he said, 'you need to know how they're getting in. When you do, you get yourself a rat-catcher dog, a Jack Russell should do it, and you sit him there. It's the same here. The rats we have in the tunnels came in through the sewers. We need to get a few Jack Russells, armed response units, and get them into position, wait for the rats to come out again. And when they do, then we catch them. Or kill them. And we don't have much time.'

'I agree, we don't have much time.'

'Get onto that?' Kelly growled into his phone. He looked at Brody, who could see it was still connected to his call. 'The Jack Russells. I heard what you said. I've just whistled up a few.'

35

One of the items Tyler was carrying was an ultra-light telescopic ladder. It looked like a weird washboard of sorts. But it extended all the way up to just beneath the silver sun. He fixed the plasma cutter to his back and began to climb, the cutter's head at the end of its barrel angled in front of him. This was no ordinary plasma cutter, but an industrial cutter used in diamond mines in South Africa, capable of searing through 2.54 centimetres, or one inch, of the thickest metal within one minute.

At the top of the ladder, Tyler pulled down the soft welder's cape over his face and set to work. He first cut through a punch hole and switched the plasma cutter off, allowing it to hang from its strap by his side.

A half hour later he was sweating and had ringed the silver sun with tightly spaced holes. The metal was not so thick, and he now knew the reason why. It was because the vault floor was a sandwich, metal plated on the outsides and mass concrete in between. A cheaper option. He next cut through the spaces between the holes with a battery-powered hacksaw, leaving a space behind so that the panel would remain in place for Clyde to cut through and manhandle it out, drop it to the ground.

Tyler came down the ladder and said to Khabib: 'It's a sandwich.'

Khabib, he noted, still avoided making eye contact with him. Instead, he turned to Clyde. 'Yo, get a move on, you know what to do, cut through that motherfucker, and Lis' – he turned to her – 'it's a sandwich, get ready to blow. Get a move on, people. Chop-chop.'

Before he finished speaking, Clyde was already part of the way up the ladder, as Tyler thought, *Khabib couldn't even bring himself to mention my name either.*

36

If there was an emergency requiring an armed response anywhere in counties Kildare, Meath and Wicklow tonight, there wouldn't be a unit available to answer it. The best, perhaps, that could be hoped for was if a regular uniformed guard with firearms training was available with access to a revolver from a designated station's weapons cache. That is, if a weapon or weapons were even stored at any regular station in the district anymore. Because, since the establishment of the specialised garda armed support units, they often were not. Now the GASU travelled in self-contained mobile armouries, these being high-end Audi Q7s, BMW X5s and BMW 5 Series saloons and estates. Most of these units, as well as those from the Dublin central and metropolitan regions, were in place now along the quays in the vicinity of tunnel openings and manhole covers within a kilometre radius of the bank. In total, this meant eight tunnels and twenty-one manhole covers. Any unit not involved was on constant mobile patrol throughout the area, ready to respond immediately to any call.

The head of armed response at Dublin Castle prayed that another major emergency did not occur. Citizens of the city, those out and about during the night-time hours for whatever reason, would without doubt never have seen so many armed response vehicles, their decals glowing bright like neon signs, as they did tonight. They couldn't be missed. And Mandy Joyce, driving home from a freelance gig at the offices of a digital newspaper, didn't miss them either. In fact, the sight of the vehicles along the quays made her heart literally skip a beat. She held a hand to her chest, momentarily wondering if she wasn't about to suffer a heart attack. But then it passed, and she felt, heard, the blood pumping through her ears, that old familiar feeling, the excitement, pure, unfiltered, unadulterated excitement, that mesmerising feeling of being in the right place at the right time.

She pulled into the kerb. Something like this couldn't be missed for long, even at this hour, not by the other hacks. At this hour, all of the daily newspapers were being printed, or about to be, and at the TV stations, most if not all of the news crews would have gone home. So too the social media junkies, the bloggers, the podcasters, they'd all be curled up in their beds.

That left only the night desks at the dailies, thinly staffed in this era of cutbacks, falling circulation and advertising revenue. Easy enough to deal with. She knew the telephone numbers off by heart. Mandy Joyce first dialled the number of the night desk at the biggest-selling daily in the country, rehearsing what she needed to say, before realising she hadn't blocked her own number. She quickly hung up again before the phone was answered, and started over, making sure her number was blocked this time round.

Mandy wasn't ringing to offer anyone the story – at a price, of course. Oh no. She was ringing to put them off the scent, to have them look as far the other way as possible. Because this one, she wanted all to herself. This one had *her* name on it.

Oh yes, it was good to be back in the game.

'Night desk,' the voice said, typical of a night-shift worker's, flat and jaded.

'I'm ringing you from Dune Beach, you know it?'

'Dune...I only know *Dune* the movie. Never heard of Dune the beach. At least I think it was a movie.'

'It was. It's also a beach, just outside Laytown.'

'In County Meath?'

'That's the one.'

'No, I don't know it, but I know Laytown. What about it?'

'Well, um...I just rang the guards, you see, and they told me not to tell anyone about it. But I think people should know.'

'Know what?' The voice was suddenly curious.

'Well, this might sound crazy...'

'Might sound crazy...' the voice repeated, even more curious, 'go on.'

'Well, there's something out on the water. Something big. I can see the outline of it against the horizon. There's a half-moon, you see. It's like a...you won't believe this.'

'Yes, I'll believe it, go on...'

'But it looks like a submarine.'

'A what? A submarine?' A trace of incredulity crept into the tone.

Mandy realised the newspaperman might think her a nut.

'There's a couple of boats coming in,' she said, sounding like what she thought was convincingly alarmed.

'A couple of boats?'

'Inflatables, you know.'

'I know. Really...I mean, *really?*' He paused. Then, 'Can you take a photo and send it to me?'

She hadn't expected that. *Shit, now what?*

'Um, yes...I can do that. Can you give me a mobile number?'

'Of course, our tips line, it's easy to remember, 087-2425242. You got that?'

'I got that,' Mandy said and hung up, quickly went onto Google, typed in *Photo, marines storming ashore in inflatables at night*, pressed return, picked the photograph she wanted from the array on offer and forwarded it. There, not so difficult at all.

Ten minutes later she'd contacted all the night desks and repeated the process. She couldn't help but smile when all was done: that should keep them busy.

Oh yes, it was good to be back in the game.

37

When Lisbeth blew the concrete in the middle of the sandwich, the sound echoed as a dull thud up into the bank, followed by a gentle aftershock that rippled through the floor. There was quite the audience to hear and feel it: duty inspectors, regional supers and a chief superintendent, along with a minibus full of uniformed mules. The news had spread, yet nothing had been announced – officially, that is. Nor would it be, not for as long as possible, or until, ideally, every rat had been captured and caged or killed. What a coup that would be for the spaghetti hats, and they knew it.

At Brody's suggestion, a sort of command centre had been set up, nothing fancy, merely a mule with a laptop and a phone line giving direct access to the command centre in Pearse Street. When the explosion sounded, the mule rang it through and updated Pulse with an announcement. The tension levels went up a notch. The armed officers dotted throughout the city centre tightened their grips on their weapons, index fingers curled around triggers, thumbs ready to switch safety catches from 'on' to 'off'.

Brody decided the best place for him and his unit to be was here, waiting for word of the first sighting of the rats. He had made sure the door of the bank was left unlocked and slightly ajar. Every second would count.

THE CONCRETE DISINTEGRATED and fell like a shower of large hailstones, hitting the floor of the tunnel, a machine-gun fire of sound, *duh, duh, duh, duh, duh.*

When it finished, they clambered back into the recess, and Tyler started up the ladder. He punched a hole through the remaining steel panel with the plasma cutter, but this time, he took a wireless endoscope camera from his breast pocket and pushed it through, glanced down, gave a thumbs-up. Khabib could see the images relayed to an app on his phone. They waited until he too gave the thumbs-up; then Tyler went back to work.

He cut through the steel panel with the plasma cutter as before, ringing it in a circle of tightly spaced holes, then cutting through the spaces in between and leaving a short strip in place for Clyde to finish off.

WHEN THIS WAS DONE, they paused as they had done before, looking up at the perfect cylindrical tunnel, at the top of which was a black hole where a silver sun had been. They were about to go where no man had gone before – at least in this bank they hadn't. Yes, Tyler felt a kick of pride. They were artisans of their craft. If they were chefs, they would be cordon bleu, carpenters, master woodworkers, soldiers, elite special forces. And God, as always, had made sure there were no alarms to go off. That man, or woman – no one knew – was a genius, that man, or woman was, well...God.

They savoured this brief moment, then started about executing part two of the operation.

Clyde went up first, and Lisbeth carried a sodium lamp to him. When this was set up inside the vault, the light glowed bright, replacing the black hole with a golden, as opposed to a silver, sun.

They were in!

They'd done it – again.

It was roughly the same size as a shipping container, the vault, and standing inside it, Tyler was aware of an uncanny sense of intimacy he hadn't experienced before. He'd known these people for over five years now. He might not like them, in fact he was completely indifferent to them, but he was a part of them. And they worked so well together. There was nothing on this earth he was a part of except this group of people. He felt sad that Khabib had changed his attitude towards him. Maybe they could talk about it later and work things out? He thought about that for a second. Nah, that wasn't going to happen.

They were talking, in low voices, and he realised he'd zoned out. He glanced around; two walls of the vault were lined with numbered deposit boxes: experience had shown him that these, collectively, were nothing more than a lucky bag, usually containing everything from property deeds and sentimental family heirlooms, most of dubious monetary value. There were valuable nuggets in them for sure, just not enough to interest them; not right now, it was too time consuming. The two other walls were lined with shelves, on them trays of bagged rings, watches, other jewellery, with little tags attached.

Khabib was standing over a stack of metal boxes in the corner. There were nine of them. This meant the notes they contained were likely of mid- to high-denomination value. Perfect.

Khabib lifted the first box and handed it to Clyde.

'Move, move, move, clean this shit out.'

And they did. All of them.

Rope was tied around the end of each box and passed down to Lisbeth standing in the recess below. She untied the box, and the rope was hauled up, and the process repeated. The rest of what was in the vault – and they didn't want everything – the bagged items on the shelves, went into a couple of canvas satchels passed down the same way. This part of the operation, the actual execution, never lasted long: mere minutes, maybe ten tops. The build-up to these minutes, the preparation, could – and often did – take many months. Tyler likened it to a drag race. Take a hand-built car, probably a hand-built engine in it too, prepared over weeks, months, who knows, put it on the back of a transporter and take it maybe hundreds of miles to a racetrack. Wait around for a couple of days, set up a pit garage, pay people to help you. And for what? A sixty-second burnout down a strip of track where the odds were high you mightn't even reach the checkered flag in one piece.

This was similar, this was their burnout, even if the odds were much better stacked in their favour. But they only needed to fuck up once.

And, like in a drag race, this went by in a blur.

'THEY'RE IN THERE. Jesus Christ. They're in there. I can hear them.'

Brody didn't know who the mule was, but he had an earpiece in, a wire extending from it to what looked like a small magnet stuck to the vault door.

Well, duh, Brody thought, *tell us something we don't already know.*

'I mean,' he said, 'they're leaving. I can hear them. That was quick. Like, that was *really* quick.'

Brody agreed, it was.

Now, all they had to do was wait for the rats to show themselves.

Easier than it sounded, and Brody could only wait, when what he wanted to do was get out of here, move onto the streets. That was his instinct. Because that's where everything happened, where information was to be found, the streets. But not now. This time, it wouldn't work like that. This time he had to wait. Word would come. He had to trust it would. And when it did, then he'd move.

Fast.

'YOU THINK THEY'LL SHOW?' Mandy asked casually, looking over the river wall, because she'd noticed that was what these armed officers were doing too. Every so often, one would lean across and look down. She wondered why they were doing that. What was going on down there? It was like they weren't looking for something out on the water itself either, but something straight down beneath the wall. Odd.

When she leaned across, she saw the mouth of a tunnel down below, one of those sewage tunnels, no longer used now except for flood overflow.

Her excitement grew. What *was* this about? They were looking for something, that was for sure, or someone.

The officer nearest to Mandy turned and gave her a weary look.

'And who are you?'

She was prepared for that.

'Just waiting for Jack. Brody, I mean. You know him?'

'Of course I know him.' The officer seemed to relax at the mention of Jack's name. 'Everybody knows him. Are you with the MCIU?'

'Yeah, I don't think he'll be too long,' she said, avoiding the question yet answering it at the same time, really saying she didn't think he'd be long, not whether or not she was with the MCIU.

He nodded, seemingly satisfied with that, and poked his head over the stone river wall again.

'They've got to show,' he said, 'maybe just not here. This isn't the only one. Tunnel, I mean.'

'Course,' she said, picking up on that and going along with it, feeling her excitement building, and doing her best not to show it. This was definitely going somewhere, oh yes. Jesus, it was great to be back in the game.

'They'd pick the shortest route,' she added, like she was a wise old oracle. 'They have to show sometime.'

'Didn't you hear?' he asked.

'Hear what?'

'They're on the move. They're coming...'

They're Coming, she thought, *what a great fucking headline.*

There was a sound of footsteps and the jangle of equipment. Mandy glanced behind her and saw an armed officer step away from a vehicle and approach.

'Mandy Joyce,' he said, 'haven't seen you in a while. Someone tip you off? Well, there's nothing to see here. Scoot.'

The officer she'd just been speaking to said, 'Nothing to see here? Isn't she with the MCIU, Enda?'

'Is she fuck,' Enda answered. 'She's a journo...'

'Gotta go, boys,' Mandy announced, doing a perfectly executed about-turn and walking quickly away across the road.

'That's impersonation,' the officer called after her. 'I'll have you for this. You had me thinking you were a mule.'

'No, I hadn't,' she called over her shoulder. 'I never said I was a police officer; you just thought I did.'

WHEN SHE CROSSED THE ROAD, the officers turned away from her, like there was nothing they could do about it now, both looking over the wall once more and down into the river. Mandy backed into a laneway and turned on the video record facility on her phone. She pointed it. The light wasn't great, but it was good enough. In fact, it suited her purposes perfectly, adding a gritty realism to the scene, she felt, perfect as a teaser for a TV news report: *Keep watching for some amazing footage in just a moment exclusive to...*fill in with Sky News, CNN, ITV, whatever. Now, wouldn't that be something. And then, after that had been milked for all it was worth, the terrestrial channels could run it.

But run what? That was the question Mandy asked herself.

Something. Something big, that's what.

So far, she was the only journo here, the only one in the whole world who seemed to know about it.

Come on, hurry up, whatever it is. Happen. Whatever it is. Just HAPPEN. My career depends on it.

38

Clyde prised open the cash containers in the recess. The contents of the satchels were tipped out onto the floor. Tyler knew gold had a certain glint to it. And there was a lot of gold pouring out of those satchels. Khabib moved next to Clyde, bent down onto his knees like he was praying, reached into one of the boxes and took out a wad of €100 notes. The paper binder around it said €50,000. Khabib tossed the equivalent of a respectable year's salary through the air to Lisbeth. She caught it neatly in one hand. He laughed. Lisbeth stuffed it in her back pocket.

Everything here would be carried out in their backpacks, pockets, hoods, wherever and however, even underwear and socks if they needed to. The equipment they had brought in they'd leave behind, or jettison, as Khabib liked to call it.

The backpack Tyler had carried his plasma cutter in rested against the wall at the end of the recess. He went over and picked it up, made sure all the pockets were empty. He unzipped the compartment at the bottom, it expanded to maybe three times its original size, and if the notes were of high enough denomination, he could carry two or three million in there at least, easy.

He reached a hand into the compartment and fluffed it out, took out the item he'd put in there and needed now to complete his work. Next to his bag was the plasma cutter. He'd already removed the detachable handle from it. He picked it up and stood, began screwing it into what he had just taken from his bag. Almost done.

He turned round.

'Hey, Khabib,' he called.

Khabib looked up, but those eyes of his were not looking into Tyler's. So be it.

'Where you want this?' he asked, and nodded.

Khabib looked to what he was holding. Tyler dropped the plasma cutter handle. That had merely been a cover; he hadn't really been screwing it into anything at all.

Now Khabib did look into his eyes. Which pleased him, it really did. He wanted Khabib to look into his eyes as he spoke.

'Thank you, Khabib,' he said. 'For everything. Really. You changed my life. But all good things must end.'

There was a moment, a fleeting moment, Tyler saw it pass behind Khabib's eyes, an uncertainty, followed by a confusion and then something Tyler had never seen in him before, a profound fear.

Pouf, pouf.

Khabib's head seemed to bounce backwards twice as the bullets exploded into the centre of his face; his usual one to the chest and one to the centre of the forehead were off the menu tonight, apologies to our guest. Tyler had also changed bullets, opting for a particular type of exploding dumdum. Which explained why the centre of Khabib's face was literally blown apart, the debris of skin, muscle, bone, along with both eyes exploding like a jet of gritty red sand. His upper body slumped back onto legs folded beneath him, because Khabib was still in a kneeling position. And where his face had been had the appearance of something to be found at the bottom of a butcher's bin, retrieved perhaps to be given out free to a good customer as a treat for their dog.

He had used the silencer again, but only because he knew the Glock within the confines of the tunnel would be ear-splittingly loud without it.

Lisbeth screamed, the sound actually louder than the Glock, her own face dripping with gritty sand and what looked like a fruit berry squashed against the bridge of her nose. It was one of Khabib's eyes. Tangled in the hair over her forehead was a shard of one of his bones. Yet she still gripped a wad of €100 notes in her hands. Tyler made a calculation. She was in his line of sight, so he could dispatch her by hardly changing position. But he knew while she screamed like this, she wouldn't be thinking of doing anything else. He allowed her to continue at it. Instead, he swung the Glock to his left, just as the hard Glaswegian seemed to be making sense of the chaos and probably coming to the conclusion that he'd better do something about it really quick or he'd be next. Which was the correct calculation to make. He was trying to do something about it, but had only taken one step, raising the lump hammer but not getting far, before *pouf, pouf.*

Two to the centre of his chest, Tyler was mixing it up this time. Clyde had always thought he was so hot. Well, see what you make of this. Tyler watched as the muscled chest that the tough Glaswegian had worked so hard to maintain was ripped apart, all that stuff held compactly in there flopping out, the colon unfurling like a water hose. But the loose stuff flew, a soup-like concoction of digested food, blood, pieces of organ offal, faeces. The smell of a ripped-apart stomach was like no other. Tyler wanted to gag. The Scotsman looked down, started bringing both his hands up, pushing them through his organs, staring as if in morbid enchanted wonderment, before collapsing to the ground, his eyes glazing over, then frozen and dead, staring ahead.

Lisbeth's screams went to a new level at that, the sound seeming to cut through and tear into Tyler's very eardrums. It hurt. It hurt bad. *Shut the fuck up.* He shot her twice in the chest too. There really was quite the mess now. And that stench…

Tyler shook his head to try to clear it as Lisbeth's dying hand reached out toward Clyde. Aw, how sweet. He poked one ear with his little finger, wiggling it about, took it out again.

The noise was still there.

But now Tyler knew the sound wasn't what he thought it was. It wasn't coming from inside his ears. It was a different sound, and it was one coming from outside the recess, yet from inside the tunnel. It was the sound of the rats squeaking. A horde of them. He looked, saw some climbing over the top of the wall from the tunnel into the recess. They ignored him, started on the bodies, two of them tucking into a piece of Khabib's ear.

Bon appétit.

Tyler had seen Lisbeth place her bag somewhere. No surprises, he found it next to Clyde's. Oh, how fucking sweet. He went and rummaged through it, found the retractable blade she kept in there for splicing electrical wire. He also found the extra block of explosive she kept and the spool of command wire. He wasn't exactly sure how to use any of it, but he had seen her prepare these often enough and was confident he could manage. He located the detonation switch she'd used. It was in the bag too, with the length of command wire she'd used neatly wrapped around it. He pocketed the blade for now and turned his attention to the cash boxes and the Aladdin's cave pile of twinkling gold and silver and whatever else was stacked in there next to it. Enough to keep a small country going for a little while for sure, sitting right there.

He couldn't take everything, he knew that; he probably couldn't take even half of it. He filled his bag with as much as he could carry, got a good chunk of the cash in there. He shifted through the twinkling Aladdin's pile, tossed out the expensive-looking items – and concentrated on the very expensive-looking ones instead: mostly watches, diamonds and personal jewellery. These he pocketed until they were all brimming. He put on the heavy jacket, the pockets bulging, and squirmed – with some difficulty – into the straps of his backpack.

So far, so good.

Now for the tricky part. The part that could go wrong, easily go wrong, could have him end up like the three in the recess only having suffered a much slower and more agonising way of getting there.

He walked ahead into the tunnel, but in the opposite direction to that which Khabib had used to get them here. He counted each step. On step ninety-seven he had reached a fork in the tunnel. To the left, it stretched off into the darkness at a right angle. To his right it curved gently away. If he was correct, if he went left, it should take him beneath the river. He would walk in a straight line over to beneath the far bank. He knew there was a manhole cover over there. He had seen it. But locating it from down here was a different matter. And what if he was wrong, what if his directions were off?

He didn't have time to stand and ponder his dilemma, that would do nothing but drain the batteries of his head torch. Although he had a couple spare, if he became lost, really lost, it wouldn't matter how many batteries he had. Not down here. Not in the tunnels. They were all the same. Once you became lost in a labyrinth such as this, all that awaited you was a cold, dark, frightening death, and one where the mind gave up long before the body.

Tyler went left, *one, two, three...*

After 185 steps, the tunnel was still heading straight ahead. Surely, he must have reached the other side by now? He looked up, swinging his head from side to side, lighting up the roof. There was no sign of what he was looking for anywhere, that manhole cover. He closed his eyes, thinking, and, remembering he'd left the head torch on, reached up, still with his eyes closed, and turned it off. If he'd had a look at the blueprints, he'd have known for sure. But he hadn't; Khabib had kept those, just like everything else, to himself. Tyler began to think he might never find that manhole cover. It would be best to head back, to try to follow the route Khabib had used. But that would not be easy; there were so many twists and turns, it was confusing. Which was just the way Khabib had intended it to be. He thought now it had been a mistake to come this way. He should have attempted to trace the route Khabib had used. He decided that was what he would do now, he'd go back and try to find it while he still had battery power for light.

A trickle of fear ran through him. Fear had a power all of

its own; it consumed you. He couldn't afford to do fear, not now. His eyes were still closed. He felt safer with them that way, like those times when Momma came mooching around outside his room. He'd never wanted to open his eyes back then either, just wanted everything to go away. But nothing ever did go away. Just like it wouldn't go away now either.

He snapped his eyes open and, just as he was about to press the head torch on, thought he saw something. Had he? He stared ahead. What was it? Another of those glowing spectres, drifting in a sea of black. Maybe he was going crazy? Or maybe he already was crazy? Momma always told him he was crazy. He stepped back, feeling his breath catch at the back of his throat, his hands turning clammy. He could almost taste his fear now, could literally smell it on the air. It was Momma, wasn't it? Had to be. But he didn't trust Momma, not when he was like this, alone in the dark, vulnerable like he was back then, a kid.

'Momma,' he said, a croaky whisper, and he was back in the darkness of his bedroom. He waited for her to open the door to enter and come to him. 'No, Momma, please,' he croaked, and the fear seemed to reach down deep inside him, so deep. He felt like he would piss himself.

He strained his muscles against the urge. He was a grown man now! Come on. Grown men didn't piss themselves.

'Go away,' he shouted. 'Go away, Momma, fuck off, you hear me? I killed you once, and I'll kill you again.'

But he knew he couldn't. He could never kill her again. He took another step forward. The spectre did not move. It stayed in place, suspended at a point a short distance away. He thought it looked strangely like a halo, as if waiting to offer him salvation. He took his hand from the torch, didn't turn it on: if he did, he would no longer be able to see the glow; it would be lost. And he wanted to, he really wanted to be able to see that glow. The part of his mind still capable of rational interpretation began formulating a thought.

As it did, his heartbeat quickened. Could it be...? Really, could it? He moved closer. Yes, yes, it could...

He stopped and blinked, looking up. It was real. There, above his head, not a spectre, no, certainly not. Again, he blinked. It was an actual halo, faint, yes, but real: a thin circle of light squeezing in from outside. He allowed himself a brief smile.

Thank you, Momma. I should never have doubted you. You led me here, didn't you? Thank you.

He had found the manhole cover.

39

It had been about an hour since they'd heard any sound from inside the vault. Brody had sent word to the mobile armed units that the assumption was that they were on the way; the raiders were leaving the bank. Soon, they would be out. They had to be.

That was the assumption.

But still, the word back from the units was that there was no sign of anyone yet emerging.

Brody didn't like it. That could mean maybe they'd already slipped the net, that, somehow, they had managed to get out without being noticed.

Brody forced himself to remain calm, even as AC Kelly began to pace about at one end of the bank, and Superintendent Ryan at the other.

He waited.

They all waited.

There was nothing else they could do.

MANDY JOYCE DETECTED the subtle change; they were getting restless. She was close enough to hear the radio through the open door of their vehicle. They were spread at a distance from each other along the wall, so they had to raise their voices to be heard. She was still standing in the lane, unseen, and could hear what was being said. She heard an officer say, 'Keep a lookout; this might be it,' and they all – she counted four of them – leaned over the wall, looking down into the water. She detected a change in posture too, a stiffening of their bodies, their weapons held higher up against their chests, from where it would be a quick, short manoeuvre to adopt what she'd heard called the tactical stance – when a cop is getting ready to shoot.

Something was about to kick off...she could feel it.

She stayed in the shadows, watching. Yes, it was better than any drug, being back in the game.

40

Tyler made his way quickly back to the recess; no need to count his steps now. It was straight ahead until he met the fork in the tunnel. The first time, walking away from it, he'd taken a left; now, returning to the recess, he took a right.

As he approached, he saw the rats; two of them were in the hollow of what had once been Khabib's face, one he guessed so small it was almost completely lost within it, nothing but its tail visible, the other bent over, its big back showing, jutting out. They ignored him. Other rats were stationed at the sides of the bodies, others sitting on top, all gorging on flesh. The smell, like an abattoir, would carry for miles, especially down here, drawing in rodents from afar.

Rats didn't faze him. He jumped up into the recess. Still, they didn't move. He knew rats had poor eyesight, very poor, and probably couldn't even see him. But stomp your foot, which he did now, and they all scampered away. As they ran past him, brushing against his legs, he took the blade from his pocket and reached behind his head. He'd grown his hair purposely long in case this day would come. He grabbed a fistful and ran the blade across, cutting it cleanly through. Tyler took his hand away, went to each body in turn, sprinkling hair on top. Then he held the blade to his palm, bracing himself, and cut it across, deep but not too deep, enough to draw blood, and enough of it. He dropped the blade and turned his hand, pooling the blood as best he could onto his palm, walked to the edge of the recess and turned it over again, at an angle, so that the blood fell down along the tunnel wall. He gave it a minute, dripping the blood over as wide an area of the wall as possible, then took one of the plasters he'd brought with him and taped it on. He went back to Lisbeth's bag, found the small disc-shaped detonator she kept spare. His biggest problem was the explosive. He'd never used any before. He took the block, like a square of cheese, from her bag too. Lisbeth was very careful about the quantity she used. He'd watched her earlier carefully unwrap a small portion, he guessed it was the end of a previous block, and weigh it on a digital scale. He'd calculated there was little more than an eighth of a block in it that time, enough to blow the roof.

But right now, well, fuck that. He was going to use it all.

He dragged the bodies of Lisbeth and Clyde over and piled them on top of Khabib's. Some rats lurking underneath scurried away. He ignored them, took the block of explosive and removed the wax paper wrapper from it, pushed the detonator in, just as he'd seen Lisbeth do many times before. He got the command wire and pushed the end into the detonator. He was relieved when it made a soft clicking sound and caught fast. Lisbeth had used a junction box as she was reconnecting wires because of the distance she needed to cover. Tyler wasn't going to worry about that either. He would spool out the command wire as far as it would go. If he ran fast enough, even allowing for the weight he'd be carrying, the shock wave should be sufficiently muted within the confines of the recess, coupled with the weight of bodies on top, to be felt as nothing more than a nudge into his back. Or so he hoped. If it all went the way he wanted this to, enough of the walls and the roof would come down. Or so he hoped, too. Yes, there was a lot of hope in this.

But he knew it would work, just *knew*. Because Momma was with him. He knew that now. You'd think she'd be angry after what he'd done to her, killing her like that and all. But it seemed like she was trying to make amends for the wrongs *she'd* done to him.

He jumped down into the tunnel, pulled on the jacket, squirmed into the backpack again. Damn, they were both heavy, but nothing he couldn't handle – he hoped. Yes, that word again. Still, seemed a shame to have to leave what he guessed was over half of the swag behind. What he was carrying would buy him another house on Melrose Avenue if he wanted it. Two of them. Maybe three. But he didn't. He had enough houses. But it could, that was the point, it could, and maybe a slice of a start-up tech company, too, with what was left over. He already had a slice of one, and it had returned his investment. He was a millionaire from that one investment alone. It was safe to say he already had enough money to do whatever he wanted to. So why the fuck was he still doing this? That was a good question. But it beat working for a living, that was for sure. He wanted to laugh, but he didn't. That was for later.

He grabbed the command wire and ran it out all the way, pulled it away from the spool. The detonator box was sitting on top of a couple of gold and silver diamond-encrusted watches in one of his shirt breast pockets. He took it out and slipped the end of the wire right into it. But it didn't fit correctly, it was loose, seemed like nothing was keeping it in place, and it slipped back out again. He worked out it had a lever on top. He pulled up the lever and slotted it in again. When he released it this time, the lever snapped onto the wire, holding it firmly in place. He pressed a small button along the bottom that had an image on it of a circle with a line running through it. He felt a vibration pass through his finger as the big button in the centre glowed green, beneath it the words, 'For Detonation'.

He paused. What if this didn't work? And what if it did? What if he blew the whole tunnel down on top of himself? What if the block of explosive wasn't enough? What if it was as about as good as a pipsqueak fart? What was a pipsqueak fart anyway? He really hadn't thought this through, had he? No, he hadn't. But he had no choice. Too many questions, too little time.

Fuck it.

He pressed the button, his back turned against the recess, dropping the detonator box, starting to run, waddling would be more appropriate: this shite was heavy.

And then...

Nothing.

Nothing?

But he didn't stop. He kept moving, the weight quickly beginning to slow him down. It wasn't easy carrying a couple of houses on Melrose Avenue on your back, after all, or a Bentley Bentayga in your shirt pocket.

He stopped, the torchlight rising and falling on the walls around him with each breath he took.

Now what? It hadn't blown. It hadn't fucking blown. He'd done something wrong. Damn. This stupid plan was not going to work. It wasn't going to fucking work. He looked back and thought he caught something, a faint pink glow, the same colour as on a winter night sky in a northern city, Stockholm or Oslo, someplace like that. It seemed to grow in intensity, changing into a bright, deep yellow, the edges altering to what looked like a singed orange. What was happening? Were the gates of hell opening? He heard a sound, like a low murmuring at first, growing stronger, more menacing. He imagined a monster stalking through the tunnel towards him.

And then there was a brilliant flash, and the earth shook, shook like an earthquake, and the shock wave came, not the gentle nudge into his back that he imagined, but one that sent Tyler sprawling against the tunnel floor, where he waited, his body pressed against the bricks, as the monster passed over him.

41

For a moment Brody couldn't make sense of it, his mind scrambling for meaning, standing frozen to the spot, not able to find any.

And what was that sound, thunder?

He looked down, and as if in slow motion, like time itself had slowed down, he saw the cracks appear on the floor beneath him. He watched, mesmerised by the sight of a spider's web of black veins spreading across the marble. He felt a sensation like the ground beginning to sway and realised that was what it was; the ground really was swaying. He stumbled, fighting to maintain his balance.

Was this an earthquake? He'd heard of earthquakes in Wales, but this was Ireland. Was it possible?

Everyone bolted for the door.

Brody didn't. He stayed, watching as one end of the room appeared to tilt, the vault shifting, the sound like a feral, ear-splitting scream, the front end rising. Then the vault juddered and dropped suddenly a foot or so into the floor, where it stayed, stuck in a huge hole.

This was no earthquake, he felt certain. No, the bank raid gougers had detonated a bomb beneath them.

Now Brody did bolt for the door.

'L ISTEN UP, EVERYBODY,' AC Kelly shouted five minutes later. He had a crazed look in his eyes.

He was in the middle of the roadway, gesticulating wildly, pointing this way and that.

'We need people there' – pointing in one direction – 'and there' – pointing in another – 'and there' – pointing off somewhere else. 'We need checkpoints set up. We need to ring the city with checkpoints. And we need an ambulance, and we need it now. This is a major incident.'

The road outside the bank was already full of mules. Brody knew they didn't need any more bodies here. The windows on either side of the bank's door had been blown out, covering the area in broken glass. A couple of mules had been caught by flying shards; blood was streaming down one fella's face; another was holding a blood-soaked cloth to his ear. Brody had checked on his own team, and all were unscathed. No one, mercifully, appeared to have been seriously injured.

Armed response units were already arriving. The sight of them seemed to calm AC Kelly somewhat. The other spaghetti hats had gathered around him, not saying very much, happy, it seemed, to have him in the driving seat.

Brody wasn't. He had a feeling about this. If this gang were such professionals, and he believed they were, why would they go and set off an explosion like that? Not after they'd already likely cleaned the vault out. Yes, they could have made a mistake, that was possible. Or they could also be wishing to create a distraction.

That second option made a lot more sense to Brody.

As AC Kelly and the spaghetti hats disbanded, he approached the open door of the bank, sturdy and still attached to its hinges, and he peered inside. A green emergency light had activated at the back, casting a murky glow across the rubble-strewn floor, the air filled by a billowing cloud of dust. But there was no sound; everything was eerily quiet.

Brody went in, tentatively made his way forward, his feet crunching on the broken glass and pieces of furniture and bits of floor tiles. With each step he was testing the floor; it appeared sturdy until he was almost at the vault, where it seemed to have the density of rotting floorboards. Brody stopped. A voice he didn't recognise shouted from behind, 'Get out. It's not safe in there.' He ignored it. The green light cast shadows about the door of the vault, sitting in the floor like the back end of a truck that had fallen into a sinkhole. On one side of it a piece of floor had given way, the green light seeping down into the tunnel, illuminating a pile of yellow bricks covered in what looked like twinkling fireflies. Ireland didn't have fireflies either, Brody knew. But he'd seen them on his travels. These fireflies were, in fact, twinkling gems and diamonds. Maybe something had gone wrong after all, he thought. For them to leave these behind. He was about to turn away when he saw something. A shape like a toy hand you'd buy in a pound or dollar shop at Halloween, sticking out of the bricks below. Except this wasn't a toy. This hand was real.

Yes, Brody thought, *something seemed to have gone wrong alright.*

MANDY JOYCE HAD HEARD the explosion, but it didn't sound like an explosion from where she was standing; it sounded like nothing more than a dull thud coming from the other side of the river. She put it down to out-of-hours roadworks. They were everywhere in the city. She watched the officer, who didn't pay the sound any attention either. In fact, he looked a little bored, pacing up and down by the river wall, hardly bothering to look over it now.

And then a panicked voice screamed from the radio.

'Bomb blast at the National & Provincial Bank, corner of Essex and Wellington Streets. All units to this location. All units to this location. All fucking units.'

Mandy's belly fluttered. Other people's misery was her excitement.

Jesus, a bomb blast. *Oh Lord, thank you.*

TYLER CROUCHED beneath the manhole cover approximately fifty metres away from where Mandy Joyce stood. His weight distribution was ungainly. He had to lean forward from his perch at the top of the ladder, his hands pressing against the tunnel wall, his chin against his chest, just enough forward ballast to stop him from toppling backward off the ladder. He hadn't thought of this being a problem. Above him, he could hear the sirens on the other side of the manhole cover, and more than one vehicle had gone racing over it, the loud jangling noise just above his head alarming him and almost sending him flying.

The sound of the explosion within the tunnels was like

nothing he'd ever heard before. They had to be responding to it.

He waited until the sounds of the latest wave of sirens faded, and then pushed. There were no connecting nuts or screws on the manhole cover, he'd already checked: it was designed to be removed using a crowbar, from above ground, that is. But from down here, all that was required was a mighty push.

Which he did now, angling his weight up through his body and into his shoulders and the back of his neck. He effectively squashed himself against the underside of the cover, wedging himself between it and the top of the ladder. He groaned, straining, hoping the step of the lightweight ladder would not give beneath him, but he felt it do so a little. Yet the cover shifted, just a bit. He took another breath and pushed as hard as he could, using everything he had. He felt it shift again a bit more, with it now a scraping sound. He moved up a step on the ladder, the manhole cover rising above him, and another step, the cover starting to slide from his shoulders, one more step and it was clanging onto the road. He straightened, his head and shoulders coming up out of the manhole cover, as if appearing out of the turret of a submarine. His upper body was now in the middle of the roadway. He anchored both hands onto the tarmac and looked both ways. Off to his right, he could see the headlights of stationary vehicles at traffic lights. On his left, a box truck rumbled by.

He needed to be quick. He started to push himself out of the manhole, but he couldn't fit with the backpack on. He went down a step again, began manoeuvring out of the straps. It was easier to take off the bag than it was to put it on, the contents acting as a counterweight. He slid the second strap from his arm and grabbed the top handle. With both hands he hefted the bag up and out of the manhole. The headlights in the distance began to move – towards him. Shit. Was he going to be quick enough?

Tyler rolled out of the manhole just in time, a driver leaning on the horn and swerving by. He counted three cars passing by him with centimetres to spare.

He needed to get the cover back in place. If he didn't, it would flag attention. He lay flat on the roadway, braced his feet against it, and pushed until it dropped into place. He got back onto his feet, hefted the bag onto his back, crossed the road, ran into a warren of back streets, where he was swallowed up into the darkness.

42

There was nothing much to be done until morning. An army ordnance team had been alerted, but wouldn't arrive until first light. A checkpoint perimeter had also been set up around the city. AC Kelly had called that one right, Brody thought. But they hadn't come across anything so far. Whoever this gang were, they'd likely be either already gone or lying low. Brody thought of the hand sticking out of the bricks. Maybe they were already dead or injured. Either way, no one would know until the ordnance boys got here and went down there and gave the area the all-clear.

Brody went home to try to get some much-needed sleep. However, when he collapsed into his bed, he couldn't sleep. Despite everything, just as with the night before, he was overthinking, and in the middle of it all, there was Ashling Nolan. He checked the time; it was just gone 2:30 a.m. Too late to ring her, but then he thought, even if it wasn't, would he have done it anyway? Somehow, he didn't think so.

He twisted onto his side. What he needed now was some sleep. *Sleep, sleep, sleep.*

He closed his eyes and willed his mind to be empty, concentrating on each in- and out-take of breath, just emptying it...*in out, in out, in out...*

It wasn't going to work, just wasn't. It was a complete waste of time. He might as well get up and wait for morning to come. But then, once he'd stopped battling it...

Brody fell asleep.

43

Tyler turned onto a street and walked along it, staying close to the edge. It was filled by boarded-up buildings, cheap B&Bs and grotty hotels. He had really hoped everything wouldn't come to this. But it had. Now, he had no choice but to play the cards he'd been dealt. Walking the streets like this, all it would take was a police patrol to stop and question him. He needed a place to lie low.

At the end of the pavement, he stood in the doorway of a boarded-up building, watching. For what, he wasn't certain. A street like this could provide opportunities, he knew; it had always done so in the past. After all, it was on a street like this he'd first met Khabib, in a topless bar in south Boston.

Damn you, Khabib, but you left me no choice.

I didn't want to kill you, man; now you're another ghost I've got to deal with.

He couldn't go back to the Airbnb. That was out, because

what God giveth, he also could taketh away. God knew everything; it was too dangerous.

A hotel midway along the street took his interest; the name over the door was Euro Inn, the 'u' missing, but it was easy to work it out. Couples were coming and going, the men an eclectic mix, the women all similar in appearance, businesswomen, just of the street-walking kind.

Which gave him an idea.

The couples never came out together. The men emerged first and quickly shuffled off, followed by the women, who sauntered off down the street, presumably on the lookout for their next punter. The first businesswoman to emerge and come his way was dressed in a cheap faux leather skirt, tight polo-neck jumper, with long bony legs in open-toed high heels. She looked at him as she passed, and he held her gaze.

'Alright, love?' Her voice like churning gravel. She slowed but didn't stop.

'Actually...' he said with a smile. 'I could do with...you know, it's been a long day.'

She stopped now and smiled too, displaying two rows of small yellow teeth in prominent pink gums.

'You looking for business, love, yeah?'

'Yes. Business. I suppose. Yes.'

'Youse want to go to the hotel there?' With a jerk of the thumb over the road towards the Euro Inn. 'Or the park up the top of the road, yeah? Same price, love. What ya want to do?'

'Well...I don't like hotels. I don't want anyone to see me. I'm, um...' His voice trailed off.

'I know, you're married.'

He nodded.

'They're all married, love.' She gave a crackly laugh. 'The

park, then, yeah? Nice and private it is. Are youse coming...'ere, coming, get it?' She gave another crackly laugh. 'You will be in a minute, love, ha ha; old Margy'll look after your every need so she will.'

He didn't answer, the thought making him want to puke. Her eyes narrowed, calculating.

'Are youse coming or not?' No crackly laugh now, all business.

He stood still and looked away, adopting a little-boy lost look. 'Just don't want to meet anyone, y'know, that's all. I really don't. I mean...'

'I know, love, you're married.'

Her heels clicked on the pavement. He thought she was about to walk away. But she didn't. Instead, he heard her step closer.

'Aw, you worry too much, a fine-looking man such as yourself. If I met you on a night on the town, I'd give it to you for free. Tell you what, I live around the corner, yeah. Will that be private enough for ya, love? Me own flat it is. The block is full of auld ones, all tucked up in bed at this hour. No one will see you. We'll go there, yeah? I wouldn't normally do that for any old Tom, Dick or Harry...'ere, Dick, d'ya get it?' Again, that rumbly laugh.

He felt he really was about to puke. He turned back to face her. In the streetlight he could see the furrowed lines across her forehead, across her cheeks and chin, her knobbly nose. What was she, at least sixty?

'I'd like that,' he said softly, playing the part. 'You're right, I do worry too much.'

'Well, you don't need to worry now, old Margy'll take care of ya. Fifty euro, love. Up front.'

'Why don't I,' he said, zipping open a small side pocket

on his trousers where he'd placed four €50 notes before heading out on the job, just in case, 'give you this.'

Her thin lips puckered as he held out the notes.

'What the fuck?' she said, like she'd witnessed a magician perform an amazing trick that she couldn't believe. 'A man of means, is it?' she added, snatching the notes and shoving them quickly into her shoulder bag. 'I'll tell ya, love, you're either gagging for it big time, or you've too much money to know what to be doing with it.'

'Maybe a bit of both,' he said.

'Maybe a bit of both,' she agreed, linking her arm into his. 'Now you come with me, a fine gentleman such as yourself, and we'll go back to my place. You don't need to show this old dog any new tricks, I'll tell you either. I know everything there is to know already.' Her crackly laugh was louder than before as she led him away.

A sign over the door of the building she brought him to announced:

Dublin Corporation requests tenants to be respectful of others at all times.
NO LOUD MUSIC. NO LOITERING. NO SMOKING
IN CORRIDORS.

They went in. 'The lifts are broken, love,' she said, crossing the deserted foyer that smelled of piss and bleach. The stench grew worse as she led him up bare concrete steps onto the second floor and out onto an open balcony, where he gulped in fresh air. Her flat was at the end of the walkway.

She opened the door and led him in, turned on a light from a bare bulb hanging at the end of a long flex in the centre of the room. A crumpled cloth sofa rested in a corner next to a window, a portable TV in front of it on a stool, behind it a rickety table with metal legs and a plastic tablecloth, a couple of wooden chairs pushed in on either side. Everything looked like it had been taken from a skip, which it probably had. A kitchen area was in a corner, completely bare of any foodstuffs, it seemed, except for a jar of instant coffee sitting on the counter by a rusting cooker. A door in the wall at one end was open, and he could see into a bathroom.

She went and opened the door in the opposite wall, stood with her hands on her hips. Behind her was a double bed, and next to it an overflowing waste bin full of crumpled tissue papers. He detected an aroma of semen and rubber, and he stifled a gag. Tyler wasn't so sure he was the only person she brought back here.

He pulled off the heavy backpack and laid it down on the floor, watching her eyes take it in, then watched as they flicked to the bulging pockets of his jacket and shirt, finally down to the pockets of his canvas work trousers.

'You're too pretty to be a labourer,' she said. 'What are you, then?'

'A bank robber,' he said.

She threw back her head and laughed.

'You're a gas ticket alright.'

'You asked,' he said, walking slowly towards her. 'That's what I am, a bank robber.'

'Yeah, right.'

'Nothing I can do about it if you don't believe me...'

'Course I don't believe you; go away outta that.'

He was beginning to enjoy this.

'As I was saying, if you don't believe me...' He stopped, turned, and went back to the backpack, zipped the top open and took out a wad of notes. 'Look.' He returned to her, held out the roll of €100 notes.

She folded her arms, looking at it.

'Is it real? It's not, is it? Monopoly money, yeah?'

'Of course it's real,' he said, keeping his voice light, playful. 'And this.' He snapped open one of the breast pockets on his shirt, took out the first thing he touched, a diamond-encrusted watch. 'It's only a Tourbillon watch. You know how much these go for? It's a vintage; we're talking €80,000 right here.'

Even if somebody had never heard of, or seen, a Tourbillon watch before, they could tell this was something special.

Margy stood still, her head bowed, looking at the timepiece. He could see the white roots along her hairline, like someone had run through it with a Tipp-Ex brush.

When she turned her head up again, he knew she knew. Margy was a cagey old fox. She'd made a mistake in bringing him back here. A big mistake.

'Why you tellin' me?' Her voice soft and fearful, almost a whisper.

It reminded him of way back then, in the darkness of his parents' bedroom, lying naked next to his mother. He reached out a hand and touched her arm. She flinched.

'No, no,' he said, 'don't be afraid, please.' He brought his hand up and rested it against her cheek, ran it softly across, feeling the hard leathery skin beneath, brought it down to rest on her neck.

'WHAT DO you mean it's not enough?' Mandy Joyce was on the phone to the night editor at INN TV News. The channel was based in Kuwait, but had recently opened a studio in Belfast, covering the whole of Ireland.

'I looked at the footage,' the editor said. He'd said his name was Trevor, his accent a strange hybrid of southern and northern Irish with a dollop of northern England thrown in. 'I mean, it doesn't actually have anything in there, does it? Where's the hook?'

'What do you mean, where's the hook? There's been a bank robbery...well, they haven't gone in yet, the guards, the police, whatever, because they have to wait until morning. They blew the vault – the robbers, I mean. They're certain of it, the guards, but, you know...'

'Yes, I know, they haven't gone in yet...Look, what's your name again?'

What's my name again? Fuck you!

'Mandy, Mandy Joyce.'

'Look, Mandy, here's the deal...'

Here's the deal? Who's this bollocks think he is, the Reuters bureau chief of New York?

'...we already have a wire report about this.'

Mandy blinked. 'You do? But how? I was the only...There was no one else there, is what I mean.'

'There didn't need to be. We have satellite imagery of smoke rising from that location; we've geo located it; it's as you say, this National & Provincial Bank. Oh, don't get me wrong, Mand...'

Mand? Fuck off.

'...this is shaping up to be a big story, yes, indeed it looks like it is, and we can see a tremendous amount of *police* activity there at the scene – via the satellite. Yes, but what you sent us, a video captured on your phone, of what? Some officers peering over a wall...Look, I'll do what I can for you, I know what it's like trying to cut it as a freelance, been there and done that, as they say, but I don't think this cuts the mustard, have to say.'

Cut the fucking mustard. And he'll see what he can do for me. *It's the other way round, shithead.*

So this is what it's come to, is it? Mandy thought. The great Mandy Joyce, reduced to grovelling about in the dirt for a wee bit of work, like a dog waiting for a scrap from the dinner table.

She wanted to scream and, before she could, stabbed her finger against the call termination button, wanting to throw the damn thing onto the ground and stomp on it again and again and again. What a dickhead. Didn't he know that part of being a good reporter was the ability to sniff out a great story. That bollocks couldn't sniff out a great story if it were a three-course meal in a Gordon Ramsay restaurant.

44

The new day seeping through the cloudy night-time sky was slowly casting the city into spindly shadows, the buildings and deserted streets taking on a panoramic cinematic aura, both beautiful and eerie at the same time.

However, along this street, it was all activity, like an action movie was in production, as the tracked bomb disposal robot trundled down the ramps from the back of the drab khaki army truck, its operator, wearing combat fatigues, manoeuvring it by means of a small handheld console.

Brody watched him from behind the second cordon tape. It was frustrating to be standing back here. Further back behind him, maybe ten metres away, was yet another cordon tape, and further back again there was a road junction, blocked off by a squad car with a revolving roof rack.

Traffic snarl-ups would be ongoing throughout Dublin city centre today.

Standing beside him, Superintendent Ryan looked like

she hadn't slept at all, her fleece jacket crumpled and her eyes red rimmed. Brody thought she was distracted, and worried too, which wouldn't be unusual considering the circumstances, but he wasn't convinced it was the circumstances alone that were responsible for this – if he was reading her right, that is. A couple of spaghetti hats stood huddled together further along. Spaghetti hats always seemed to stand apart like that at a time like this, these two whispering to each other. One of them eyed Brody and dropped his head. On the other side of Brody was Voyle, shuffling his feet because he always found it hard to stand still. Brody was convinced he was on some spectrum or other. Which would account for a lot of things. Next to Voyle was Marty, standing stock-still because he was well able to, patiently waiting for whatever it was to come his way, and then he would deal with it. Which left only Considine…speaking of whom, where was she? In answer to this silent question, he noticed a tall figure out of the corner of his vision, and he turned to see Considine crouching under a cordon tape, come up on the other side, and walk quickly towards him.

'Some little gobshite,' she said, panting, 'told me I couldn't drive through. I had to walk.' She pointed vaguely. 'All the way from back there. I got the little bollocks's number. I'll deal with him later.'

'You got his number,' Voyle said. 'He was cute, was he?'

'Fuck off,' Considine snarled. 'I'm not in the mood.'

Voyle was about to say something in answer to that, but Brody grabbed his arm and squeezed. Voyle shut his mouth again. *Business as usual between these two*, Brody thought.

He watched the tracked robot trundle into the bank. Brody would like to see what the operator could see on that console of his, but the military brass had ordered he was off-limits.

'How long more?' It was Superintendent Ryan.

'I don't know,' Brody answered, stepping away from the cordon tape. She followed. 'We can only wait,' he added. 'It's hard waiting, I know. By the way, everything all right...with you, I mean.'

She didn't answer right away. Her shoulders slouched. *Something isn't right*, he thought, *that's for sure.* She rubbed a hand across her eyes, like she was wiping away tears. He didn't know how to react to this. The new super had maintained a frosty distance since joining the unit, even if she seemed to be mellowing lately. He wasn't going to fling his arms around her, that's for sure. Instead, he'd go halfway. He rested a hand gently on her elbow.

'Want to talk?'

'Damn. I didn't intend to...I thought I could run with it a little longer. I'll be alright.'

But something told him she wouldn't. He made a decision.

'Let's go and talk about it. Come on.' He nudged her gently, but she didn't move.

'No, Jack, that's okay, but thank you. We have a job to deal with here. That's the priority. We're on company time, remember.' She paused. Then, 'I have cancer, that's all.'

What? Had he heard right? But he knew he had. And *that's all*? She'd said that. Like, for real. Jack didn't know what to say, so he said nothing.

'Shite timing,' she said with a forced grin.

Brody wondered, was she telling him because she had no one else to talk to? He'd been thinking lately that he knew nothing whatsoever about her private life. Maybe that was because she didn't have a private life.

IT DIDN'T TAKE LONG, a half hour, that's all, for the all-clear to come. A bomb disposal officer in a blast suit had gone into the tunnels via the hole blown in the floor. The robot couldn't get down there. No explosives were found, but he did find something else.

BRODY, Superintendent Ryan, and Chief Superintendent Walter Shanahan went down into the tunnel. They kitted out in hazmat suits first, as the bomb disposal officer had advised.

The body parts seemed to be strewn over a large recess built into the side of the tunnel. They shone their torches from here down into the tunnel itself, where Brody spotted bone fragments and…he blinked, a brown boot with the stump of a foot protruding from it resting in the centre, sticking out of the water that was not deep enough to carry it off.

'What the hell happened here?' he said.

He could tell by their expressions that neither Ryan nor Shanahan had a clue either.

He looked up. Brody wondered if the part of the ceiling they were standing under might collapse. Maybe. But they'd have to take their chances.

'We need forensics,' he shouted up to those above, 'the whole shebang. Dr McBain too. Can someone get onto that.'

'Onto it,' a voice he didn't recognise shouted back.

'I think we'd better get out of here,' the chief super said, looking increasingly nervous. 'What you think?'

They didn't object.

They went back up the ladder they had come down, placed there by the ordnance officer and secured at the top by stretch cords to anchor hooks in the wall.

Brody was the last to step off it. Just as he did, the section of floor he was on began to give way. He moved quickly away just as it broke free, falling down and bouncing against the ladder, twisting it like a child's toy, and landing on the rubble below.

45

Mandy Joyce was furious. She wanted to scream. She wanted to go to the top of the highest building and shout from the rooftop: *This isn't fucking fair.* Here she was, behind the cordon tape at the end of a narrow street that itself was behind a cordon tape where the press was gathered. She couldn't even be there, because she no longer had either a press card or accreditation from any news organisation. Instead, she had to stand next to a couple of dubious-looking characters, the only people about at this hour of the morning, both smelling of sherry and other things she didn't even want to think about.

'Wha's the story, love?' one of them slurred, his mouth completely hidden behind a shaggy, unkempt beard. She folded her arms, ignoring him.

'Something I said, love,' he said, 'was it?'

'Get lost.'

'Get lost yourself, ya minging auld bitch.'

'Here, enough of that now,' the young guard manning the cordon warned.

Up ahead, a woman appeared before the clambering press horde and gestured to the pack. Despite the hour, the word was out. They were all present – except for Mandy, of course. She bit her lip as she recognised the woman, what's-her-name from the garda press office. Mandy caught the eye of the young guard. 'Listen,' she said, 'can I go through? Please. I'm a journalist. Really. I'm working freelance, that's all. Mandy Joyce. You may have heard of me. I worked with All Ireland News.'

'No. Never heard of you,' he said smugly.

A bit too smugly, she thought. Which told her he probably had heard of her but just didn't want to give her the pleasure.

'If you're a journalist,' he added, 'then why aren't you in there?' With a nod to the press pack behind him.

'Well, that's what I'm trying to do if only you'd...'

'Where's your press card?' he cut her off.

'I-I, I don't have one. I mean, I've applied for one, it takes a little time, that's all, but I will...'

'Ah-hah...' The uniform held his palm up like he was stopping traffic. 'That's enough. From all of ye. Listen, if ye don't behave yourselves, ye'll all have to move along. Now, I won't tell ye again.'

Mandy blinked. *Jesus, he's lumping me in with these two cretins.*

What's-her-name had started waving what Mandy guessed were press releases about through the air. Hands gestured wildly for them, some snatching them straight from her grasp like loaves of bread at a disaster zone. What Mandy wouldn't give to be in there right now. Instead, all she could do was watch: this comeback of hers wasn't working out the way she had hoped. Just when she thought she was going somewhere, was about to break through the churning surf of the foreshore and enter the wide-open ocean of journalistic opportunity beyond, she'd been tossed into the water as she discovered her boat was still tethered to the shore.

It's not fucking fair.

The bearded one gave her an odd look, she thought.

'The state of you,' she said, 'what would your mother think?' And she walked away.

HE OPENED the fridge door and looked inside. Disgusting, that was the only word for it, like it hadn't been cleaned in years, which it probably hadn't. A tub of cream cheese now sprouted what seemed to be an assortment of green mushrooms. He didn't even know green mushrooms existed. He pulled open the freezer door. The interior was caked in ice, within it a box, printed along the side, *Value pack southern fried chicken, 2 steaks.* He found a knife in a drawer, hacked the box out from the ice. Underneath the sink he found a frying pan, surprisingly clean, and from the fridge again he took a tub of reasonably fresh-looking margarine. He cooked the chicken in it, leaving it over the flame for a good twenty minutes, until the outside was burned and he was completely certain it was cooked through before daring to put it in his mouth. He found half a loaf of sliced bread in a cupboard and ate a couple of slices with the chicken. When he was finished, he pushed the empty plate away.

What now?

He'd bolted the door. If someone were to come, he wouldn't answer, just hope they'd go away again. But, as yet, no one had. He had a feeling that no one would. Because he didn't think anyone came to this place. There were no mementos, nothing on the walls except peeling paint and mould stains, no family photographs. Margy, if that was even her real name, was nothing but a sad old whore whom no one would even remember. Perfect. He could stay here for a couple of days, wait until he worked out what to do next. This depended on what was happening outside, on whether his plan was working or not. He couldn't see any reason why it shouldn't, at least not in the short term, and that would buy him enough time.

Speaking of which. He was sitting at the table. He got up and went over to the settee, sat down and turned on the TV. There wasn't a remote that he could see, so he leaned forward, pressed a button and started going through the channels. He found one airing a news documentary, *repeat* written in the top corner of the screen: some discussion on long-term projections for electric vehicle sales or some shite. He wasn't interested. He was interested in the ticker tape running across the bottom of the screen carrying the news updates. It revealed there was a trade union dispute somewhere. It was followed by an asterisk. Then sports. Sports always followed the news the world over. Which told him the ticker tape was near the end of its cycle. The weather would be next. It was. He waited for it to finish, then...

BREAKING NEWS.

The cycle was starting all over again. Tyler leaned closer to the TV, clenching his hands, tensing up. The tape began:

Gardai have confirmed that human remains have been

discovered in a sewage tunnel system running underneath central Dublin following an explosion in the early hours of the morning beneath a branch of the National & Provincial Bank on the corner of Essex and Wellington Streets. Significant internal damage was caused to the building. It is believed raiders entered the bank vault via a tunnel, but it is not known if anything has been taken, as yet. A garda spokesperson said early indications are that the raiders may have died in the explosion in what appears to be a botched robbery attempt. He added that gardai are at the very early stages of their investigation and will know more when forensic results are available. Keep watching this channel for further updates throughout the day.

Tyler punched the air. 'Yes,' he said.

So far, so good.

He could relax – a little. No one was looking for him. If he could believe what he'd just read. And he didn't know if he could. Maybe they wanted him to get comfortable, get complacent, make a mistake.

Nah, that wasn't it. It was just like they said, the very early stages of the investigation. He was cool...still, just to be sure, he'd wait it out here just a little while longer.

He got up and went to the bathroom, stood in the doorway, looking at Margy lying on her back in the bathtub. It could have been anyone. But it wasn't. It was her. He guessed this was the story of her life, always in the wrong place at the wrong time. She hadn't put up any resistance, not after he'd bounced her head against the bedroom doorjamb a couple of times, that is, dazing her. Then he'd just...squeezed. That's all. It was over in mere minutes, almost like she'd wanted him to do it. In death, the old whore looked peaceful, younger, almost happy. He smiled.

But yet, he worried. Because they didn't seem to go anywhere, did they? Those people he killed. They seemed to hang around, as spectres and shapes, trapped in a halfway house of tormented souls, a type of purgatory.

Or maybe they were just waiting for him?

Tyler stood there, watching Margy's stiff body, started biting his nails.

A MOBILE COMMAND CENTRE, this a long-wheelbase truck specially converted in Germany for the purpose, had arrived at the scene. AC Kelly stood at the top of a surprisingly spacious room inside it, his jacket off, the sleeves of his shirt neatly rolled up to above the elbows, a map of central Dublin on a PowerPoint on the wall behind him. He was performing a real-time continuous assessment, two civilian IT specialists sitting at computers at a table along the side of the room updating a sidebar on the PowerPoint with information. The door was open, and senior officers from throughout the region, as well as commanders of a variety of specialist units, were coming and going.

It was clear to Brody, who was standing by the steps outside the command centre, that while everyone was striving to give their best impressions to the contrary, no one really had a clue what was going on. But what was important was to look like they did; that was half the battle.

He was watching the bank, waiting. When he saw him emerge from the doorway of the building, clutching his familiar battered medical case, Brody approached. The white-haired, bespectacled pathologist loped along like a giraffe towards his car parked on the other side of the cordon tape. By the time Brody reached him, he'd already placed his bag into the boot and was about to get in behind the wheel.

'Doc,' Brody said, 'a word.'

Dr McBain glanced at him. 'Brody, I'm in a hurry. It's like happy hour in the city, and it's not even' – he glanced at his watch – 'lunchtime. Has the world gone crazy?'

'I don't know. But, at the moment, if anyone knows anything about what's going on, it's you.'

'Oh, that old flattery will get you everywhere, old chestnut. You know I can't tell you much until I've got results. I haven't got results. Not yet. What can I tell you? Nothing, that's what, except that there's pieces of at least three people down there, that's all. I've arranged to have the bigger, we'll call them portions, removed to the lab. Everything will have to be removed and sifted through. I've taken swabs of blood splatterings too, even though strictly speaking I should have left that for SOC. I've gone beyond the call of duty, Jack.'

'Well, that's something.'

'It is?'

'Yes, of course.'

'There you go, then, happy to oblige.'

And with that, the doctor sat into his old Toyota and reached for the door handle.

'Doc, this is more than a happy hour, it really is.'

'Sorry, Brody, it's all the same to me. I'm a scientist; my brain doesn't discriminate, you know.'

'I know. But I need results. As in fast, like really fast.'

'Faster than the results for the next poor blighter, is it?'

'Yes.'

'Um.' The doc didn't seem too impressed. 'Why? They're

all dead. No one survived that blast, did they? It's not as if you're chasing anyone.'

Brody thought about that. Maybe the doc had a point.

'Still, I need those results. And I need them fast.'

He watched as a little vein began to throb in a corner of Dr McBain's forehead. *Oh-oh.* He always handled the doc carefully. He'd learned he had to. The doc had two speeds, cruise and ballistic. Brody, in surprise, saw the throbbing vein disappear again.

'Okay, Jack. For you. I'll drop them off myself at the laboratory, detour back there before my next job, have someone make a start right away.'

'Thank you.'

The doc nodded and closed the car door.

Brody started to walk away. He wondered if the doc was mellowing in his old age. Perhaps.

But he doubted it.

A TEAM of officers had been detailed to collect and view CCTV from throughout the city centre. That was their only job, nothing else. In fact, there were so many officers, drafted in from outlying stations, that some had to be accommodated in the headquarters of the Department of Justice, a venerable red-brick building overlooking St Stephen's Green. But this job was even more difficult than looking for a needle in a haystack, or a grain of sand on a beach, whatever, because at least then you knew what you were looking for. This team didn't. And as far as Brody was concerned, in all likelihood, it was a complete waste of time too. These raiders – he'd call them that – were professionals, and he was certain they weren't going to allow themselves to get caught on any CCTV cameras. Still, this raised the question, if they were so professional, how could they have managed to get themselves blown up like that? So?

The more he thought about it, the more Brody thought it wasn't really making sense, especially as it appeared they'd already been into the vault. They'd effectively gotten away with it. They'd been killed *afterwards*. Why? No, not making sense.

Steve Voyle emerged from the mobile command centre as Brody approached. 'What's happening, boss?'

'A very good question.'

He came down the steps and stood next to Brody.

'And the answer?'

'I don't know. Short and simple.'

'At least you're honest.'

'Thank you.'

'Any suggestions on what we do in the meantime?'

'Hm...' Brody said. 'Maybe. You ever watch nature programmes, Steve?'

'Nature programmes?' Steve shrugged. 'No more than anybody else, I suppose.'

'Same here. But I remember one, a few years ago now, called...what was it again...?' Brody closed his eyes, thinking, opened them again. 'Yes, that's it...*Nature's Deadliest Killers*, that's it, on the lions of the Serengeti. One in particular, a wily old female, who had the highest kill rate in the pride. And you know why she had the highest kill rate?'

'Because she killed more prey than any of the others, duh.'

'Very smart, Steve. Yes. But *why* did she have the highest kill rate?'

'Something tells me you're about to reveal the answer, boss.'

'I am. She did nothing, that's why. Like, she'd just sit in that long grass for hours and hours, biding her time, doing nothing but waiting. She'd sit there longer than any of the others. Most of the other lions would get frustrated and break too soon and try to chase down an antelope or whatever. Their kill rate was something like one in five, usually bringing down the old and sick animals, or the very young. But the wily old lioness was different. She'd just sit or lie there, waiting, and waiting, until...*pow!*' Brody grabbed Steve's arm in a pincer grip. 'She'd break cover.'

Steve jumped.

'Okay, boss, Jeez...so you're telling me you're a lion now, is that it?'

Brody released his arm.

'Not in so many words, but that's the general drift.'

Steve shrugged again.

'Fine,' he said. 'Fine, boss, whatever.'

ENGINEERS SPENT the day surveying the damage to the bank. They deemed the structural integrity of the building and surrounding infrastructure to be sufficiently compromised to place the area off-limits – for the foreseeable future. A work crew was sent into the tunnels to carefully remove the debris – including bones and body parts – placing these into builders' bags. It was difficult work, and it was still in progress by the afternoon of the next day.

A press conference had been arranged for the afternoon of that second day too, just as the clearing work in the tunnel was finishing up. The builders' bags had already started being removed to an industrial facility on the outskirts of the city where the contents would be sifted through and any evidence, body parts, whatever, removed. AC Kelly thought it a good idea if the conference was held at the end of the street with the bank as a backdrop. Brody thought Kelly had missed his calling as a film director. Kelly wanted a member of all units involved represented, and he choreographed the front row line-up in an ascending order according to size from the middle out. Which meant that Brody, at six foot three, should have bookended the line directly next to AC Kelly, who, not being particularly tall, would act as a central low point. But Brody managed to get himself excused, telling the AC he had something to attend to in connection with the case. Anyway, he also told Kelly, it might be better to have Considine take his place. She was a striking-looking woman and would be a good advertisement for an all-inclusive, modern police force. Kelly liked that idea and agreed.

As the press conference began, Brody slipped away.

46

Tyler watched the screen change from one that contained a shadowed studio with pundits sitting around a table, that word 'Repeat' in the top corner, to a close-up of a newscaster speaking to camera:

'We now take you live to a press conference taking place outside the branch of the National & Provincial Bank where a serious incident occurred last night.'

The image changed again to one of a line of cops. What was this, a beauty contest? Tyler almost laughed at the thought.

He had a good feeling about this, he really had.

The small one in the middle began to speak, all gold braid and epaulettes. The *man*. But Tyler was really interested in the female who was standing next to him. Because she really did belong in a beauty contest. A Miss California maybe, or Daytona Beach. He should know, he'd seen enough beach babes in his time. Just like them, this girl stood out. But she was no beach girl, she was a cop. Tyler felt himself starting to get turned on, at the same time listening to what the little guy in the middle had to say. It didn't sound like a lot:

'Thank you for coming. You will appreciate this is an ongoing, active investigation, and there are certain aspects of it that I'm not at liberty to divulge. Not yet. I wish to begin by revealing that gardai, while pursuing a line of enquiry following the discovery of a female shot to death at the Herbert Park Platinum Hotel a couple of nights ago, have established a link to other similar incidents that took place on the continent. By similar incidents, I mean the shooting dead of a lone female in a hotel room in the cities of Antwerp, Valencia, London, Nice and Milan. At the same time as each incident occurred, a bank in the city was robbed, the culprits entering via a sewerage tunnel running beneath the bank building and then, by using both explosives and cutting equipment, gaining entry to the vault.'

Tyler heard a loud murmur run through the press pack. The cop continued:

'What we are also dealing with here in Dublin is a secondary, much larger explosion, which caused a significant amount of internal damage to the building behind me, resulting in a partial collapse of the ground floor and a collapse of a section of tunnel ceiling beneath. Officers who subsequently entered the tunnel found human remains within the rubble. We are currently investigating the possibility that the raiders themselves died during this operation, that they perhaps made a fatal error and blew themselves up.'

'The raiders died in this explosion, is that what you're saying?'

'Yes, we believe so, but like I say, the investigation is at a very early stage, I'll remind you.'

'How many raiders were there, do you know?'

'We're not certain. Three, maybe four.'

'How much did they get away with?'

'If I could just clarify, it doesn't seem like they have in fact got away. We're not certain of the amount, but it's substantial.'

'Any clue as to the identity of these raiders?'

Tyler had started to zone out, thinking that if they knew anything, really knew anything, they would have said it. They'd already shot their load. They knew nothing. His plan was working.

But then he heard something, what sounded like his own name being mentioned. He wasn't certain. He looked behind him.

'Mother, is that you?'

There was no reply.

He could see through the open bathroom door the top of Margy's head poking up over the rim of the bath. Had her head been like that before? He stared. He wasn't certain. Well, had it been poking over the rim of the bath or not?

He heard his name again. But from a different direction. He snapped his head around. He saw then. It was coming from the television, from the mouth of that pygmy officer in the middle.

Tyler froze.

'...his name is Abraham Jackman, a Canadian national wanted in connection with the murder of his mother in Beavertown, Ontario, when he was just fourteen years old, back in 2001. We believe Mr Jackson may also be connected with the murder of the female found in room 532 of the Herbert Park Platinum Hotel. We did not release this information previously, as it would have risked compromising the operation that we mounted to try to thwart the bank robbery.'

'And Mr Jackman may have been involved in this bank robbery too? Is that what you're saying?'

'Yes, that's what I'm saying.'

'How can you be so sure he's even still alive, then?'

'We can't. We don't know the identities of any of the bodies down there.'

'And if he was involved, it's possible, likely even, that he's dead?'

'Yes, that's a possibility.'

'And what about your operation to thwart this bank robbery? It wasn't very successful, was it? Meanwhile, a known killer may have been prowling the streets. How can you explain that?'

'Our major crimes investigation unit were responsible for discovering this link. I'll pass you over to Garda Considine; would you care to elaborate?'

Tyler felt a flutter, like he was a spotty teenager again. Only back then he was on the streets of the Lower East Side, peeping through the windows of the cars parked in alleys and laybys near the waterfront. Voyeurism didn't do it for him anymore. He'd graduated to more extreme tastes, much more.

Considine, that was her name? He said it softly to himself, 'Con-sid-ine.'

He watched her lips as she spoke, fulsome and natural. This woman was perfect.

'Thank you, Assistant Commissioner Kelly. We decided that releasing any details before now would not serve any purpose. We had a full murder investigation underway, still have. I would like to stress that members of the public were not placed at any increased danger. We needed to protect our operation, but we did not do it at the expense of public safety, just to clarify.'

Tyler had felt a jolt of elation at the sound of his name being announced on TV. But then, strangely, he began to zone out. The moment had passed. He wasn't interested in it anymore. Which surprised him, the recognition he thought he'd craved was nothing more than a one-off hit and a huge anticlimax. He watched the California beach babe cop's lips moving, but he no longer heard her words. Right now, all he was interested in was this woman. What was her first name? Then he realised he couldn't be certain she really was as good as she looked; he was watching her from a distance on a small TV screen, after all. But if she was...Because girls like her did it for him. They always had. Plus, more than anything, she reminded him of Desiree.

Now Desiree, she was a California beach babe, only a very bad one. He'd met her at engineering college in New York, all inked arms and neck, *Sazzy* in cursive script over her right eyebrow. *I mean, who the fuck did that?* He saw her on his first day as he walked across the gleaming polished floor to lecture hall 2A. She was going there too. Desiree lounged back in her seat, flicking a pencil between her fingers, chewing gum. The lecturer asked them all to introduce themselves. When it came to her turn, she said, *Desiree Lopez. I want to work in earthquake and war zones, whatever, wherever shite happens. I'm not interested in building highways or shopping malls.*

Tyler had asked her out right after. She'd said no. He'd stewed on it. He asked her out again. She said no again. He stewed some more. He asked her one more time, and one more time she said no. But now he'd annoyed her, she told him, *Now fuck off, pretty boy, and go wank into the mirror...*

He knew where she lived. He waited for the right time. He waited almost two years. But he waited. He knew she liked to sunbathe on the roof of her building in summertime. He went there one day in late July and threw her off it. Simple as. Anything else would have had people talking. Because they knew he'd never forgiven her for snubbing him like that. But people fell off roofs during summer all the time. A couple of drinks, a joint, a pill, whatever, not a good combination. They said the crown of her head hit the pointed top of a bollard. They said her head split open like a melon, the bollard pushing up through between her shoulders into her chest, her legs flopping down to the ground, making it look like she was devouring the gold-embossed, black-painted piece of metal. Which she was, in a way.

It was quite a sight.

Funny thing, he never felt Desiree was out there, not like the others, not like Momma. She wasn't following him around, whispering to him in the dark. Maybe even in death she wasn't interested in him. Or maybe it had something to do with her having virtually no head. Maybe. Now there was a thought.

Tyler sat back. He had a little time. They thought he was dead. And it would take them that little time to work out that he wasn't. Or maybe they never would. And a lot could happen in that little time.

He watched Considine flick some stray strands of hair from her face. He liked the way she did that, graceful, erotic almost. And he liked that sense of vulnerability she exuded. It wasn't that it was obvious, but it was to him. She wore no make-up, her hair tied back in a ponytail, nothing fancy. The collar of a sweater went halfway up her neck beneath her windbreaker. Almost like she didn't want to come across as what she really was, as nature intended, which was a beautiful, sultry, alluring, sexy female. He could see all that. But he really wanted to see so much more.

He felt himself starting to get hard.

BRODY RANG Dr McBain's office. The pathologist's secretary haughtily told him he could not be disturbed. 'He's very busy; he hasn't even started his autopsies yet,' she said.

Brody glanced at the clock on his office wall; just gone 1 p.m.

'Get him to call me as soon as, will you, please?'

'And who will I say is calling?'

Brody peered at the clock again. At its centre, about where the hands were anchored, was the manufacturer's name, *Wrights of Bristol*.

'Wright,' he said. 'Sergeant Bristol Wright.'

'Go away outta that,' she said, the haughtiness disappearing. 'You're Jack Brody.'

'Exactly,' he said, and hung up.

Snotty bitch, he thought, letting on she didn't recognise him. Although, he considered, it probably suited Dr McBain to have someone such as herself manning his phones as his first line of defence.

He got up from behind his desk and walked over to the window, looked out. There was a handful of cars in the car park, one of them Superintendent Ryan's Audi, he saw. He left his office and went up the stairs. Her office door was closed, and he listened outside. There was no sound. He tapped gently on the door.

'You in there?' he said softly.

There was no reply; he was about to turn and go away again when he heard her voice.

'Yes, come in.'

She was in the small kitchen area, leaning back against the sink, her arms folded.

'They miss me at the press conference?' she asked.

'I don't know. I left just as it started.'

The sunlight streaming in through the window behind her backlit her. She was silent and still, and Brody thought there was something otherworldly about her in this moment. She reminded him of a painting, by one of those Dutch masters, Rembrandt maybe, something like that, although he was no expert.

She unfolded her arms and slapped her hands against her thighs.

'Right.' She stepped out of the annexe. 'Where are we with this? I really need to focus.'

She went and sat behind her desk.

'Sit down, Jack; you're making me nervous...by the way, I didn't mention anything about the other thing to anyone. Not yet. Did you?'

The other thing.

He shook his head as he sat. 'No, course not.'

'Thank you...Now, tell me, like I say, where are we with everything?'

Superintendent Ryan listened to what Brody had to say, then told him to get everyone back to HQ for a unit meeting.

―――――

BRODY HAD a phone call to make. He made his way to his office, closed the door and sat behind his desk. He logged onto his computer, found the number he wanted, and dialled it using his desk phone. Brody felt sure he'd have to work at getting the person he wanted, follow a trail of telephone numbers until he eventually tracked him down.

But that wasn't what happened. When he dialled the number of the Paris Police Judiciaire and in his Leaving Cert French explained what he was after, he was told, *Oui, il est lá.* Pascal Dórea was there.

He was off to a good start. The gendarme transferred his call.

'*Bonjour,*' the voice on the other end of the line said.

Brody had never spoken to the famed criminal profiler before. It was Voyle who had always dealt with him in the past.

'My name is Sergeant Jack Brody, of An Garda Síochána, the Irish police.' He spoke in English.

'*Oui,*' Pascal Dórea began. Jack was grateful when he switched to English. 'Yes, Steven has told me about you.'

Brody wondered if he should thank him for speaking in English, but decided this might be a little patronising, so didn't.

'I'll get straight to the point, Mr Dórea...'

'Please, call me Pascal.'

'Thank you. Pascal, then. It's a follow-up to the profile you provided for Inspector Pierre Jousten of the Belgian Police. You remember?'

'Of course. The hotel killer.'

Jack outlined what had happened in Dublin, told him that the body parts found in the tunnels were being analysed, that he was awaiting results, and the debris in the tunnel had been removed to be sieved through at a secure location.

'It's just,' Jack said, 'none of this is making a lot of sense to me, that's all.'

Pascal Dórea was silent for a moment. Then: 'You don't believe he's down there, do you?'

If was as if Pascal Dórea was able to literally read his mind.

'In your profile, you said if his activities were discovered by the other gang members, the hotel killings, it would have serious consequences for him.'

'Yes, of course, they would kill him, no?'

'Exactly,' Brody said, 'that's why I was thinking, what if he got there first? What if he killed *them*?'

'Very plausible.'

There was the sound of fumbling. Brody imagined the profiler was taking a cigarette from a pack, then the sparking of a lighter, finally a long draw on a cigarette.

'Yes, very plausible indeed,' he said, exhaling. 'Anything is possible. Because he is able to read situations. He is acutely aware. He would be able to sense it very early on, any difficulty. You think this is what he has done. Clever.'

'We found a pubic hair, a DNA match to an Abraham Jackman, who killed his mother back in 2001, then disappeared. Ties in with your assessment of possible intimacy between the two.'

'I am aware of this information. It is available through Interpol. I'm impressed with your work.'

'Thank you. But he left that behind for us to find.'

'Then it would make sense.'

'What would?'

'His leaving it behind, yes. He may have wanted, how you say, some recognition. It is a common trait, this desire for recognition, one I am surprised did not manifest itself before now, although maybe it did and was missed.'

Brody heard the profiler take another long draw on his

cigarette, then breathe out the smoke again. It sounded like a wind blowing down the phone.

'And if he didn't,' Brody said, 'die, that is, in that explosion, what then? How can I find him, is what I want to know. Would you have any ideas? Before he uses the time we waste thinking he's dead to leave the country. Then it'll be too late; he'll simply disappear.'

'I do not know where he is, of course,' Doréa said, 'but I know what he will do. To me it is very obvious.'

'And what is that?'

'A woman. He will seek out a woman. This would be natural for him. His relationship with his mother defines him, no; it both nurtured and destroyed him. It is through this prism that he seeks all understanding.'

Brody thought about that.

'A woman.'

'Yes.'

'But how will he meet a woman in...' Brody fell silent. 'Aw, a sex worker, you mean?'

'*Oui*. The perfect solution for him.'

Yes, it was. It made sense. If Abraham Jackman was out there, he was holed up with a woman, a prostitute, someone he'd likely picked up literally off the streets. And that was where Brody needed to start. An unfortunate woman who'd soon be dead, Brody had no doubt. That is, if she wasn't dead already.

'One other question,' Brody said.

'*Oui*.'

'The pubic hair we found. Without it, we would never have known this person's identity. Would he really have risked it, and just for what, recognition?'

'Yes, of course. You must remember, you are not dealing with a normal person, no.'

Brody nodded. No, he was not dealing with a normal person. Everything that didn't make sense to him did make sense to this person. Like looking into a theme park mirror, everything stretched and distorted.

AN HOUR OR SO LATER, they were seated around a desk at the top of the unit room. There was Voyle, Marty, Considine, Brody and Superintendent Ryan.

'I'm waiting on results back from the doc,' Brody said. 'I'm working on the assumption that this Abraham Jackman character won't be one of the bodies down there. We'll see.'

'What?' Voyle said. 'You don't think he's one of them?' His eyes narrowed. 'Then why...oh, I get it, you think...shite, he blew it himself.'

'He's dangerous. Very dangerous.'

'Goes without saying, boss.'

'But I'm saying it anyway. I don't know what, maybe he doesn't know himself. I spoke with Pascal Dórea, your friend. That explosion, it was chaotic in a way, completely out of character for this crew. I think it's a cover. He's out there.'

Brody ran through the conversation he'd had with Pascal Dórea.

'A prostitute,' Considine said when he finished. 'Really?'

'Yes, really. That's what we think. A perverse sort of mother figure, Oedipus complex and all that. It makes sense when you think about it.'

He could see they were thinking about it. No one objected.

'Dublin isn't so much a city as a small town, when you know where to look,' Brody added. 'And, specifically, we're looking for a prostitute who's suddenly gone off radar.'

'He may not be out there.' It was Marty. 'He may've been killed in the tunnel.'

'Maybe.'

'Don't you think you need something a bit more to go on than that, boss?'

'Maybe,' Brody repeated, realising Marty might have incubated as a cop, but he was increasingly hatching as a legal eagle. Soon, the powers of analysis, reason and rationale would replace instinct and his cop's nose.

He'd be great down the Four Courts.

'Nicola,' Brody said, 'you're with me. Marty, with Steve. Everyone happy?'

'That's an existential question,' Marty said. 'I'd have to think about it.'

Superintendent Ryan cracked a grin.

'That's funny, Marty,' she said.

MASSAGE PARLOURS, brothels, housewives doing a bit on the side and, what a kerbside sign on Talbot Street called *Tantric Happy Endings Upstairs* – whatever that was about – were out. Brody wasn't interested. He was interested in the coalface of the city's illegal sex industry, those who walked the pavements or stood on street corners at the western end of the Quays or along Fitzwilliam and Merrion Squares or the Grand Canal off Leeson Street. Yes, Dublin could be very much a small town if you knew where to look.

When Brody and Considine arrived at Benburb Street

along the Quays, three women stood huddled together down from the main gate of what had once been the largest military barracks in Europe, known originally as the Royal Barracks. Following Irish independence, it became Collins barracks. Now it no longer was a barracks. Instead, it was part of the National Museum of Ireland. The area in the vicinity had once been the grittiest and grottiest of the city's red-light areas. Hundreds of soldiers going through it every day might have had something to do with that. Now it was becoming increasingly gentrified and hip, but the world's oldest profession still clung on.

'It's the day trade,' Considine said.

'Doesn't look much,' Brody answered. 'Business slow?'

'It's not what it once was down here. Yes, slow. Punters are going online too, sex cams, you know, stuff like that. And don't forget robots. Once they come along, well, can you imagine, boss?'

'Robots?'

'Yeah, robots. Sex robots.'

'How come you know so much about sex robots?'

She winked. 'How come you don't?'

He opened the door and got out of the car.

The three women began quickly moving away.

'Girls,' Considine called, 'we're the guards. And we'd like a word. Come back here now. Don't have me chase you. Come on.'

THERE WAS a ferry sailing to France every evening at 7 p.m. from Rosslare harbour in County Wexford. Tyler planned to be on the one sailing the next evening. Failing that, at the very latest, the one the evening following that. He felt overcome by a strange sense of freedom. Like that time when he'd run into the woods after killing Momma. He'd run for what seemed a full day without ever stopping. He was sure he had stopped sometime, but it felt like he hadn't, and he could never remember having done so. He'd just run and, with each stride, had never felt so completely, utterly and wonderfully free, for the first time in his entire short life. When dawn broke the following day, he walked across a dry brook bed into the United States of America.

It was that easy. He made it to Buffalo that night, and the next day he was eating hotdogs from a cart along the East River in New York City. Quite a feat for a fourteen-year-old, but then again, he was no ordinary fourteen-year-old. He realised very quickly that cops rarely bothered a fourteen-year-old. You just had to have your story straight and always look innocent: *My mom's waiting for me in the mall car park, officer...*Of course, being a good-looking white kid, well dressed and polite – always polite, that was important – you could get away with virtually anything. He got taken under the wing of a Hispanic gang in Washington Heights. They weren't much older than him. They gave him a place to stay and fed him – but for a price. He ran drugs for two years and then sold drugs on the drugs supermarket that was Amsterdam Avenue. Like a lot of the drug dealers on the avenue, it paid his way through college. Until he'd dropped out, that is. Not that he had any regrets about that. He didn't.

Abraham strode onto the sales yard and stopped next to the two-axle RV.

A salesperson appeared almost instantaneously.

'Hello, sir, how can I help you today?'

'I'd like to look at that,' he replied, pointing to the motorhome.

'Hm, oh yes, the Dethleffs Globetrotter. A beautiful example of...'

'You take cash?' Abraham interrupted.

'Cash.' The salesman coughed, a nervous reflex, not a reflex to clear his throat. 'Well now...' But he didn't sound too certain.

'That's okay,' Tyler said, 'don't worry, I can try somewhere else. Sorry to have bothered you. Thing is, I just sold my old one, private sale. Cash. I wasn't going to say no, was I? I'm actually on my way to the bank to lodge it right now, if I can make it in time, that is. I was passing, saw this...a Dethleffs Globetrotter, eh.' He nodded to the camper. 'Nice. Probably better off not buying right now anyway, best not to be too hasty, eh?' He made to turn away.

'Um, one moment. Your accent,' the salesman said, 'I can't place it?'

Tyler had been trying to play it down, inflecting it with just enough of what he thought was an Irish brogue.

'My accent? Well, Galway's where I was born and reared. But I spent some years in the good old U S of A. New York.'

The salesman smiled, a car salesman's smile, stretching from one ear to the other but never reaching his eyes. 'I was going to say, cash. Well, that's no problem.' And smiled again.

Tyler felt an almost irresistible urge to wipe that smile off his fucking face.

'Cash is king, as they say,' the salesman said, 'and if you won't say anything, then neither will I.'

'Oh, you don't have to worry about that. I just want that

beauty. I won't say anything either. Now, can I have a quick look, see how that baby works?'

'Of course. Certainly. This way.' The salesman gestured towards the vehicle and smiled that soulless smile of his.

'Youse ar' too early, love, biznis doesn't pick up 'til around night-time, yeah, especially when da pubs close.'

Voyle and Marty were standing on Fitzwilliam Square, at its centre a gated green area surrounded by red-brick Georgian townhouses long converted into offices and high-end medical and dental practices. Swish cars were parked against the kerb. The woman was standing, pressing herself in against the wrought-iron fence, as if seeking to hide beneath the overhanging branches of a large tree there.

They had just introduced themselves and had assured her they had no interest in her street-side activities. That was not why they were here.

'But I'm curious?' Marty said, 'if there's no business, why are you here?'

''Cause,' she said, 'you'll always git some auld john, so youse will. Suits me fine. I don't like da night. What's it youse want, love? Youse are gettin' in da way of what biznis der is. And' – she nodded vaguely towards the buildings opposite – 'they don't like da attention. Wha' ya lookin' for?'

'That's just it,' Voyle said, 'we're not really sure what we're looking for. Let's start with this, how about if you know of any girl not showing up lately.'

'Ya mean missin'? Dat wha' yer sayin'? Is one of da girls missin'?'

'Maybe,' Marty said. 'I don't know.'

'C'mere till I tell ya, youse don't know much, do youse, love? Missin' since when?'

'Yesterday.' It was Voyle.

'Ah Jaysis, sure dat's no time at all. Maybe she's gone on da gargle. I go off on it meself too sometime.'

'Do you know if anyone's missing or not,' Marty said, 'even in that timeframe?'

She cocked her head to one side. 'I heard alright wan of the udder girls mention yesterday dat she was 'upposed ta meet a girl who she owed money ta. But the other girl didn't show up ta collect it. If I'm owed money, I'd show, so I would.'

'You know who this person who never showed is?' Voyle asked.

'Nah, but Chrissy will, dat's da udder girl's name. I can give her a call if youse want?'

'Yes,' Voyle said, 'I would; that would be great, thanks.'

She held out her hand. 'Not on my bleedin' phone, I won't. I've no credit.'

'Oh.' Voyle looked at Marty, who suddenly seemed very interested in looking at his shoes.

Voyle sighed, reached into his pocket and took out his own personal phone, handed it over. She scratched inside one nostril with an index finger, then punched in the number onto the keypad with the same finger, pressed the phone to the side of her face.

When she finished, she said, 'Her name's Margy, lives in da Basin Flats. Youse know where dat is, yeah? And she didn't show up down at Sister Clancy's for her dinner. Ya know Sister Clancy's? She does da fifty-cent dinners on da North Strand. Chrissy says Margy has never missed her dinner der. Ever.'

'The Basin Flats,' Marty said, 'they the ones in Inchicore?'

'Yeah, da top floor, don't ask me which wan. Chrissy don't know neither. Something's up alright, if youse ask me. Chrissy owes *her* bleedin' money. We'se all show up when owed money, don't we'se?'

'Yes,' Voyle said, 'I suppose we do.' But not having ever owed anyone money, he didn't really know. 'Now, what's *your* name? You never gave us that. And your telephone number too, thank you.'

Her name was Bridget McCann. He wrote it along with her telephone number into his notebook.

'My phone,' Voyle said then, 'and we'll be on our way.'

'D' I not give it back ta ya, love?'

'No, you didn't.'

'Must'a slipped me mind.' She handed it over. 'Silly me. Sorry, love.'

Voyle gingerly took it, put it in his pocket.

He thanked Bridget McCann for her help, and he and Voyle returned to their car.

As they did, Brody and Considine were heading back to the Phoenix Park. The state phone rang. Considine was driving, so Brody answered. It was Dr McBain.

'My secretary said you rang. Jesus, Brody, I've told you before, you watch too much *CSI: Miami*. It doesn't work like that. It takes time. How many times have I...?'

'And I told you, I don't watch *CSI: Miami*, or any other CSI, for that matter.'

'Don't get lippy with me, me lad.'

'Have you anything?'

'Four bodies. That's what's down there. Three with heads, one without. That answer your question?'

Brody was silent.

'Yes, in case you're wondering, Jack. You heard me right, four bodies, three...'

'Yes, yes, three with heads, one without. Well, and where are the heads?'

'Oh, here and there. The angle of the explosion, the compacted environment increased the shock wave, with the neck really not standing a chance; the head in each case was simply plucked off. Very interesting, I must say, from an anatomical standpoint. I can see myself presenting a tutorial on this in the near future. And before you ask, samples did return matches on the Interpol database. Hair and blood samples found, returned for this Abraham Jackman you're interested in. The other three pinged as...'

Brody was silent again. Shite, it seemed Abraham Jackman had been down there after all. He was dead. 'This is a lot to take in,' he said. 'Can I ring you back?'

'You can do what you want, but it doesn't mean you'll get me.'

'I'll take my chances, just a couple of minutes, okay?'

The phone went dead as the doc hung up.

Brody listened to the sounds of road noise from outside.

'He's down there?' Considine said. 'Like for real, Abraham Jackman?'

'Seems like it.'

'In that case, doesn't that mean our suspect is dead?'

'Seems like it,' Brody said again, as if in a daze, feeling the wheels of this investigation begin to spin in the mud, going nowhere.

THE DETHLEFFS GLOBETROTTER was what you'd expect for €85,000, every last euro of it. Abraham had handed the money over in a paper bag he'd found at the whore's flat. The salesman counted it out, and Abraham noticed, as he bent over the cash, a tattoo on the back of his neck. Teardrops. Interesting. Teardrop tattoos usually signified the person had taken a life. One teardrop, one life. It usually went beneath the eye. But that wasn't a hard and fast rule. Seeing it reassured Abraham. He felt confident this man was part of the international brotherhood of businessmen, just like him, who choose to make their money from nefarious means: the gangsters, the thieves, the killers. A second-hand car business offered a perfect cover for laundering cash. Yes indeed, no wonder this man had taken the cash; his initial reticence, Abraham guessed, just a ploy to reinforce the illusion of being a legitimate businessman.

As Abraham stepped out of the portacabin that served as a sales office, they both exchanged a look, a knowing look, both the keepers of secrets. There was nothing that made it more certain that a person would keep a secret than knowing they had a secret themselves. They both could sense it in the other.

Abraham walked away, and the portacabin door closed, as if he'd never even been there in the first place.

THE DETHLEFFS GLOBETROTTER drove smoothly and virtually without sound. Tyler would drive it all the way to the south of Spain and arrive as fresh as when he'd first sat into it.

These Irish roads were not suitable for such a wide and long vehicle. Once he got onto the continental roads, he could set the cruise control, and this baby would almost drive itself. He negotiated the access road into an industrial estate just down from the flats complex where the whore had lived. He wasn't going to draw attention by driving it into the flats complex itself. Anyway, to do that would be like tying a goat to a pole in a field full of coyotes. Even here, in this industrial area, mightn't be too safe either. But he wouldn't be here long. He only had to collect the bag of used notes and the other stuff, the jewellery and gems, that was all. The gems and jewellery he would conceal in the roof cavity, while the bag of cash would remain with him. He would place it, open, on the co-pilot's seat beside him, a shirt or some other items of clothing on top. A framed photo would be placed on the wide dash, facing the door, his face photoshopped onto the body of a family man with an attractive wife and kids. It would be the first thing any official would see if they came snooping around. On the other side, at the port of Calais in France, he would offer up his passport as he drove through the green channel. It should warrant nothing more than a customary, even disinterested inspection, and even if it did warrant more, one glance at that photo on the dash was usually enough. Then it would be *Continuez*, maybe with a doff of the hat. Although the egalitarian French rarely engaged in such deference.

'HER NAME IS MARGY, boss; she didn't show up to collect some money she was owed.'

'Address?'

'Basin Flats. Inchicore, nothing else.'

'Could be nothing else too,' Brody said. He thought about it. Then, 'Swing by and take a look, will you?'

'We're already on our way there,' Marty said.

'On second thoughts, where exactly are you?'

'The top of Camden Street.'

'We're much closer, Parkgate Street, at the junction for our turn-off. Inchicore is only ten minutes away. Basin Flats, yeah?'

'That's the one.'

'We'll look after it, Marty, okay?' Brody noted the time on the digital dash, almost 6 p.m. 'You and Steve head home. You can stay on the clock until ten o'clock. Just make sure you answer your phones if I ring.'

'You're a fair man, boss, you know that?'

'Would you be saying that if I wasn't telling you that you could stay on the overtime clock?'

'Aw now, boss, what kind of question is that? What do you think yourself like? Of course not.'

Brody laughed. It was good to laugh, and he terminated the call.

He replaced the phone back into its cradle.

'Inchicore,' he said to Considine.

'I heard.'

'Which way is quicker, you think?' he asked. 'About-turn and go over the bridge, or straight on and cut through Ballyfermot?'

'About-turn, unless...I give it a little pinch of the blues and twos, and we cut straight ahead.'

'Give it a little pinch there, Nicola.'

THREE CARS BEHIND, Mandy Joyce moved as close to the vehicle in front as was possible. Any closer and the encounter would be classed as intimate. She could see the driver eyeing her in the rear-view. It was an elderly man, she was relieved to see. A young fella might be unpredictable, give her the finger, or worse still, hop out and give her the silverback gorilla chest-slapping routine. Young fellas were too quick now for all that. But this old codger's road-rage days were well behind him. She gave a reassuring smile and raised her hand in a *oops, sorry about that* gesture. The man reverted his eyes to the road ahead. Mandy could almost hear him praying for the lights to change.

But then she saw lights, and they weren't those she'd been waiting for. It was the unmarked, with Brody and Considine in it, up ahead. The blue lights inside the back window had started flashing, and there was a loud, piercing *whoop* sound. Just one, and then the Focus was moving out of the line of traffic, the vehicles in the next lane bulging into the oncoming to facilitate it.

And then it took off.

What the fuck is happening?

Mandy could only stare as the unmarked Focus cleared the junction and sped off ahead, to Timbuktu for all she knew.

Shit, shit, shit.

The light up ahead was still on red. Then it changed to green, but the car in front with the old codger driving hardly moved. *For fuck's sake.* She leaned on the horn. The car moved now, but very slowly. She'd had enough, swung the steering wheel of the Clio and nudged into the next lane. It was her turn to be the source of other drivers' irritation. She ignored the chorus of honking horns, pushed her way into the lane, and joined the flow of traffic moving ahead.

TYLER CLOSED the flat door behind him and walked quickly along the balcony towards the stairwell. He wore a baseball hat pulled low over his eyes. He met no one, saw no curtains twitching. The bag of cash was slung from his right shoulder, the gems and jewellery in a cloth bag he'd found in the whore's flat, hanging from his left shoulder. He went down the stairs and out, turned right along the pathway leading to the road. At the corner, just as he reached the road, on the other side of which was the industrial warehouse where the camper was parked, he saw a car turn sharply into the flats complex. He turned as it passed, like he was glancing behind him, as if someone had called his name, but his eyes followed the car, noticing the two occupants, the male passenger, but his view of the driver was obscured. A cop car, he could almost smell it. He reached the corner and paused, looked back. The car was moving slowly in front of the flats. He saw it stop before the block next to the one where the whore had lived. The doors opened, and the occupants got out. Abraham felt a sharp tingling sensation in his belly and gulped.

It was her. The California babe cop from the press conference. He couldn't believe it. He watched her walk round the back of the car and stand on the pavement next to her colleague, hands clamped onto her waist above two perfectly shaped hips, the same windbreaker she had worn at the press conference riding up to reveal a perfectly shaped butt. There was only one word for this woman:

Exquisite.

'I want you,' he muttered. 'I want you so bad.'

He glanced to her colleague, a little taller than she was, but he reckoned they both were over six feet. The colleague was tough looking, firm build, no excess, tight haircut. He reminded Abraham of the SEALs who'd come into San Diego from the Naval Special Warfare Centre in Coronado when he lived in that part of California for a time. This SEAL type had an air about him, a fluidity of movement, a presence. It wouldn't be a good idea to mess with this dude.

Abraham turned and walked to the kerb, waited for a break in the traffic, and lumbered across the road towards the industrial park.

THEY SWUNG into the Basin Flats from Kylemore Way. Considine slowed the Focus. There were four blocks of flats to their left.

'Now what?' she said.

Brody looked in his door mirror. There was a man a little back they'd passed, a bag slung from each shoulder. Too late to ask if he knew anything about Margy. The man began walking towards the Kylemore Road.

Considine pulled in and parked in front of the second block.

'Anyone ring the local station and enquire if they know Margy who lives in the Basin Flats?' Considine asked. 'Seems like a good idea.'

'It does,' Brody agreed, opening the door and getting out; when Considine was standing next to him, he added, 'We'll do that next.'

They stood looking about. Brody noticed a shop further down the street, right next to the fourth and last block, a wire mesh security grille over its windows, a bunker containing bags of coal in front, and next to it a metal cage with yellow cylinders of gas inside. He nodded.

'Let's try there first.'

Little shops like this existed in all deprived areas of the city. A place where groceries could be obtained on the 'tic', entered into a ledger, and paid for later, usually when the social welfare money was collected once a week. Places like this were indispensable in a place like this.

It was gloomy inside. A Perspex screen stretched all the way along in front of the counter. Behind it sat a white-haired man in a plaid shirt and cardigan. Brody was surprised. He'd expected someone younger, maybe ink on his arms, possibly a shaved head, a don't-mess-with-me attitude. You'd need someone like that around here. The man was sitting on a stool and didn't get up.

When Brody spoke, the man said, 'I can't hear you. Speak up. And into the holes. There.' He pointed.

Brody noticed then a cluster of holes drilled into the Perspex at about head height. He bent slightly to speak into them.

'We're looking for a woman called Margy,' he said.

'And who're you? The guards?'

'Yes, the guards.' Brody made to reach into an inside pocket of his jacket.

'I don't need to see your card,' the man said, 'or whatever it is you have there. I have enough to be looking at. And you can tell Margy she owes me for the cornflakes and bread she got a couple of mornings back when you see her. Will you tell her that?'

'And your name is?' Brody asked.

'William Finnerty. It's over the door. Didn't you see it?'

'Look, Mr Finnerty, this Margy. Can I just try to narrow it down a bit? See if she's the one we're looking for?'

'I'd say it is, alright. You wouldn't be the first. Margy, the prostitute, that the one? There's not many of them about.'

The old man said it without expression or emotion, Margy the prostitute, like Margy the nurse, or Margy the cook. Just a fact, like the name over the door, or the price of tomatoes...Not that he had any tomatoes; Brody couldn't see any.

Brody exchanged a glance with Considine.

'Where exactly does she live, Margy?'

'Block three, just down from here. The very top floor, end flat along the balcony. Great views.' The old man scoffed. 'Me shit there is.'

BRODY KNOCKED ON THE DOOR. When he got no reply, he banged. The door of the next-door flat opened; an old lady, a *very* old lady, fragile as a small bird, poked her head out.

'What's all the commotion?' Her voice no more than a whisper. Brody had trouble hearing her.

'Sorry for troubling you; we're looking for Margy.'

'Margy who?'

'Margy,' Brody said, 'who lives in here.'

'Does she?'

'That's alright, love,' Considine said, stepping over. 'You go on inside where it's warm, and we'll try to keep the noise down.'

The old dear looked at them fearfully, then stepped back inside her flat.

'You'd better,' she said, 'or my Bobby will see to yez when he comes home from work.'

She went in, and the door closed softly.

'I'll see if I can't get someone over from the corporation asap to open this door,' Considine said, already scrolling through her phone for the number.

By the time someone at the corporation could find someone with a key, twenty minutes had passed. That someone had already clocked off work and had to go back to the depot to collect it. Brody had no choice but to wait, because summoning a car from Ballyfermot to have someone with a great big key attend would have taken as long. The door to the flat was too secure to kick in.

IT WAS ALMOST as if fate had intervened. He truly believed that. Like it had intervened in the past. He hadn't intended to kill Momma, or Khabib for that matter, or Clyde or Lisbeth. He hadn't intended to run into the forest. He hadn't intended to end up in New York. He hadn't...and on and on. Fate had led him on a wild ride to this very point now. It had looked after him, cared for him, given him everything he had ever wanted and more, so much more. He almost laughed. His bag of cash alone was the equivalent of a small country's budget. Fate had spoiled him. He trusted fate.

And now it had sent him – her. California babe. Could he resist it? Dare he resist it?

His plan – roughly, because he didn't really make plans – was to lie low and make the ferry crossing tomorrow night.

By the time they finally realised his body was not, in fact, down there, he'd be in the south of Spain. All that would be left behind was a conundrum of epic fucking proportions, a fertile ground for conspiracy theories and endless real-life crime dramas. He liked the idea of that.

That was his plan.

That had been his plan.

But then she had driven past.

He knew where she was.

At this very moment.

Fate, you make it impossible to resist.

You always have.

I don't really have a say in any of this, do I?

THE MAN from the corporation wasn't happy.

'I was just about to have me bleedin' dinner when I got the call. Had to go back to the bleedin' depot and then out to here. She's probably gone off for a couple of days, won't be happy to have you two ploddin' about her gaff.'

'Just open the door,' Brody said, 'good man.'

'What d'ya think I'm tryin' to do. Aw, there you go.' He pushed it open. 'En-bloody-tray.'

Brody was about to lead the way in when he realised he'd made what could be a fatal mistake. He stopped. Suppose Jackman was in here? They were defenceless. Neither he nor Considine was armed. But then Brody thought that if he was in here, they'd probably already be dead. Made sense. Jackman wouldn't have observed any niceties. Brody was satisfied – as far as he could be – that the man wasn't here.

'How long will yiz be?' the corporation man wanted to know. He was trailing behind Brody and Considine as they entered the flat. Brody went into a bedroom. The blankets were disturbed on one side of the double bed. There was a smell in the air, a masculine smell. No surprises there, considering Margy's profession. But this was fresh, and it was the only scent; there was no feminine trace to indicate Margy's presence.

'Boss, in here.'

The corporation man, who was behind Brody, stepped out of the room. Brody crossed to the bathroom where Considine was. He heard the corporation man following, muttering to himself.

Brody stood in the doorway, looking at the body lying in the bath, waxen and deathly grey, staring at the ceiling with frozen, glassy eyes.

'Jeez,' the corporation man squealed, 'is she dead?'

Brody didn't answer. He'd let the corporation man work that one out for himself.

BRODY CLOSED THE DOOR, making sure the latch was off so they wouldn't have to summon the corporation man again. While he rang it in from the balcony outside, Considine went down to get the crime scene tape from the car.

NICOLA OPENED the boot and pulled up the floor cover. The roll of crime scene tape was in a compartment next to the spare wheel. She grabbed it and lifted it out, was about to close the boot again.

'Detective Garda Nicola Considine.'

She slammed the boot shut and swung round.

'Yeah, that's me; who's askin'?'

'Special Constable Dwight Harper, Royal Canadian Mounted Police. Can I have a word?'

Nicola took in the man standing before her, about five ten tall, she guessed, good build, Hollywood good looks with a smile to match.

'Special Constable what? Royal Canadian Mounted Police? Where'd the feck you pop out of?'

He pointed to behind him. 'Assistant Commissioner Kelly is over there. We need you to move away from here immediately. You're compromising the entire operation.'

'What operation?' She looked up. 'And Brody's up there.'

'We know. Please, the suspect will be here at any moment. You must move...'

Considine's mind whirred. Who was she to compromise an operation? It was typical she hadn't been told. Nor Brody.

'Now. Please. Come with me. He'll be here any moment. The suspect.'

He jogged a little way ahead and stopped. 'Come on, please.'

'Okay, okay.' Explanations could be sorted out later, she thought. She followed, forgetting to close the boot.

About twenty minutes before, Mandy Joyce had thought she saw something that looked like the unmarked Brody was travelling in turning to the left. It was way up ahead. She still had two sets of lights to work through before she reached the turn-off point. When she reached it, she cursed. There were, in fact, three left turns, all in close proximity to each other: one to the Basin Flats, one leading to a garage forecourt with a tyre shop behind it, and the last running along by a row of bungalows, which looked like sheltered housing of some sort. It could be any one of these three roads. Which one? She'd already passed the turn-off for the Basin Street flats before she'd realised and now hastily turned into the garage forecourt. She crossed it and went along by the tyre shop behind. There was no sign of Brody's car. She came back out again, parked by the shop and got out, walked over to the wall and looked over it along the roadway running in front of the bungalows. The car wasn't there either. Damn. Mandy went back to her car and drove out and started back towards the city. She had to go back almost into Inchicore again before she could get into the other lane, swinging round a roundabout and heading back out.

Fuck, this was going to take forever.

The road dipped as it went down the incline into the flats before levelling out again. She looked ahead, but she couldn't see the car. Was this a complete waste of time? It was then Mandy felt the adrenaline rush she'd been riding begin to leave her, like a wave crashing to shore and the water receding back out to sea. She stopped in the middle of the road, closed her eyes, her hands gripping the steering wheel, feeling like she wanted to cry. *No, no, no,* she told herself, *pull yourself together. Not now.*

She opened her eyes again, took a breath, and drove on, her right foot involuntarily twitching against the accelerator pedal, her hands trembling on the steering wheel. She took another breath, then another, and yet another. It was starting to get dark outside. She concentrated on turning on the headlights, thinking that she hadn't had the car serviced in ages, distracting herself, calming herself. It worked.

And then she saw it. Or so she thought. A little way ahead. Was that the car? The one Brody had been in. Unless they were high-end models, cars were all the same to Mandy, but this one looked like the one. And it was missing its hubcaps. She could swear the car he'd been in was missing its hubcaps too. And the colour was right, green. The boot was open, but there was no one about.

From the corner of her eye, she saw a couple moving quickly along the street away from it. She pulled in and looked back. It was one of Brody's team, the tall blonde. Considine, that was it, always wore jeans and boots and a windbreaker with GARDA written on the back. Yes, that was her. She looked at the one with her. A man. Not Brody, that was immediately obvious. She noted the way he was not quite alongside her, yet close enough that he seemed to be herding her before him without her even knowing it.

What was going on there? Mandy could sense it. Something was not right.

AT THE TOP of the road from the flats, the Mountie came alongside her.

'Almost there,' he said. 'Just the other side of this road here.'

She followed him across the Kylemore Road into an industrial compound, where he pointed without breaking stride to what looked like a fancy camper van.

'The command centre. That's it.'

They reached it, and he flew up the steps, flung open the door and stood just inside.

'Detective Garda Considine is here,' he called out.

She went in and looked along his outstretched arm to the top of the vehicle.

'Kelly will explain everything to you,' he said. 'He's right there.'

She looked. And blinked. AC Kelly wasn't there. No one was there. She and the Mountie were the only two people here. Mountie?

It suddenly dawned on her how odd this was. She hadn't even asked for his ID. Nor had he offered it either.

'Fuck,' she said, realising she'd made a mistake, a very big mistake.

And then she felt something nudge her sharply into the back of both her knees, breaking her posture, sending her sprawling to the floor.

Her cheek was flat against the carpet. It smelled of pine and talc.

'You don't surf, huh?' he said, standing over her. 'You made that easier than expected. If you did, you would have rolled with it. Listen up, make a move, and I'll kill you, got it?'

Considine turned her eyes upward, her face flat against the carpet, said nothing. Then she saw it, a piece, a proper piece, a semi-automatic she guessed, with a silencer attached, just like Shisha had described.

'Got it?' he repeated. 'I want you to say it.'

Considine said nothing. She wouldn't give the bastard the pleasure.

SOC OFFICERS from Kilmainham station arrived at the same time as the technical bureau. The bureau was based at Garda HQ and served the whole country. They had arrived within ten minutes. Brody had often to wait twenty-four hours for them to arrive when down country. He was about to take up the offer of a hazmat suit from one of the technics, Andrea Wilson was her name, when she asked casually, 'You on your own?'

Brody took the plastic-wrapped suit.

'No, I'm waiting on Nicola Considine. She went down to get the crime scene tape. She must have found a witness or something.'

'I didn't see her down there. You driving a Focus, green?'

'Yes.'

'The boot's open.'

'It is?'

'It is.'

Brody dropped the hazmat suit and ran along the balcony towards the stairs.

CONSIDINE WAS FEELING a lot of things, scared, stupid, naive, but more than anything, really fucking angry.

'Go fuck yourself,' she spat, spittle literally falling from her mouth.

'Feisty, aren't you,' he said. 'I didn't expect that. I thought you'd be a lot more...I don't know, docile. I'm not sure how I feel about it. You hear me? I don't know how I fucking feel about it.' He stepped back, swung his leg and kicked her savagely in the side. She felt the pain rip through her, but she didn't scream, she wouldn't scream, *she wouldn't scream.*

She clamped her mouth shut and braced for the next one. But it didn't come.

Instead, she felt her arms being yanked behind her back and duct tape starting to be wound round and round her wrists.

'You're not like the others,' he said. 'No. You're more like Momma.' He came round and stood in front of her, kneeled down and peered intently into her eyes. 'Aren't you, more like dear old Momma?' He touched her cheek lightly. 'But so much prettier. I thought up close you mightn't be. But you are, you're even prettier. In fact, you're beautiful...Momma.'

His eyes seemed to float about in his head, Considine thought, yet not seeming to move at the same time, staring into hers; strange eyes, greyish black, like a wolf's. He raised the corner of his mouth into a half grimace, half smile, clenched his fist and started to bring it down onto the top of her head. She turned her head away, bracing for the impact. But he didn't punch her. Instead, he tapped hard on her head a couple of times. He laughed.

'What? You in there, Momma? Eh, are you? In there? You're just never going to leave me, are you?' He grabbed her hair savagely and pulled. 'Get up.'

It felt like boiling water had been poured over her head as Considine got to her feet. But she didn't scream, *she wouldn't scream.*

He pushed her roughly in the centre of her back. 'Get in there.'

It was a bedroom, and she fell onto the bed. And then he was winding duct tape around her ankles. He folded her legs back and wound the duct tape between her ankles and neck, trussing her so that it was impossible to move. Finally, he wound the duct tape around her mouth, then cut it and tossed the roll onto the floor.

'Momma, you're never going to give me any peace, are you now? There's only one answer to that, Momma. Later, okay, later...'

He stepped away, and Considine heard the bedroom door bang shut. She was no longer angry now. She was too afraid to be angry. Now she feared for her very life.

She heard the engine start, and felt the camper begin to move, swaying gently as it turned in a complete circle. It travelled forward and stopped. She could hear traffic. The camper swung right and moved ahead, building up speed. They'd left the industrial compound, she felt certain, and were driving along the Kylemore Road.

Oh, sweet Jesus, please help me.

BRODY RACED from the apartment block and reached the Focus. He stood, looking all about. There was no sign of her. He got on the phone and rang her number. It went to answering machine. He didn't leave a message. He looked all around, desperate.

Where the hell was Considine?

'SHE WENT THAT WAY.'

The voice came from towards the back of the Focus. Brody looked as Mandy Joyce walked between the Focus and the orange Renault Clio parked there.

She pointed ahead towards the Kylemore Road.

'She was with someone. They looked to be in a hurry.'

'With someone? With who?'

'A man, never saw him before. I don't know. Funny thing, he was just behind her, but he seemed to be leading her...if that makes any sense.'

Brody jumped into the Focus. Shit, the keys weren't in the ignition. Of course, Considine would have taken them with her.

Wait, he told himself. There had to be a good reason for her to take off like that. But what? Maybe an accident on the road outside, someone looking for help? Somehow it didn't sound like it. He rang her phone again. And again, no answer.

Yes, there was a good reason for this, but he felt sure it was a bad good reason.

'I want your car,' he said, 'alright?'

Mandy was excited by the turn of events. 'Of course,' she said. 'But I'm going with you.'

Another's misfortune was her opportunity, after all.

THEY DROVE for what seemed like forever, but Considine knew for much of that time they were idling in traffic. The camper slowed and turned to the left sharply. She felt it rise and fall gently; she imagined it was going over a speed bump. Then it moved smoothly up through the gears. After a while she heard seagulls squawking and a ship's horn blowing, somewhere nearby, the sound seeming to shake the very air itself. They had to be close to Dublin Port. She knew security was tight here – very tight, so she calculated they were not in the port itself, but very close to it. The camper stopped, and the engine died.

For a moment it was deathly silent before she heard his footsteps approaching. The door opened. He smiled and stepped over to the bed. He pushed her so that she was lying on her side, facing him.

'Momma, you only understand one thing, don't you? No use being gentle with you, Momma. That was my mistake. Maybe this time you'll get the message. I don't love you, Momma, you hear. I don't love you.'

He reached down and gripped her arm tightly, flopping her onto her back. He took from a pocket a shiny rectangle of metal, flicked a finger against the side of it, and a blade extended from the top. A flick knife.

Considine saw him extend his arm. So this was how it would end for her. Here on this bed, in this fancy camper. He leaned forward, resting his knees onto the bed, and she felt the blade touch the side of her neck, nothing more than a mere kiss. Then she watched as he swung the blade up, catching the light as it did so, and glinting. He began to bring it down, and she screamed, the sound nothing more than a muffled croak from behind the duct tape. She closed her eyes and braced herself, waiting for it to tear through her flesh and into her body...

BUT IT NEVER DID. Instead, she felt it cutting through her windbreaker, ripping the material down the centre, the same with the plaid shirt she had on underneath. She snapped open her eyes and saw him popping the buttons of her jeans, pulling open her belt. He gripped the knife with his teeth and began tugging on her jeans. They began to slide down over her hips, over her thighs. He yanked them down until they were around her knees.

He stood back and began unbuckling his belt.

Oh dear God. Oh God. Please. Not that. Please, please, not that, anything but that...

THE LITTLE ORANGE Renault seemed to have an engine problem; it was losing power and could barely keep up with traffic. Brody realised he was wasting time. He wasn't thinking straight. He was panicking, that was what he was doing. And he couldn't afford to panic. Not now.

Considine was gone, and he hadn't a clue where she was.

He pulled the car in against the side of the road and stopped, squeezing the steering wheel like it was a living thing that he wanted to kill, feeling his nails digging into his palms underneath.

He fought against an almost overwhelming desire to howl in sheer frustration.

'It's probably nothing,' Mandy said. 'Are you listening?'

He released the steering wheel and sat back. 'Yes, I'm listening.'

'But just a moment ago, before you came out, I saw a camper van emerge onto the Kylemore Road opposite the flats. There's industrial warehouses or something in there. A real fancy motorhome. Probably a coincidence. But it was about the same time. Just sayin'.'

Brody angled his head at her as if coming out of a trance.

'A camper van.' He focused on that information. It was rational. It could be something. It *could*.

'Okay. Tell me while I ring it through. What was it like? It can't be hard to find. A fancy one, you say.'

'Yeah, like those big American yokes. Not many of those about, I'd say.'

'No,' Brody agreed, not many of those about at all. This was worth looking into.

CONSIDINE WAS SO scared she could hardly breathe. Nothing had ever made her feel this way before. Nothing. Not high-on-coke knife-wielding gougers, not armed robbers, not blood-filled syringe-wielding junkies, not drunks twice her size trying to grab her or punch her in the face.

She felt his hands on her, turning her over onto her belly like she was a cloth doll. She was still trussed up, her legs pinned up behind her, ankles taped together to her neck. She tried to see behind her but couldn't. He cut her legs free, and they flopped onto the bed, then he quickly pushed them wide apart. She felt the blade cut through her knickers and his hand pull these away. She was utterly exposed. She tried to kick out, but he slapped her hard across the face. She saw that he was naked, and felt a hot hand on her buttocks. She wanted to recoil, and he slapped her across the face again, harder this time, dazing her. Then she felt a finger slip inside her, but not into her vagina, instead into her anus.

His other hand moved across her buttocks. Considine blinked back the tears. He took his finger out of her, and both his hands suddenly seized the cheeks of her buttocks in a painful grip, the thumbs pulling aside her arse cheeks.

Oh, sweet Jesus no, please, no...

'Momma, you dirty little bitch...'

She felt him against her anus. *GOD! Please. NO!*
'Move away, you sick bastard. Leave her alone.'
Considine heard the voice. A female voice, sounded like. Or could it be him altering his voice, playing with her? She detected a faint aroma, a delicate, expensive perfume. The same voice spoke again.
'Stop, I said. Leave her alone. Now!'
There is someone else in the camper! In the room!
'Turn her onto her side.'
What's happening?
'Why?' she heard him say.
'Just do it!'
Considine felt his hands fumbling on her; they were clammy. He placed her onto her side like the voice had told him to, and now she could see the other person. It was a woman, who stepped away from the door further into the room. She was petite and beautiful, very beautiful, wearing a loose-fitting jumpsuit. Considine noticed a small mole by her right eye. In her right hand she held a small, stub-nosed pistol.
The man spoke, and Considine could hear it, the unmistakeable fear.
'Chi Chu? How the hell did you get here?'
'A tracker app, bitch, bargain basement at that. You think someone wasn't hovering around on every job you've been on. Like we trust *you*? No, bitch.'
'Look, Chi Chu, this is not what you think.'
'This is not what I think, is it? Don't tell me what I'm thinking, you sick fucker. Get over by the window. Move.'
'Look, Khabib was going to kill me. You know that. Is that why you're here? I know he was going to kill me…I had to do it…don't you see…I had to. I had no choice. Who sent

you, God, was it? Please. You and me, Chi Chu. Like old times. We walk away. Come on, we go wherever you want, anywhere you want. Just you and me, Chi Chu, what do you say?'

She scoffed. 'You idiot. You think you can escape God. Come on. And tell me, what about her?'

Chi Chu pointed the gun at Considine, then back to him again.

'What about her? She's a nobody, that's what. Just shoot her. I'll skip my fun. We just walk, like I say.'

'Skip the fun? It's kinda different to the other fun you like, isn't it? The fun like in Paris? And London. Valencia. I could go on. And what's this *momma* shit I hear you on about? You were saying it just now. Like for real, you were going to do it to her *that* way? Oh, you sick fucker.'

'Look, I've got a problem.' He tapped a finger against his temple. 'It's in here.'

'It's been in there a while is what I hear. Bit late for that, *Abraham*, honey.'

Chi Chu never referred to him as Tyler.

'What's that mean? I can get it sorted. I told you. It's just some weird childhood shit. You know my story, don't you? I mean, it's tragic. I just need to sort it out, that's all.'

'It's tragic alright, I'll grant you. But we all got our own stories.'

'Look, can I put on some clothes? I'm naked here.'

'That didn't bother you a moment ago.'

'Well, can I?'

'Get over by the window and bend, with your hands against the bottom of the glass. Do it.'

'Why? What're you going to do?'

'I want to milk you, honey, what else.'

'What? You do? Like, you did back then? You mean... you're getting off on this too? You want to, for real, milk me?'

'Sure. Now just do it.'

'Why the gun?'

'Just do it, I said.'

He went over to the other side of the bed, glancing behind him uncertainly, then stretched out his hands, the palms touching the bottom of the glass, and bent over, just like she'd said.

Considine watched this woman, Chi Chu, step up behind him without a sound, saw her switch the gun to her other hand, swapping it for the knife that he'd been holding earlier, and she had now. Chi Chu glanced at her and smiled, placed the gun into a pocket of her jumpsuit. She reached out and wrapped the hand around his scrotum, readied the blade in the other, directing it at a piece of flesh, but not touching it. Then in one quick movement she rammed it in and sliced the blade across, wiggling it about in places like she was cutting through gristle. In shocked disbelief, Considine watched his scrotum drop off and fall to the floor. He howled like a wild, demented animal. A cascade of blood fell from him as he stumbled, howling, turning, reaching his hands down between his legs, like placing them into a red waterfall, his eyes wide, confused and petrified all at once. He began to slide down against the window to the floor. He seemed to howl forever, but, in reality, it was less than a couple of minutes; then gradually it subsided and stopped. Considine watched his eyes half close and then stay that way. But he was not dead, his chest rising and falling slowly as the blood continued to drain from his body.

When Considine looked about the room, she saw Chi Chu was no longer there.

There was more of those yokes about than Brody had thought. Ireland had a housing crisis, after all. For some people, Brody was discovering, camper vans seemed to offer a solution. It wasn't that they were ubiquitous, no, it was just that when you actually went looking for one, you realised how many of them were actually out there.

Too many to do stop and searches on, that was for sure. One patrol pulled over a forty-foot American import on the Nangor Road. Brody could have told them that was a waste of time. The Nangor Road was out by the airport, too far away. It took the unit pulling it over almost a half hour before the driver could find a space the beast could actually fit in.

Brody didn't know, of course, if the camper van Mandy had seen pulling out of the industrial yard had anything to do with this. But it might. He summoned a helicopter from the garda air unit, call sign Alpha Sierra Two. As it happened, it was already in the air, returning to base from a mission, but still with forty minutes' worth of fuel on board.

Brody had to think quick. He reckoned if that camper van Mandy had seen did have something to do with Considine's disappearance, it couldn't have gotten far. He guessed it was within, at most, a fifteen-mile radius, probably a lot less. And, probably too, it would be parked up somewhere. Could Considine have been transferred to a car? Maybe, but he discounted that. Because if that were the case, then whoever took Considine would have used the car in the first place, not a great big camper van. The use of a camper van was an ominous sign.

Brody felt a rage laced with a sense of panic start to flow through him.

He bit his lower lip until it hurt, until he could feel a trickle of blood. It helped him concentrate.

He spoke directly to the observer in the helicopter, told him to coordinate his sweep of the area radiating out from the Basin Flats in Inchicore to a maximum of fifteen miles. 'You're looking for an American-type camper van. It's probably parked in an out-of-the-way location. Don't worry about main roads; mobile units have got them covered. Understand?'

'Roger, ground unit, understand. Stand by.'

Now Brody, as before, could only wait.

HE DIDN'T HAVE to wait for long. The helicopter, loaded with the latest surveillance, tracking, geolocation and camera equipment, had everything but the ability to time travel. It located a vehicle fitting the description Brody had provided in an area of the East Wall, at the back of a railway yard on the other side of the fence from the Dublin Port cargo terminal. It was also not far from the location where the body of the motorcycle cop had been found a couple of days before. When Brody realised this, he knew everything was all connected. The camper van was part of it.

He went with an armed unit to the scene and followed them inside.

'Nicola,' he shouted, 'you here?' There was no reply. A door was open towards the back of the vehicle. Brody followed the armed unit in. It was a bedroom. And a bloodbath.

'Jesus Christ,' he whispered, taking in Considine lying on the bed, her hands tied behind her back, jeans pulled down around her knees. He saw the heavy smear of blood on the windowpane. He looked along the other side of the bed, saw the figure lying slumped between it and the window. The scene was one from a horror movie. He set about freeing Considine, turning his back to the armed mule, doing his best to preserve her modesty. She pulled up her jeans and bounded off the bed. The floor between the window and the bed was drenched in blood, lying in the middle of it near the slumped body what looked like a mould of wizened pale jelly.

'Thank you, Jack, thank you, thank you, thank you.'

He turned and helped her to the door. They went out of the room, and she mumbled something, then stopped.

'What is it, Nicola?'

'One minute,' she said, her voice suddenly clear and strong.

She went back into the bedroom.

'No, Nicola, we need to get out of here. I've already conta...'

She had gone to the other side of the bed. He saw her stand over the man – Jack didn't know whether he was dead or alive – and begin to raise...

'No, fuck's sake, Nicola, don't.'

...her leg.

Before he could reach her, she'd started stomping her booted foot down onto his head, again and again. It made a dull, squelching sound as it made contact each time. He ran and pulled her away.

'Fuck's sake, Nicola, no...'

'You bastard,' she shrieked at the prostrate body. It

shifted sideways and fell backward, one shoulder against the wall, the other the floor, the head turned up, mouth and eyes half open. A death mask.

As Brody hustled her out of the room, they met two uniforms rushing in.

'Too late. About-turn. Out.'

The crime scene was already contaminated enough by everybody's size twelves.

PORTABLE ARC LIGHTS were set up, and a forensic team worked through much of the night. Brody eventually left as dawn was licking the sky with a pale light, when the identity of the body lying in the camper was confirmed as that of Abraham Jackman. The public office at Crumlin garda station had contacted him to say that the camper van had been reported stolen. It had been taken from a sales lot on Mayo Road owned by a character with a dubious criminal record. Was there a connection? Maybe, but Brody would never know. He took the details of the injured party in this and thanked the officer for telling him. No cash or jewels, nothing, had been found in the camper, but the vehicle would be taken to the maintenance depot at the Phoenix Park and gone through with a fine-tooth comb.

Brody eventually collapsed into bed a little after six. His eyes snapped open again just gone nine. He strangely didn't feel tired, but he didn't feel rested either. Adrenaline, he knew, was responsible, but he could only run on this for so long.

When he got to the Phoenix Park, Marty and Voyle were already in the unit room. He could tell by their demeanours they had taken the news about Considine hard. Voyle and Considine had a fractious relationship, but underneath it all, there was a strong bond.

Brody stood in the doorway.

'Any word?' he asked.

'They kept her in overnight,' Marty said. 'But she has no injuries...' Marty held his gaze, as if to say, *No injuries, what does that mean, boss? She mightn't have physical injuries, but what about on the inside?* 'They released her about an hour ago. She was collected by her father.'

Brody nodded. 'Okay, I'll be in my office.'

He went upstairs, listened at the top of the corridor that led to his office, couldn't hear anything from the floor above where Superintendent Ryan's office was. He sat behind his desk, kept the door open, logged onto Pulse. There was nothing from Dr McBain's office. Probably because the pathologist would not have attended the scene until first light this morning. SOC had provided photographs, including close-ups of boot prints in the blood about the victim's body and also on his head outlined in red. Shite. That could make it awkward for Considine. There was quite a bit of technical detail, measurements from the bed to the door, and the space between the window and the bed – sixty centimetres – and the angle of the body and the direction of the scrotum. *The direction of the scrotum?* This was listed as evidence with a tag number 7 placed next to it. Brody blinked. Like for real, *direction of the scrotum*? He wondered what Dr McBain would make of that. According to the SOCO, this indicated that the victim had been turned the other away from his attacker at the time...*the most likely posture is that he was bending over.*

It was a lot to take in, much more than he'd have guessed

would be available for...he glanced at the clock...9:53 in the morning. It was good work.

The incident had been placed on Pulse through the operations centre in Castlebar under a case number linking it to the bank job, which in turned linked it to Interpol, which in turn linked it to the incidents on the continent, adding yet another layer in a growing spider's web of international crime.

Brody had to admit, this case was a bit like trying to lift mercury with a fork. He didn't get to solve every case in his career. That was impossible. And this case wasn't solved, not really, but it would be solved enough for it to be claimed as such by the spaghetti hats on the six o'clock news. He thought of Mandy Joyce. Of course, if she were correct, the six o'clock news was no longer relevant, or not as relevant as it once had been. The news was now forever accessible via apps, selected by algorithms, and available on the phone you carried in your pocket. No one needed a TV now. Anyway, why did he even care? He was starting to get a headache.

But one thing he was certain of, this case was not solved, not completely, nor, he doubted, would it ever be.

As they said, you couldn't win them all. That would be impossible. But if you could win enough...

'Miss Wendy Zia Yang?'

'That's right.'

'Have you travelled from a third country as part of your journey to New York today?'

She smiled. 'Yes, I came in from Singapore last night.

Stayed at the Shelbourne Hotel in Dublin. Travelled down to Shannon today to make my flight.'

The immigration pre-clearance official at Shannon airport smiled. He looked at her passport again and then back at her. As he handed it over, he dropped his voice.

'Will you be coming back through again?'

She took her passport and smiled. 'Yes, of course, I will.'

'It's just, well, maybe you could give me your, um, phone number, and you and I, maybe we...'

'Yes,' she said, 'maybe we could. Am I free to go?'

He nodded sheepishly. 'Of course, you're free to go.'

'I'll be through again. What's your name?'

He pointed to his name tag. 'Danny, right there.'

'I'll look you up, Danny, okay.' She added, lowering her own voice, 'Maybe I shouldn't say this, but you're cute, Danny.'

She walked through into departures, leaving the pre-clearance official feeling on top of the world, staring after her. She swished her hips like she was walking down a catwalk, just for Danny.

That was how it started.

That was how it always started.

That was how it had started with Abraham too. But how was she to know he was nuts? Danny was normal; he'd have to be working in a job like that. And that job opened up a world of infinite possibilities. God would be very happy when she told him.

Yes, she'd look up Danny next time she was through.

47

The under-sixteen coaching class at the Northside Boxing Club had attracted more youngsters this week than during any time over the previous four or so months Brody had been running them. He knew the reason why. It wasn't because he was an inspirational coach, although Brody liked to think he was doing a good enough job. No. It was to do with the grudge rematch between Stephen Dempsey and Joshua Obianagha. It was finally going to happen. Tonight. Which might create problems. Because both parties had taken along a posse of supporters.

'What we going to do now?' Jimmy Nugent, reformed drug addict and hard man who'd set up and was in charge of the club, said. 'Obianagha's going to clobber him. He's way the better boxer. Dempsey's followers won't like it.'

'I know,' Brody said.

'Look at them.' Jimmy nodded to Stephen Dempsey's gang. 'Like ferrets ready to go down a rabbit hole.'

Brody could suggest to Jimmy that he run them all out. But then what? They'd throw a brick through every window in the place? Or wait around for Joshua's supporters to leave, and then jump them?

'Right, lads,' Brody said, knowing there was no choice but to get on with this. He went up the makeshift steps, which consisted of two upturned milk bottle crates, into the ring, went under the ropes and stepped into the centre. 'Dempsey. Obianagha. You both ready? Come up.'

Dempsey went in first. He was pumped, immediately began pacing about in his corner like a caged animal, punching one hand off the other, occasionally turning to his supporters and thrusting his arms into the air in short, sharp movements, riling them up. They roared in return. On the arm of one of Dempsey's young supporters, Brody spotted a tattoo of a white wolf. He knew it was a white supremacist emblem. So young, he thought, so hateful.

In the other corner, Joshua was dignified. As he always was. He stood, hardly moving, his face blank. He had already worked out his strategy, Brody knew; now he just needed to focus and carry it out. Which was what he was doing, slipping into the zone, emptying his head, focusing. Brody thought they were both evenly matched in weight, roughly fifty kilos apiece, both junior flyweights. Joshua's arms were longer, however, and he had a greater reach. He was a harder puncher too. Brody hoped he'd make it onto the national Olympics team next time round. Depending on how he did then, he could turn professional if he wanted to.

'Step in,' Brody called. They both did. 'Touch gloves.' They both did. 'And keep this civil.' Joshua nodded. But Dempsey was impassive.

Brody raised his right arm and brought it down between them both.

'Box.'

Dempsey immediately sent in a low blow. Maybe too low, Brody wasn't certain; he let it pass. But it caught Joshua off guard. He shuffled backwards. Dempsey followed, sending in a flurry of jabs, swarming Joshua, giving him no chance to use that long reach of his, or to utilise his strategy. Which, in its own way, was clever. Joshua was backed onto the ropes, and Dempsey, already wide eyed and bloodied, his jabs like a massed artillery barrage, was constant and unyielding. He'd been working hard for this moment, Brody realised. Yet it was an impossible pace to maintain. But maybe he wouldn't need to, because in the midst of his jabs, Dempsey sent in an uppercut that scored a direct hit, bouncing Joshua's head back, disorientating him. Joshua turned to the side, lowering his head, squeezing his gloves against the sides of his head, looking for respite. The artillery barrage continued, and Brody didn't think he was going to make it. He prepared to step forward, to stop the fight and give a count. But at that moment...

Ding, ding.

The lad was literally saved by the bell.

Dempsey gestured to his supporters as he strutted back to his corner.

Joshua sat slumped on his stool. One of his ring buddies, a couple of the older lads in the club, doused a cold-water sponge onto the back of his neck and the top of his head, while the other spoke into his ear.

Brody wondered if that would be enough. If it wasn't, he'd have to end the fight.

He beckoned to both boxers to resume, and stepped into the centre of the ring again. They came out. Dempsey was provocative, baring his chest. He stood, daring Joshua, slapping his gloves against his chest. It was then Brody heard it.

So slight it would be easy to miss. But he didn't. He watched Dempsey closely, very closely. He couldn't get this wrong; he had to be completely certain. Joshua came forward, and Dempsey brought up his fists, the movement just that little bit slower than it should have been, without any proper smooth rhyme to it. Dempsey lowered his head and brought back his right arm.

'Stop,' Brody shouted, raising both arms, crossing them over each other, a signal to both boxers to cease. He was taking a chance; he wasn't certain.

'Wha' ya do that for?' Dempsey demanded, his gum shield causing him to slur his words. 'I was just 'bout to finish him off.'

'I know you were,' Brody said, then, without warning, grabbed one of Dempsey's gloves. The lad immediately attempted to pull it back again, but Brody's grip was too strong. A simple strip of Velcro held the glove in place. Brody pulled it apart and took the glove off. As he did, an egg weight – so called because it looked like a small egg, except it was made of metal – fell out and bounced onto the floor of the ring with a dull thud.

A collective *Oooh* went around the room.

'You have one inside the other one too, don't you?' Brody began pulling at the other glove.

The room fell completely silent; Dempsey's raucous supporters staring on in what looked like disbelief, while Joshua simply looked confused. Such deceit would be incomprehensible to him. Brody removed Dempsey's other glove. The lad didn't resist this time. Sure enough, another egg weight dropped out; this time, Brody caught it before it fell to the floor.

The audience stayed silent. If Brody was to take anything

from this, it was that they all appeared disappointed, even Dempsey's supporters, which was good. As for the lad himself, he stayed standing in the ring while Brody and Joshua stepped out, his shoulders slumped, head bowed. Jimmy Nugent went in and wrapped an arm around him, led him away. He wasn't so tough or loud now.

A LITTLE LATER, when they were the only ones left, Jimmy Nugent said to Brody, 'He told me his father gave them to him. I'm going to have a word with that bollocks, I swear to God I am.'

'You think that'll do any good? Like, seriously?'

Jimmy looked to be thinking about it.

'Aye, I do. The lad was holding back tears. He's not as tough as he'd like you, or himself, to think.'

'I never thought he was tough in the first place,' Brody said. 'Bullies never are.'

'Ach, Jack, that's a bit unfair.'

'I don't think so. He would have fucked young Joshua up, that's what he would have done. Don't make excuses for him.'

'Well, if I don't, who will? I was like him one time. You have kids, Jack?'

'You know I don't.'

'No, actually, Jack, I don't know whether you do, or you don't.'

'Okay, sorry, Jimmy. And what? Meaning if I don't have kids, I can't understand, is that it?'

'You're being a little defensive there, Jack.'

'Am I?'

'Yes.' Jimmy smiled. His face didn't lend itself well to smiling, everything off-kilter. 'I think this might just be the wake-up call young Dempsey needs. He's a sensitive lad, really. It's his home life; he's just mirroring the behaviour he sees. Trust me.'

'Very Freudian.'

'Sarcasm doesn't suit you, Jack. I know you have a heart.'

'I could haul him in over that, seriously.'

'And will you?'

'No.'

'Jack?'

'Yes?'

'I really appreciate you doing this, coaching the kids, I mean. I don't think you have any idea the positive effect you have on them.'

'Yeah, but I didn't like it, Jimmy.'

'I know.'

'Right. I gotta go. See you next week.'

Brody started towards the door.

'Yeah, see you next week,' Jimmy called after him.

EPILOGUE

The night air was cold when Brody went outside, the sky cloudless, with no moon, the city lights obscuring the stars, adding a strange, translucent sheen to the heavens. He thought of Mandy Joyce. He should be at the Guinness Storehouse about now, attending the official launch for her podcast, *Sewer Rats*, produced and completed in record time and already downloaded over a hundred thousand times on pre-orders alone. Mandy had reinvented herself: podcasts, whoever would have thought?

A set of headlights flashed from further along the street. Brody paused, looking towards them, and they flashed again. He walked along the street towards the car parked there. As he drew near, he recognised it.

Well, well, he thought.

But something was missing. That kick of excitement that used to be there before. It was absent. He could see Ashling Nolan, behind the wheel, reach across to open the passenger door. He got there first and pulled it open, placed his head in the doorway.

'This is a surprise. That was me you just flashed?'

She laughed. He'd always loved her laugh. But this time something was missing too. This time it was different, just *different*.

'Of course. I don't just flash at anybody, you know. I remembered tonight was your coaching night. Thought I'd surprise you. Can you sit in, Jack, please?'

There was something about her tone that he caught, a sense of earnestness maybe, he wasn't sure.

'Of course.' He did, and for the first time since he'd known this woman – not that long, granted, but long enough – there was something he hadn't experienced before, an awkward silence.

'Look,' she said, then, 'the last night...'

'It's okay, Ashling, you don't have to explain, really, it's fine.'

'It is?'

'Yes, of course.'

'I wasn't going to explain,' she said.

'Oh.'

'Not really. Okay, I may have been a little lacking in empathy. You are married to your job, like I said, but maybe that's because, look, there's no easy way of saying this, but maybe that's because you don't have much else going on in your life apart from your job. And I'd never considered that before. Not until the last night. But then I did. Now, Jack, you do have something going on in your life, if you still want it, that is. You have me.'

Jack stared ahead, saying nothing.

'Aren't you going to say anything?' she asked softly after a moment.

Jack didn't know what to say. He suddenly felt like he

didn't want to say anything. He was just tired, so very, very tired.

'It's been a hectic few days,' he said. 'Can we talk about this another time?'

He turned towards her and saw her pout her lips. She did that a lot. And he realised he didn't like it. She did it when she didn't like something. He also realised that Ashling Nolan had shown a tendency to make decisions for him in this relationship. And he'd just gone along with it. She thought it was a good idea for her to show up outside the boxing club at this hour and get into a dialogue, and he was just supposed to go along with it? He'd been happy to go along with everything in the past. He remembered that night after he'd met her, he'd asked himself the question whether or not he was in lust or in love with her. He didn't know the answer then, but he felt he did now. Lust, that was the answer. But lust was like a shooting star, it burned bright as it blazed a trail across the sky, magical, mystical, ethereal – while it lasted. And then it was gone.

For Brody, this shooting star had burned itself out. It was gone. He knew it because he felt it. And he felt nothing.

Ashling seemed to sense the moment.

When she spoke, he realised she was holding back tears.

'Jack, I've something to tell you.'

The words she said seemed to rock the very ground beneath him.

'I'm pregnant.'

In the pause that followed, a car drove by, its lights shining in, revealing them so close together, side by side, but yet so far apart.

WE HOPE YOU ENJOYED THIS BOOK

If you could spend a moment to write an honest review on Amazon, no matter how short, we would be extremely grateful. They really do help readers discover new authors.

ABOUT THE AUTHOR

I hail from Mayo in the west of Ireland, although I spent much of my life away, in the US, UK, Europe, Jersey in the Channel Islands and various parts of Ireland.

In my younger years I was incredibly restless. I left home and school at 16 and spread my wings. I've had over forty jobs, everything from barman, labourer, staff newspaper reporter, soldier in the Irish army, station foreman with London Underground, mason, and many more besides. I returned to education as a mature student in the early noughties and hold a BA in history and sociology from the National University of Ireland at Maynooth, and an M.Phil from Trinity College Dublin.

Since 2005 I've been a civilian employee of the Irish police, An Garda Síochána. However, I've been on extended sick leave since 2015 following a mystery illness which struck while travelling in Spain. It almost killed me. The doctors never got to the bottom of it and they call me the Mystery Man. But every cloud has a silver lining. It has given me the time to write. Although I've been writing all my life, most of my output languishes in the bottom of drawers.

Under my real name, Michael Scanlon, I was initially published for the first time in 2019 by Bookouture with the first of three crime novels. Working with Inkubator is another great opportunity for me. This time I'm using a pseudonym, as the style of J.M. O'Rourke books are so different, and also, I really like the name!

I hope readers like them.

ALSO BY J.M. O'ROURKE

The Detective Jack Brody Series

The Devil's House

Time of Death

A Deadly Affair

Bad Blood